I0831718

Blood on White Roses

Kimberly Thompson

Kingdom Builders Publications LLC

Kingdom Builders Publications, LLC

Printed in the USA

SECOND EDITION

ISBN 978-0-692-96565-8

Library of Congress Control Number 2018935319

Authored by
Kimberly Thompson

Editor
Kingdom Builders Publications Staff
Lakisha Forrester

Cover Design
LoMar Designs

Cover Illustrator
Shanquita T. Foster

PROLOGUE

I'm not going to sit around and pretend to be Little Miss Perfect. I know I can be a tad bit egocentric, a tiny bit childish, and maybe a real bitch but I'm not gonna change for nooobody or nothing. I'm a complete package and you either accept that or kick rocks. Not everyone is going to like me, but I can understand the hate. I'm beautiful, my family has money. I have my own car, popularity, and a fantasy for a boyfriend. You call it superficial, I call it a hell of a life. After all, who wouldn't want to be me like me or walk in my shoes? Popularity runs in the Carlisle family like hardwired DNA. Mom was a sexy, sassy volleyball player. Dad was the basketball star everybody wanted to be around, because of his down to earth demeanor and hilarious jokes. Even my siblings, Apollo, Dite, and Ares are well known at school. It's only Athena that chooses to blend into society like an antisocial chameleon. My sister, Dite, is already starting to act just like me and I honestly couldn't think of a better role model. I know I've participated in some harmless teasing to some of my classmates. But, somebody was gonna be the punch line sooner or later. We used to call Sybil Florentine "Piggy" and Rayanne Greyman Ray GAYman, ha!), but, somebody is gonna be the punch line sooner or later. Ok, so maybe Sophia Carlos didn't deserve the picture of her I plastered on her locker of her with an exaggerated lazy eye in middle school. It was wrong, but it was just so damn funny! It's not her fault God gave her a left eye that was too lazy to look completely straight. Honestly, some people just need to learn to take a joke. You can either be the comedian or the punch line and I made sure I always came out on top. I'm glad I have Marley and Lauralee (who can be awfully annoying and clingy at times) as my friends. I had a third best friend, Callista. I used to call her my "Calli Doll." She stabbed me in the back and our friendship fell apart, all because of her selfishness and jealousy. I regret ending what we had, and no feeling is worse than regret. I've made mistakes, but hear me when I say, Minnie Carlisle shall never change.

-Minnie C.

CHAPTER ONE

"There's nothing worse than having a worst enemy who knows you like a best friend."

Sometimes, I wonder how one city can have so much mischief and scandal. Our lives seem to be never-ending soap operas. Or better yet, one big novel; and the jerk who wrote it made sure to include as much drama as possible. You would think that most people would try to keep their lives as drama-free as possible. Those are the people who definitely aren't from Angel City. Our governor, Lorenzo Giovanni, tries his hardest to make Angel City appear like the most perfect city in America. He does that mainly so that people will be more likely to move here, thus, generating more revenue for the city. Plus, having a near perfect city helps his public image. Tourists often come to see our main attraction, TresAngeles Field, located on the outskirts of Angel City. The reason why it's so popular is because it's a huge, supposedly haunted field that mysteriously only seems to grow white roses. Anyways, in the process of trying to force Angel City to become a utopia, Governor Giovanni has made the city quite boring. There's never anything new or exciting, which could explain why a lot of us Angeleans practically feed off any piece of good news or scandal that comes our way. That's not my style, though. Drama and scandals are definitely two things I don't wanna feed off of throughout my life. I just try to skate by each year living in this city with as little conflict as possible. If only life were that easy. It's mid-February of my senior year at Angel City High, so most of the petty and childish drama is long gone; and I hope the remaining three months go by smoothly. My favorite part of the year has always been February. The weather is brisk and serene. The atmosphere is filled with romance. Spring is beginning to bloom from beneath the slushy snow. Around this time of the year, my already huge ego takes a trip around globe, because of all the roses I've received from Nate and other secret admirers lurking around Angel City High on Valentine's Day. As I'm sitting on a chair in the middle of the second floor hallway, I'm looking mighty gorgeous if I do say so myself. I'm wearing my favorite, pink Aeropostale top, which lets me show off a little cleavage, along with my best blue jeans and a pair of pink, wedge heels to top it all off. I know my boyfriend, Nathaniel, will appreciate it greatly. He loves the way my perfect, size nine derriere looks in these jeans.

As I am taking a sip of the grape soda I picked up from the vending machine, I notice my cell phone is vibrating as I'm getting a call from Cassidy Paris, a childhood friend of mine.

"Hello, Crybaby Cassie," I answer.

"How long are you going to hold that against me?" He chuckles a bit. "I was just a little kid. All kids cry."

"Not like you did that day at the beach," I tease before laughing loudly.

"Yeah, whatever," He responds, pretending to be upset. At least I think he's pretending. The male ego can be so easily bruised.

Cassidy and his father, Benjamin Paris, moved from Angel City to a more rural part of North Carolina when Cassidy and I were really young. In fact, we were hardly a year old. Since Benjamin, my father, and my Uncle Danny were all good friends during their frat boy days, Benjamin made sure to continue close contact with our family. So, we got to visit one another often throughout the years. But every time I used to ask why Cassidy left Angel City in the first place, the adults would get silent, exchange odd looks, and no one would give me a straight answer. Eventually, I lost patience and just stopped asking.

"I hope you come visit again soon. I want you to see how much I've grown," Cassidy remarks slyly.

I can't help but to smile. "Behave yourself, Cassie. I have a boyfriend, remember?"

His tone changed from seductively playful to serious. "Who dares to date my Minnie?"

I paused for a second. Cassidy has always had some bad memory. "I told you before. I'm dating Nathaniel Jacobs. Remember?"

"Hmph, y'all are lasting longer than I thought," Cassidy responds with an evil chuckle. "Is he still a douche?"

My grey eyes rolled. Cassidy had a habit of calling all of my boyfriends a douche. "Cassidy, Nathaniel is not a douche."

"Maybe not a douche, but certainly a dimwit. How would you know, anyways? You're probably too busy drooling over his six-pack to notice."

I can't really argue with that, especially since Cassidy knows I love guys with muscles. "So what if I am?"

"You can drool over mine. I bet mine looks better."

"Cassidy!" I lifted my head with a smile. I glance up for a quick second and notice my best friend, Marley Aprilson, walking towards me.

"I gotta go, Cassie. Talk to you later." I say to him.

"Goodbye, beautiful," He retorts before we hang up.

By the time I place my phone back into my pocket, Marley is standing right beside me. She's wearing a pair of grey Oxford jeans with holes in the knees, navy blue flip-flops, and a white t-shirt with a yellow smile face on it. Marley obviously dresses for comfort, not for the runway. She describes her style as being "humbly adorable."

"Hey, Minnie. How's it going?" She cheerily greets as she tucks her short, chocolate colored hair behind her ears and straightens her cherry red glasses.

"Good. I just got off the phone with Cassidy, actually," I answer as I stand up to walk over to throw away my soda can. A few boys check me out as I do, but none of them have the balls to step to me. Nobody dares to flirt with the girlfriend of star quarterback, Nathaniel Jacobs. He's basically the king of Angel City High and being queen feels oh so nice.

"Mmhmm," Marley suggestively hums.

I grin. I know Marley thinks I should date Cassidy instead of Nate. She says we are "ultra-compatible." I tell her to get her mind out of the gutter and to stop reading those cheesy horoscopes that she finds in the daily newspaper. Marley's very intelligent which is why I don't understand why she believes in zodiac signs to base people's compatibility. They're just a load of hooey, like the messages you get in fortune cookies.

"Cassidy Paris and Minnie Carlisle are just old friends," I remind her for the trillionth time.

The bell rings and a crowd of people hurry to get to their third period class.

"Old friends can spark new flames," Marley sings. She shoots a grin right back at me and her set of orchid pink braces show.

As Marley and I are walking to our U.S. Government class, I notice some girls giving me the side eye from across the hall. Normally, I'd easily crush them with a witty retort but they're so irrelevant that I just decide to roll my eyes at them and continue with my day. Jealousy is a serious disease, people! We also pass by my older brother, Apollo, and his friends standing beside his cobalt blue locker. Apollo, who is now 19, is currently spending his fifth year at Angel City High since he managed to fail English his sophomore year. I wave at him and he smiles and nods his head at us.

"Your brother is kinda sexy," Marley whispers. Although I know

Apollo is girl crazy like most young guys are, I know he wouldn't take Marley up on her offer if given the opportunity. She's, uhh…not his type. Although Marley says she's saving herself until marriage, she looked ready to pounce on Keegan Hunter when he walked around the neighborhood shirtless with Nate after a few rounds of basketball.

"Hmmm, that vow of celibacy you made in 8th grade wearing off, eh?" I jokingly remark.

"Oh, no. I'm not trying to catch anything. I don't want to be like Phyllis James," Marley jokes.

"You mean SYPHILIS James," I corrected. I remember when Syphilis first tried to start problems with me because we both liked Nate at the same time. This petty broad was determined to make me suffer all because Nate wouldn't date her. Can I help that Nathaniel actually has taste? However, once I found out from her jilted ex who may or may not have sent me pictures of her medical records showing that she had two STDs, let's just say I ended that rivalry very quick. Embarrassed and diseased, she transferred to another high school. It's some people you just don't mess with.

We finally arrive at Mr. Whittaker's class and open the door. Since the tardy bell hasn't rung yet, not a lot of students are in the class yet. This means Marley and I get first dibs on where we want to sit. I chose two seats on the far side of the classroom, closest to the window. This is good because now I can text with a lesser chance of him catching me. Marley chooses the seat to the right of me. An added bonus is that I get to stare at the trees and the birds and butterflies outside; wishing I was out there with them and not trapped in here forced to learn about some stupid war I'll never need to know anything about. I highly doubt some loon is going to hold a bazooka up to my head and kill me unless I can recite the Bill of Rights to them by heart. As the tardy bell rings loudly, the rest of Mr. Whittaker's class rushes in. I see many familiar faces, nobody truly important like Marley. The second semester of the school just started last month and I can already tell the class is going to be a bore just by who's in it. Last to enter the classroom is the one, the only, the pregnant, Callista Arden. Despite already having spent a month in this class with her, I still have this same, anxious, tense reaction. Upon seeing her, my heart begins to sink to my stomach joining the slightly burned pancakes Dad cooked for breakfast. I slid down halfway in my seat.

"Minnie, it's gonna be alright. Maybe she won't say anything to you today," Marley reassures. I shoot her a look that says, "Yeah, right."

"She's seventeen and pregnant. I'm sure she has more important things to focus her mind on. You know how Callista is; her mind has always been all over the place."

I slowly slid back up in my seat. You see, Callista, Marley, and I became best friends when we met in kindergarten. Everything was peachy until around eighth grade. I started to develop and fast, making the hormone driven boys around me go crazy. The way I see it, Callista didn't like the fact that she wasn't developing as fast as I was and hogging all of her wanted attention; and that's when she changed. She began to distance herself greatly from me and decided she'd rather be besties with a slut and a delinquent. Her clique began to belittle Marley because of her "hippie" looks and stick figure." Rebecca Hardwick called Marley "mosquito tits" once. I shamefully admit that I laughed a little at that one. However, the vast majority of Callista's anger has been directed towards me. She spares Marley from her wrath for some reason. I have always tried to salvage our friendship, part of me still wants to. By freshman year, Callista made it clear she didn't wanna be around Marley or me any longer. It's nothing worse than having a worst enemy that knows you like a best friend. Seeing her just makes things awkward and tense. Callista's arctic blue eyes quickly lock onto Marley and me and she grins evilly as if she's planning to make this the worst class period for us ever. She and her posse sit down a few rows over from us. They begin to whisper, giggle, and casually glance over at us. My fists clench with frustration. Mr. Whittaker claps to get everyone's attention and stands up in the front of the classroom.

"Good afternoon, students. Let's begin today's lesson by opening up to chapter five. Before I begin, let's go over some of the main ideas of this chapter." He lectures as he writes an assignment in black on the dry erase board.

After he is finished writing his assignment, he continues on with his lecture that causes half of the class to suddenly develop narcolepsy. The other half is zoning out and completely engaging in their own private worlds. I glance over and notice Marley's knocked out cold, which is unusual because she's always been the type to pay extra attention in class. The way she pokes her tongue out slightly through her thin lips when she's thinking extra hard on an assignment amuses me. I decide not to awaken her. I know what it's like to be awoken out of the best of sleeps, since I share a house with two sisters and two brothers. I look over and notice that Callista's posse has also wandered into a beauty sleep, meaning that for the moment, she has no one to gossip about me to. However, when she happens to catch me glancing at her, she crosses her eyes and sticks up her middle finger. I can't help but to remember how many times she would make that face in middle school. I feel my cell phone vibrate suddenly against my thigh. I cautiously take my iPhone out of my pocket and see that I got a text from Nate: "Can u meet me in the hall, Babe?"

I smile and quickly reply, "Yes." Then, I quickly raise my hand.

"Yes, Miss Carlisle?" Mr. Whittaker asks.

"May I go to the restroom?" I make sure to say it extra nice and feminine so he doesn't get suspicious. He sighs deeply, as if I'm interrupting the most important lecture he's ever given in his entire career.

"Yes, you may go. Try to hurry back."

I speed walk out of the classroom and am careful not to stumble in my wedge heels, as I snatch the pink bathroom pass off of the hook by the door. I turn around, close the door softly, and notice that Nathaniel's already walking towards me. Both of his hands are in his pockets and he flashes a pearly white grin from ear to ear as he greets, "Hello, Mrs. Jacobs."

CHAPTER TWO

"All I can do is hope things will change and apologize when you find out the truth."

Nate referring to me as his "Mrs." will never cease to send a rush of goosebumps marching up my body. Sometimes, I can't believe we've been dating for a little over eight months now. Yeah, we've had our ups and downs, but all in all, it's been perfect. I run up to him and wrap my arms tightly around him, embracing him in a hug. Occasionally, Nate forgets his own strength and when he attempts to bear hug me, his muscular biceps nearly break my tiny waist in half like a toothpick.

"Nate...oh, my God. Please, stop squeezing me," I gasp.

"You should let me do more than squeeze you, Minnie," He remarks as he releases his grip and places me back on the ground. Once I'm grounded, Nate plants an unexpected and very passionate kiss on me. I go along with it and kiss him back until I start running out of air.

"Wow, you sure are affectionate today," I remark as I push him away from my body. Nate returns my remark with a sly smile. I already know what's on his hormonal mind, because I suddenly feel something long and stiff poking my upper thigh. I give him a skeptical look.

"Nathaaaaniel," I groan. When he gets horny, he can be a really difficult person to reason with.

"Wilhelmina, you're driving me craaaaazy. When are you gonna let me?" He whined. I raised an eyebrow. "Let you what?"

"Let me touch you, please you...make you scream," He answers as he kisses on the right side of my neck. As good as it feels, I refuse to give into Nate's tempting offers until I feel the time is right.

"Nate, I've told you a thousand times. I'm waiting to have sex. I'm just not ready for that yet," I explain for the 200th time.

Truth is, sex kind of scares me. I could flirt and tease all day long but the idea of going to the next level with Nate throws me off a bit. I'm afraid of it hurting or losing it to the wrong person. I wanna wait until I'm absolutely, positively sure I love Nate to give my body to him. I've always hated when Lauralee called it "making love" because it made me question if I really loved him. Call me cheesy if you want, but I think sex should be like a mystically intense, whirlwind of passion with the one you love. Maybe I've been watching too many romance films. The neck kissing ceases and he jerks his head up so now we're eye to eye. Judging by his facial expression, he was damn mad. Being an affluent only child and a Mama's boy, he's really not used to NOT getting what he wants.

"Minnie, all this playing hard to get is getting old, REALLY old. Now, I am a man and I have a lot of unfulfilled needs. If you don't satisfy them, someone-"

His lecture is interrupted by Callista exiting Mr. Whittaker's classroom. With her being pregnant, none of the teachers question her when she says she needs to go to the restroom or get water. She gets a nine-month pass. When she saw us, her eyes narrowed, and she grinned. Why can't she just mind her own business and stay out of mine for once?

"How's it hangin', Nate?" She greeted in her sultry voice.

Nate lets go of me and places his hands back into his pockets after he fixes his silky, auburn hair. "Hey, Callista. You look nice today, as usual."

Nice? This girl was huge and waddling like a watermelon on two stilts. Before she got pregnant, she used to grace campus in things such as, camouflage shorts, combat boots with spikes, and T-shirts with crude sayings, such as "F.U.C.K. the police" and "I just might slap this chick." Now, all of a sudden, she looks "nice." Oddly, Nate wasn't looking at her with eyes of desire. It was more like a look of admiration. I think that's what scared me the most.

"You don't look too bad yourself," Callista compliments.

They smile at each other and I personally couldn't stand it anymore. I turned to Nate. "I'll talk to you later."

His expression went from happy to serious. "I know we will. That's all we ever flipping do," He seethes before walking off to return to his class. Although I hadn't even turned around to face Callista, I could feel her staring daggers into my body. Without turning around, I growl, "What do you want, Calli?"

She fake laughed. "Calli? As in your "Calli Doll?" How…cute. You still call me that as if I'm the same "Calli" you knew back in Ms. Sampson's kindergarten class." I turned around to face her. "You are the same girl. I know you are."

She put her left hand on her hip and flipped her long, platinum blonde hair over her shoulder; something she tended to do when she was about to say something a tad bit bitchy. It amazes me sometimes how well I still know her.

"No, I'm NOT the same little dork you knew all those years ago, Minnie Carlisle! I used to follow you around everywhere you went and now that I don't, you and all your egocentricities can't stand it! Other people may think you're hot stuff but I know how you really are. God…I don't know why I'm still bothering with you. Why do I try anymore? People like you don't change," She growled. By the tone she used and the way her eyes were glaring at me, I could tell she had years of pen up resentment towards me, however, the feeling was not entirely mutual.

"You know how I really am? Oh please, Calli. I think you're just jealous because YOU'RE the one who couldn't finish high school without getting pregnant and not knowing who the father is."

She took a few steps back and she looked as if she was about two seconds from completely ripping my head off with her bare hands.

"You BITCH!" she seethed, placing a nasty emphasis on the word "bitch." "You think I'm doing this because I'm jealous!? You just don't get it do you!? You never did and never freaking will! Minnie, you're just-"

She stops in mid-sentence and took a few steps back towards the classroom door, visibly a mixture of upset and infuriated. As she reaches for the doorknob, I say to her, "Just tell me what this is about, Calli. I can't fix a problem if you won't show me what it is."

Back turned to me, she mumbles, "I've been trying to show you something for a while now. There's so many problems, I-I don't even know where to begin. All I can do is hope things will change and apologize when you find out the truth."

She swings the door open and re-enters the classroom. I take a few seconds to calm myself down before I follow in right behind her. I guess I forgot my own strength because when I closed the door, it slammed loud enough to interrupt Mr. Whittaker's lecture, awaken everyone in the class, and even startle Callista a bit. Mr. Whittaker glared at me.

"If you don't mind, can you please take your seat, Minnie?" He ordered, annoyed with my interruption.

It must suck for him that he can't run a classroom or his marriage. Yeah, Mr. Whittaker, we ALL know about Mrs. Whittaker's affair with the hot, Latino janitor. It's not so hush-hush anymore. I was too embarrassed at the moment to give a sassy response so I just sauntered back to my empty, beige desk on the opposite side of the classroom. Marley looks at me with a mixture of fatigue and confusion. After I sat down and slumped back into my seat, Marley turned to me.

"So…what happened?" Marley yawned as she took her long arms and stretched them high into the air. She winces a bit. Marley's left arm always seems to be hurting. I ask her about it sometimes, but she never wants to talk about how her arm got injured. I leaned a little closer to her and whispered. "Callista and I just had a mild argument. Nate was there too, but that's not even the part I care about. There's something she's not telling me, Marley. I just know it. I can practically feel the secrecy in my soul."

A somber expression overcomes Marley's face and she glances away from me for a split second. I shoot an eyebrow up at her in suspicion, as if to say "What is it?" When you've been best friends for so many years like Marley and I have, you are able to speak without talking and still know what the other is saying. Marley insists that it's nothing. I didn't persist for information as my mind was already racing. I thought back to when the three of us were in the hall. I kept trying to piece together what it could be that Callista wanted to tell me. I remembered how seductively Callista was trying to act towards Nate. I remembered how star struck Nate was when Callista came into the hall. I sighed. All I could do was hope and pray Callista wouldn't stoop that low to get back at me. Then again, as Callista's former best friend, I know first-hand of how relentless and reckless she can be. Maybe this is only the beginning.

CHAPTER THREE
"You don't mess with Jezebel!"

Since we both were in the mood for some company, Marley invited me to her house afterschool. Just when Marley and I were about to enter my car, I heard my best frenemy, Lauralee Giovanni, call out to us. She was running towards us in her five inch, sunflower yellow stiletto heels. Her yellow and black fashion belt accentuated her tiny waist in her thigh length, body-hugging, peach cocktail dress that hung delicately off her left shoulder. Lauralee has always been the diva type; the one who dresses up for everything. Some girls think she's just flaunting her status as the Governor's daughter around, but I know she doesn't do it intentionally. She can be a little oblivious regarding the impression that she gives off to people.

"Hi, Minnie! Hey, Rosemarley. You're looking cute today," Lauralee gasped as she moved her long, dark brown hair out of her face.

"Hello, Lauralee," Marley seethed. Marley has made it obvious she doesn't like that name, but Lauralee calls her that anyway because it "sounds more girly than Marley." Lauralee is the most feminine girl I know. Everything must be colorful, cutesy, and girly. Must be nice to live in Lauralee's world. You get to sleep on a bed of sunshine, the roads are made of one-hundred dollar bills, and it rains milk chocolate every Tuesday.

"Where ya guys headed?" Lauralee happily inquired.

"Well, if you MUST know, Lauralee. We are going to Marley's house," I playfully snapped.

"Well," Lauralee thrusts her left hip out and snapped her fingers. This is a little game we play. We love to get sassy with each other. That is, until the sassiness turns into aggravation, and she makes me want to shove her into speeding traffic. "If you don't mind, I'd like to join you, you arrogant shrew."

I smiled amusingly at her. "Oooh, you're getting extra sassy today, hmm?" In response, she grinned and twirled her hair. "Can't handle it, Artemis?"

"I can handle you just fine." I turned to Marley, who seemed to have grown impatient of our game of going back and forth. "Marley, do you mind if Lauralee tags along?"

Marley's fists clenched. "Why can't she drive her OWN car and go to her OWN house?"

Lauralee and I were taken aback by Marley's out of the blue bitchiness. Sometimes, Marley can be a really moody person, even if it's not her time of the month. I always found it odd how Marley's mood could switch so quickly. It doesn't take much to set her off sometimes.

"My car is getting repaired and I just wanted someone to hang out with, if that's not too much to ask, Rosemarley. Geez." Now Lauralee had an attitude to match Marley's.

Marley sighed in frustration. "Fine, then. You can come. Happy?" After that polite little statement, Marley rushed into the passenger seat, slammed the door, and turned her head away from us. Lauralee simply rolled her eyes and got into the backseat. I bet that you can guess it was a pretty silent ride to Marley's house, with the exception of my radio blaring. We walk in and Lauralee's facial expression clearly said that the house was not up to her standards. Dirty dishes in the sink, crumbs on the counter, the carpet was dingy, stuff was thrown every which way but right, and someone definitely needed to dispose of the garbage. Lauralee looked mortified.

"Someone needs a cleeeeaning seervice." Lauralee sang under her breath.

"Not everyone is as rich as you, Lauralee." Marley snapped. "You two want something to snack on?"

The wooden cabinets squeaked as Marley opened them to find food. Even I must admit that the Aprilson home needed some miracle work and fast.

"My mom's been favoring booze over actual groceries so there's not much to snack on around here. We have cranberry juice and popcorn," Marley informed.

We just stood there and stared at her silently for a few seconds. "That's it?" I asked, hoping she would find something else…anything else.

"Unfortunately, yes."

"Unbelievable. I'm STARVING and all you have is juice, popcorn, and freakin' booze. Teeeerific," Lauralee complained; the spoiled, rich girl was coming out of her now.

Although it wasn't the gourmet feast we wanted to have, we sat in

Marley's living room and snacked on the juice, popcorn, and the pack of Twizzlers Lauralee found at the bottom of her peach Gucci purse. Unfortunately, we had to sit through her complaints about how badly she was craving a turkey and Swiss sandwich on slightly toasted rye bread. Seriously, she couldn't have sounded any more like a diva. We were peacefully watching reality TV shows until a picture of the Aprilson family caught Lauralee's eye.

"Hey, is this your fam?" She stupidly questioned as she is holding the picture in her left hand. Noooo, everyone has pictures of OTHER people's families in their houses. C'mon, think Lauralee.

"Yes," Marley apathetically answered. She seemed as if she wanted to change the subject already. I got off the burgundy colored couch to stand beside her and examine the picture. The four of them seemed really happy together. Marley looks exactly like her father, Donald. She inherited his height, his brown hair, and his forest green eyes. Marley always was a Daddy's girl. Ophelia and Marley's sister, Lydia, look almost like twins with their round faces, long, sandy blonde hair, and blue eyes. To the left of the family photo was one of a pregnant Ophelia, Donald, and a young Lydia. Ophelia is smiling radiantly as she holds her huge tummy. She's practically glowing with happiness. Donald has two fingers sticking up behind Ophelia's head, giving her "bunny ears," while Lydia is making a kissy face at Ophelia's large baby bump. It made me think that maybe there is some maternal love buried deep inside Ophelia for Marley, if not, why would she be so happy to be bringing her into this world? She looks overjoyed to be having another one of Donald's children, as if it were an honor. There's an older picture of a young Donald and Ophelia, arm in arm. She's smiling radiantly from ear to ear in her garnet and black cheerleader uniform, and he's holding her snugly around the waist while in his dirty, football uniform as he plants a big smooch on her left cheek. The beautiful cheerleader and the popular, football jock. They were cliché, but they sure looked happy together. From what I've heard, Ophelia was hell on earth when she was a teen. "She would've made Regina George look like a girl scout. My big sister was materialistic, rude, ruthless, and rebellious. Everyone who went to school with us witnessed the wrath of Ophelia Carter," Marley's uncle, Terrence described. Finding true love in a gentle guy like Donald must've turned her into a better woman. A classic love story, almost straight out of a fairytale.

"Sometimes, I can't believe you're Lydia Aprilson's baby sister," Lauralee comments.

"Not the first time I've heard that," Marley grumbles, attention still on the television screen.

"Funny, I never see her come visit."

"Because she rarely does."

Lauralee continued to glance back and forth between Marley and the family picture. Call it women's intuition, but I knew she was about to say something messed up.

"You know…you'd be a whole lot prettier if you dressed like Lydia. She's so gorge," She commented.

Women's intuition never fails. Marley turned off the television and stood up. When she removed her glasses and tossed them onto the nearby coffee table, her face clearly said that she was livid. Lauralee didn't look worried at all. I guess she had yet to realize that she just insulted Marley. Marley detested being compared to Lydia since their mother compares the two all the time. Ophelia always placed Lydia on a pedestal, but for all the wrong reasons. "Lydia's so beautiful. Lydia's hair is so long and straight. Why'd you have to get your father's frizzy hair, and why'd you cut it? You look like a lesbian. You're too skinny. Look at your sister, she has meat on her bones. Those hips will get her a billionaire someday. Lydia has friends. Lydia goes out. Lydia dates. Lydia's popular." The comparisons go on and on. Basically, Ophelia only struts her around like a trophy, because Lydia is more like she was when she was a teen—popular and beautiful, and that all that seems to matter to her. I don't mean to disrespect Marley, but she could never step into her sister's shoes. I think that's one of the reasons why people comparing the two is such a soft spot for Marley. In Lauralee's simple mind, all she had done was give simple advice. I took a small step backward when Marley began to slowly walk up to her with her fists clenched.

"Look here, Lauralee. I don't appreciate being compared to her and I especially won't tolerate it witcho uppity self. Now you can take that picture, and get the hell out of my house, before I slam you across the face with it."

With every word that erupted out of her mouth, Marley took steps toward Lauralee, pushing her every now and again. Lauralee began to look confused and terrified as she took steps backward in an attempt to gain distance away from her. It was like seeing Marley turn into a different person. I've never really seen her so angry. Lauralee didn't start to defend herself, until she ran out of room to get away as she was backed into a full length mirror hanging on the wall.

"What the hell is the matter with you, Rosemarley Aprilson!? Get the hell away from me!" Lauralee frantically screamed.

She dropped the picture on the floor as she closed her eyes and pushed Marley with all the strength she had in her petite, 5'2" body. I tried to step in to stop Marley from retaliating.

"Marley! Marley, don't do this!" I yelled, but all she did was push me to the floor to move me out of her way. Marley slapped Lauralee hard across the face then grabbed her by the shoulders and pushed her violently into the mirror, causing pieces of glass to shatter amongst the floor. Lauralee screamed for me to save her as she and Marley both fell to the floor, and Marley began relentless punching that pretty face of hers. Coincidentally, Ophelia walked through the front door and once she saw what was happening, she dropped all of her belongings to help me break up the chaos. Ophelia grabbed Marley and I helped Lauralee to her feet once she was free.

"Let…me…go, Ophelia!" Marley commanded as she struggled to break free of the hold her mother had on her. She would've succeeded if her mother wasn't abnormally strong for a lethargic, middle-aged alcoholic.

"Enough! Snap out of this, Marley!" Ophelia commanded sternly, slapping Marley upside her temple. Marley stomped furiously on her foot in return. Ophelia winced deeply in pain but refused to release her daughter from her grip.

"That girl is INSANE!" Lauralee shrieked as she wiped blood from her mouth and tears from her eyes. The top of her dress now had a few blood spots on it.

"Yeah, I'm insane, bitch! You don't mess with Jezebel!" Marley yelled back.

Lauralee and I exchanged confused looks with each other. Who in the world was Jezebel? I gently grabbed Lauralee by her arm and helped her to the door. Before leaving, Lauralee threatened, "My father will have your head for this!"

"Ooooh, I'd love to give your Dad head, Lee." She taunted as she stuck her tongue out. Then, she started to manically laugh. This is going to be one of those days that friends just never talk about ever again. I'll classify this event as officially "being swept under the rug."

"You sick, twisted psycho," Lauralee seethed as we walked out and I closed the door behind us.

CHAPTER FOUR:

"Your friend needs to be institutionalized."

As expected, it was a very long and very silent ride to the Giovanni mansion. I really didn't know what to say to Lauralee. I tried my best to prevent her from getting hurt, but Marley made sure hurt would happen anyway. Of course, Lauralee was especially silent. Who wouldn't be after badly losing a fight? You'd think with all of her father's money, she could've bought herself some boxing lessons. As clueless and as annoying as Lauralee can be, even she didn't deserve to get beaten up for it. Lee's not a fighter, she's a diva. She's a perky, prissy, rich girl who doesn't have a violent bone in her body. Then again, I thought Marley was on the "peace, love, and harmony" status until I saw her fist harmonizing with Lauralee's face. That's not like Marley at all. I wonder what's gotten into her.

"Your friend needs to be institutionalized," Lauralee growled, breaking the ice.

"She's not a lunatic," I responded as I parked at the black, iron gates at the entrance of her home. Security guards eyed me as I did so, making sure nothing suspicious was happening.

"Are you freaking BLIND!?" She snapped. Someone's a little testy.

"You just pushed her buttons a little. Family is a sensitive topic for Marley because her family is all screwed up," I defended.

"So that gives her full right to attack someone like that!? Yeah, she seemed reeeeally sensitive when she pushed me into that damn mirror. I got cuts from that stupid glass! Have I introduced you to cuts numbers one through five right here on my arms? Stop acting stupid and defending that crazed hippie!"

I turned towards her. I understand she was pissed because she had just gotten that tail beat, but now she was just irking my nerves. "Quit yelling at me," I growled, staring at her intently. For a moment, I had completely forgotten about the security guards who would hop on me at a moment's notice if I laid a finger on the daughter of their precious Governor.

"Stop being so freaking stupid then." The harshness in her tone lowered to a soft-spoken, yet stern tone of voice.

"Then get out of my freaking stupid car before I introduce you to my knuckles numbers one through ten like Marley did." I smiled evilly at her, knowing she wouldn't have a witty response to that. She yells, "Ugh!" before she hastily got out, slammed the door, and stormed towards the entrance gates. They creaked as they began to open for her and she continued to stomp furiously across the exquisitely, manicured lawn and past the large, marble water fountain and flag post which held both the American flag and the NC State flag.

"And quit slamming my doors!" I yell after her, once I had rolled my window down.

"Go to Hell, Wilhelmina!" She yells back from the distance, hair flowing wildly behind her.

I purposely broke the speed limit just so I could get home as soon as possible. 25 mph was just NOT fast enough to get home soon enough. I hope there weren't any ticket-happy police officers around. I was in no mood to deal with anymore drama.

"Well, look what the cat dragged in." Apollo teases once I walked through the door.

I playfully nudge him and hug my youngest sibling, Ares, before I went to raid the fridge for some real food. If I saw a single Twizzler or a kernel of popcorn, I swear I would've screamed.

"We had spaghetti. I saved a cinnamon bun for you, Minnie," Ares smiled, letting the gap from his missing front tooth show. I've always been his favorite sibling.

"Suck up," Apollo mumbled, playfully ruffling Ares's flaming red hair.

"Jealous, much?" Ares and I retort simultaneously.

As I reheated my leftovers, Ares and Apollo went back into the living room to finish some kind of weird, zombie shooting game they were playing on the big screen television. I decided to take my food into my room to have some peace and privacy. However, I didn't get any of that because I found my two younger sisters, Aphrodite and Athena, playing in my room. Aphrodite was using MY curlers, had sprayed MY perfume, and was polishing her pudgy toes with MY Supreme Scarlett nail polish. Athena was sprawled out on MY bed mesmerized by the Animal Planet show she was watching on MY TV.

"AHEM!"

They both jumped suddenly as they didn't even notice I was standing in the doorway.

"Heeeeey, girl! Come on in!" Dite exclaimed. Was she inviting me into my own room when she wasn't even invited in it herself? Like, she wasn't even civil enough to excuse herself or apologize for using my stuff without my permission. Brat.

"Hey, Minnie," Athena calmly greeted. Our mother snuck in on us. "Awww, my three girls bonding. How nice."

I placed my food down on my night stand. "Mooom, don't they have their OWN room?" I whined.

"Don't be like that, Minnie. You all don't bond like you used to. Just be nice, Pumpkin." She responded before walking off. So in an effort to be a good, eldest daughter, I did the "sisterly bonding" Mom wanted us to do. Since Dite went with "Supreme Scarlet," I adorned Athena's nails with "Blueberry." This was "daring" to her since Athena likes everything so plain. After uncurling her hair and telling story after story of her teenage drama as she did so, Dite decided to try on a pair of my custom made heels, in which she almost broke both her tiny ankles since I'm like a shoe size and a half bigger than she is. I finished off my plate of leftovers, popped in a romantic comedy for us and halfway through the movie, my sisters fell asleep snuggled up next to me on my big, soft bed; which I must admit, gave me that warm, fuzzy, big sister feeling.

CHAPTER FIVE:

"I'll tell you someday, when the time is right."

Marley and I don't have classes on this particular day but we do have the same lunch period. The large, dark grey cafeteria was bustling with hungry students waiting in line. So much chatter was swirling around me, sometimes I found it hard to hear myself think. My stomach began to growl more as I had become submerged in the scent of French fries, chicken sandwiches and the freshly baked chocolate chip cookies from the sweets section. Unfortunately, I was standing behind Bryce Oliver, who was infamous for his terrible body smell. He smelled like he bathed in a tub boiling with sweat and old garlic. Funny part is, the moron actually thinks we call him "B.O." for his initials. However, even after enduring the torment of standing behind B.O., getting my food and settling down at one of the long, grey tables, there was still no sign of her. I was thinking that she may have gone off campus for lunch without me. Then again, Marley has no way to leave school without using the bus or me. Of course, she could get Ophelia to pick her up, but Ophelia would probably chew her ear off, so she'd rather use her mother as a last resort for a ride home. Normally, you need to get special permission to leave campus during lunch period, but we seniors find a way around everything. After all, the senior class is always the most favored out of everyone in the school, so we pretty much do what we want. Nate came to keep me company, which absolutely made my day. He's actually nice to be around when he isn't acting like a complete horn-dog. Unfortunately, Callista also has this lunch, and she kept glancing over at us the entire time. But, I hardly even cared. Nate and I were so preoccupied with joking around that we didn't even notice Marley rush up to the table before she sat down with her blue lunch tray.

"Heeeey, what's up, Marzo? Lookin' a little rough there, eh?" Nate pointed out as he quickly grabbed for Marley's fries and shoved them into his greedy mouth.

Marley took her glasses from off her face and began to clean the lenses with the edge of her shirt. "You could've just ASKED for some French fries, Nathaniel."

He continued to munch on the stolen fries. "Yeah, I could've," He replied with his mouth nearly full. Whatever salt remained, he sloppily licked off his fingertips.

Yes, he can be a prick sometimes, but he's mine. I looked over at Marley. Not to be mean, but Nate wasn't really lying about Marley looking rough today. Her shirt looked as if it had been pulled and tugged on, not to mention it was also inside out, her hair was a big, brown mess, and a small amount of glittery lip gloss was speared across her right cheek, which was weird because Marley doesn't like glitter lip-gloss. She says it's "too much" for her. I'm pretty sure her bra was on a little wrong because she did look lopsided, if you know what I mean. Well, Marley's super flat-chested so she could get away with not wearing a bra as long as it wasn't cold.

"Marley, are you ok?" I asked as I reached across the table and removed the smeared lip gloss from her cheek with a napkin.

"Uh, yeah. Why do you ask?" She answered as she began to fix her frizzled hair and bra.

"I'm just worried about you," I replied softly. She looked as if she had been mugged in an alley or something.

After Nate finished off the handful of fries he'd taken from Marley's tray, he whispered in my ear that some of his football buddies were waiting on him outside of the cafeteria. He kissed me goodbye, which probably wasn't his best idea since he still had traces of salt on his lips. As I watched him leisurely stroll towards the cafeteria's exit, I noticed he took the time to playfully slap Callista on her right shoulder. She returned the favor by slapping him on his derriere gently. They smiled at each other as they made eye contact. Callista began to smile and blush more and smoothed her blonde hair behind one of her ears, exposing the three piercings she had on each ear. After making her smile, he continued on his walk to the cafeteria's exit. I swear if she wasn't pregnant, I'd…I'd…oh, who am I kidding? Callista grew up with 4 older brothers, she'd take me without breaking a sweat. I know I can't attack her, so instead, I just remain in my seat and let my anger stew inside me. Marley took time away from fixing her hair and clothes to notice what was happening with my emotions. However, before she could make a comment on it, Lauralee rushed up to our table and took a seat to the left of Marley.

"Geez Louise, Minnie. What's the matter with you?" Lauralee questioned.

Hell, I should be asking her the same question. She seemed awfully giddy for someone who got thrashed into a mirror less than 24 hours ago. However, something was off about her as well. Usually, Lauralee dresses as if she's in the running to become Miss North Carolina or something. Today, the only make up she had on was the concealer she was using to cover up her black eye, there was not even a trace of lip gloss on her. I know how much Lauralee adores her long hair so it was odd that it looked as if it had been hardly brushed today. She was wearing a faded, denim skirt with a turquoise blouse that was slightly wrinkled with half of the buttons undone. To top off her fashion statement, she was wearing a pair of slightly worn out silver flip flops. Something was definitely off about these two.

"Sooo, umm, Lauralee," I started. She directed her attention from her Smartphone to me upon hearing her name, "How was your morning?" I figured I'd start off with an easy question and slowly work my way into what was really going on.

Her big, hazel eyes lit up. "My morning was fantabulous!" She happily sung out. Judging by her clothes and oddly happy mood, I was beginning to think Lauralee started off her morning with great sex. The suspense was killing me; I had to know.

"How was yooour morning, Rosemarley?" Lauralee inquired.

Marley stared at Lauralee with such a shock as if she was surprised that Lauralee was even talking to her. I can't blame her. "Umm, it was fine, I guess."

I decided to just come right out and ask. I couldn't take this anymore. "Lauralee Marie Giovanni, did you have sex this morning?"

My question must've really caught her off guard because the smile completely vanished off her face and her eyes bulged out. "Umm, why do ya ask?" She even sounded guilty. She's such an awful liar. She's lucky she has her parents wrapped around her finger or else she'd get away with nothing.

I raised my right eyebrow at her. "Curiosity." For a second she just looked at me before unleashing a smile so wide, her dimples showed.

"I guess the cat's out of the bag now."

Marley showed apathy towards Lauralee's news, but I let out a loud, happy squeal. Amused, curious, and annoyed students glanced over at our table. Lauralee and I didn't mind the attention, but Marley buried her head in her arms on the table out of embarrassment.

"Oh, my God! Who was it!?" I squealed, squeezing her delicate hands in anticipation.

Unfortunately, the bell rang, signifying the end of our lunch period. Darn, just when lunch was starting to get good. The cafeteria filled with sounds of students laughing, talking and the clashing of their lunch trays. Marley, who hated being late for anything, picked up her neon green backpack and said goodbye to us before walking off towards her next class. Lauralee and I remained seated.

"Well, the janitors will be cursing us out soon if we don't move. Are you gonna tell me or not, Lee?" I eagerly inquired.

"I'll tell you someday, when the time is right." Lauralee calmly answered. With that, we both grabbed our belongings and hurried to our next class.

CHAPTER SIX:
"Who is Violet Jacobs?"

After school, Nate and Callista's sickeningly flirtatious behavior was still tormenting my thoughts. I was tired of feeling disrespected and tired of worrying so I decided to take charge of my relationship and end this behavior once and for all. I whipped my iPhone out of my back pocket and quickly dialed Nate's number. Lucky for me, he answered on the fourth ring.

"Hello?"

"Hey, Nate. It's me," I replied, as if he didn't have caller I.D. on his cellphone.

"Oh, hey. What's up?"

"Nothing. Hey, I wanted to talk to you. Could you come to my house for a minute?" He was probably anxious now, thinking he was in trouble. He paused for a few seconds or two before answering, "Uh, sure, Minnie. I'll be there in-"

Before he could finish his sentence, I heard the voice of a woman shout out, "How about Violet? Violet Jacobs has a nice ring to it, Nathaniel."

"Mom, I'm on the phone with Minnie!" Nate shouted with annoyance in his voice.

I took a deep sigh of relief. I was just glad it wasn't the voice of Callista. After a few seconds, he came back and replied, "Yeah, I'll be there in ten." Then, he hung up the phone. I freshened up a bit and made sure I wore the Victoria's Secret perfume and the jeans that Nate absolutely loves on me. I decided to talk with Nate outside on our porch because with four nosey siblings, privacy comes rare. On my way out, my Mom warned me that dinner would be ready in about fifteen minutes. Not many people were outside this evening, so Nate and I would finally get the chance to have a private and intimate conversation, something we hadn't done in a while. I closed my eyes for a few seconds to enjoy the soft breeze that passed by every now and again. Nothing is more calming than a gentle breeze grazing across your skin, tickling each tiny hair as it passes by.

"You're really enjoying that wind, aren't you?" A voice commented.

I reopened my eyes and turned my head slightly to my left to see that it was Nate. He was dressed in blue jeans with a red, Polo shirt and red and black Nike's. Thank God red is his favorite color because he always looks so damn delicious whenever he wears it.

"Yeah, it feels good." Another breeze floated by, teasing Nate's hair.

"Hmm, lots of other things feel much better than the wind, Minnie," He suggestively hinted as he walked up to me and locked his Dodge Challenger with the push of a button. I wrapped my arms around his neck and he wrapped his around my waist as we embraced in a long, warm kiss…with tongue. He pulled away from the kiss first, which is something he never does.

"You really shouldn't tease me like this, Minnie," He whispered into my left ear. "I'm tired of my left hand being my best friend, you know."

I had more important matters on my mind than Nate's high libido so I pulled my body completely away from his and uttered the four words every human hates hearing, "We need to talk."

He placed his hands in his pockets and exhaled deeply, already preparing for an unfriendly conversation. "Is this about Marzo's fries? I was just joking around, ok? Next time, I'll ask."

I carefully examined his facial expression to be sure he wasn't being sarcastic or humorous. When I realized he was dead serious, I couldn't believe it. Was he stupid enough to think that I would have taken the time to summon him over here to talk about some damn fries?

"No, Nate. This isn't about Marley's fries. It's about Callista Arden." He sighed deeply with annoyance. "What about her?"

I smoothed my hair behind my ear. "The two of you are a little too close for my standards. You guys are constantly flirting and what not. Like today when we were at lunch-"

Nate cut me off by giving himself a face palm and accompanying it with a loud groan. I guess he didn't want to be bothered with talk of Callista Arden. "It was just a little nudge on the shoulder and a slight slap on the cush! Geez, you're acting like she got on her knees in front of everyone and started suck-"

I rushed up to him with my eyes glaring at him and my right index finger pointed inches from his face. I was trying my best to not get all emotional and irrational on him, but I was NOT about to lose my boyfriend to a jealous, ex-best friend of mine. "That's not the point, Nathaniel! The point is you are flirting with a girl who you know is out to get me and doing it right in front of my face! You're making me look stupid and humiliated and it seems as if you don't even give a damn! I'm starting to wonder if the two of you have a little "thing" going on…"

Instead of the apologetic, comforting response I was hoping to receive, I got the exact opposite. Nate angrily swiped my finger out of his face and kept a tight grip on my wrist. I knew he wouldn't hit me. Nate grew up watching his grandfather abuse his grandmother, his uncle, and his mother. He'd never stoop to his grandfather's level, and he swore his life to it.

"Look, I'm getting sick of this. First, you deny me the sex that I deserve. Then, you accuse me of having some kind of affair with your best friend. Listen to this, Artemis Wilhelmina Carlisle, and you listen good; I am NOT in love with Callista Arden!" He seethed, staring me dead in the eyes.

I snatched my arm swiftly, causing him to release his grip. I could feel my eyes slowly watering. Great, now the waterworks would start kicking in. "You just told on yourself, Nathaniel! Never did I say or hint you were in LOVE with Callista. So, are you? Are you in love with her?" I sobbed. I didn't know if I felt more angry or sad. I felt like screaming, but I was afraid that if I started, I wouldn't stop until I was hauled away to a mental facility.

He placed his hands back into his pockets and lowered his head. Because of his hat, I could hardly see his face. "You're being a childish bitch, Minnie." He stated after a few moments of silence.

I didn't even know how to respond to that so I said nothing. I simply stood there with tears rolling down my cheeks and my hair blowing across my face as another breeze crept by us. Nate continued to be silent and avoid eye contact with me as he slowly pulled his phone out of his pocket and began to text.

"Who are you texting?" I quietly asked as I wiped tears my face.

"Keegan," He quickly answered, referring to the running back of the Angel City Bulldogs and his best friend since 7th grade.

I knew I'd be walking on thin ice if I asked anymore questions about Callista so I decided to ask another question that was prompted by what Mrs. Jacobs said earlier.

"Who is Violet Jacobs?"

His thumbs abruptly stopped typing and he quickly lifts his head up to look me in my eyes. "What?"

Nate being thrown so off guard by my question triggered an alarm in my head. I stepped a little closer to him. "Violet. Your mother mentioned someone by that name earlier."

"…She's no one of importance to you," He coldly responded as he finally put his phone away.

His secrecy over whomever this Violet person was made me just want to dig deeper. Since they shared the same last name, I assumed they were relatives and not yet another girl he was flirting with who just so happened to have the same last name as him.

"Is she a relative?"

"Yeeeees."

Yes! That made one less girl to worry about and one less behind to kick. Now that I was feeling more confident, I continued to dig.
"Mmmmhmm. Have I met her?"

He let out a small laugh. "Ha! No, not yet."

"A distant cousin, perhaps?"

Nate rolled his baby blue eyes. He walked up to me, tucked my hair behind my ears, and kissed me on my forehead, causing me to smile.

"I gotta go, Babe."

As he began to walk back towards his car, I yelled, "Wait! Where are you going?" He didn't even turn around to face me when he answered. He just stopped and replied, "I have a bet to win."

I was now very confused, but I was not in the mood for more questions and more arguments. It was probably just some idiotic, manly thing he and Keegan were up to. The only thing I wanted to do now was go inside and eat dinner with my family and maybe talk to Cassidy or Marley later. Oooh, maybe I'd call Lauralee and badger her until she tells me who she lost her virginity to.

"Don't do anything stupid!" I called after him.

He didn't reply. He just hopped in that lustrous, garnet car, made a U-turn, and sped off towards the sunset. God, please don't let him do anything stupid.

CHAPTER SEVEN

"They were hitting me where it hurts most—my heart."

The next day, Lauralee decided to do something nice and volunteer to drive Marley and me to school. Cassidy, who had a dentist appointment later that day and was fortunate enough to be able to stay home from school, called me early that morning. I never mind when he calls me. It's nice to chat with a sane and normal person every once in a while. As I waited on Lauralee to arrive in her customized, cotton-candy pink Hummer H3. By the way, I've always found it odd that someone as feminine as Lauralee chooses a Hummer instead of a Ferrari or some other fancy, luxurious sports car. Anyway, I let Cassidy know about everything that happened yesterday, and let's just say he damn near exploded through the phone when I told him about Nate grabbing my wrist. I let Cassidy know about everything. I told him about how Callista was pushing all of my buttons and was doing jumping jacks on my very last nerve. I told him about Nate's borderline-unfaithful, flirtatious behavior and all the secrets he seemed to be keeping from me.

"Damn, Minnie. Well, if he's being such a jackass, why not just dump him? See? I told you he was a douche," Cassidy reasoned.

"Is that how you really feel or do you just want me to kick his balls?" I responded as I hopped into the cream colored leather seat of Lauralee's car. The color of the seats matched with her steering wheel cover and the cream and magenta colored floor mats she had placed on the black floor of her car.

"I want you to kick his balls, dump him, then kick him again, but when you do it the second time, draw for blood," Cassidy happily replied. He and Nate have never really liked each other. Every time Cassidy came to visit, they'd argue all the time. I remember the really heated argument they had once over a simple baseball game when we were younger. So, it's not surprising that Cassie wants to see Nate suffer one good time. Can you imagine how pissed Cassidy was when he found out Nate asked me to be his girlfriend? I clip my phone into the phone stand on Lauralee's pink and black dashboard and switched it over to speakerphone so that I can finish my hair and makeup on the way to school.

"Whoa, whose balls is getting kicked?" Lauralee pipes in as she turns down the music playing from her state-of-the-art, surround sound system. I'm beginning to think there is a thing as too spoiled.

"Who was that?" Cassidy asks, answering Lauralee's question with another question.

"Lauralee Marie Giovanni, the one and ooonly! Hiya, Cassidy!" Lauralee happily sings. She's disgustingly perky in the mornings. Ever since her Mom got pregnant, I think she's been raiding her coffee stash since she's avoiding caffeine during her pregnancy.

Cassidy laughs. "Hey, Lauralee. You know, sometimes I wonder how YOU ended up being friends with the Governor's daughter." Lauralee and Cassidy laugh. I smile as I reply, "You're such an ass, Cassidy Paris."

Lauralee and I finally pull up in front of the Aprilson's home and she loudly honks her car horn, causing a dog to bark in the nearby area. I wrap up my conversation with Cassidy and hang up the phone. As we are waiting for Marley to come out and join us, Lauralee decides to open her big mouth yet again and comment, "I truly don't know whyyy you just don't get it on with Cassidy. Shoot, I'd love to have a crack at him. He's a nice catch and good looking to boot."

Her saying that reminded me of how many times Marley has said similar things to me. "We are just friends. Besides, I have Nate."

Lauralee sprayed on some Hawaiian Ginger perfume as she replied, "You know, I may not be good at math or science-y stuff, but I AM smart enough to tell when someone is being shamefully cheated on."

Ugh, must she constantly give her two cents on EVERYONE'S situation? I know she thinks she's just stating the truth or sharing some friendly advice, but she doesn't realize that it sometimes comes off as offensive. This explains why she doesn't understand why some people do not particularly like her.

"First of all, I'm NOT being "shamelessly" cheated on and-"

"Umm, I said shamefully, not shamelessly," Lauralee corrected.

"I don't care! That's not the point, Laura! The point is that I'm not being cheated on at all! Nate loves ME, ok? Oh, and how in the blue hell can you analyze MY relationship when you don't even have a man!?" I scolded. It's always your single friends who swear they know everything about relationships, including yours. The day I see Lauralee going on a date is the day I'll start taking relationship advice from her.

Ok, so I know I was a little harsh on her. I really didn't mean to get that way. It's just that this whole Nate and Callista thing was really driving me up a wall. They were hitting me where it hurt most, my heart. I could tell I hurt her feelings a little, just by the look in her eyes. I do consider Lauralee a friend, but sometimes she just irritates me like a younger sister who you know admires you, but still aggravates you to no end. I guess after a certain period of time, friends naturally begin to irk each other without meaning to.

"I'm sorry, Lauralee. I didn't mean-" I started.

She put her right index finger up to my face, indicating that she wanted me to stop talking. She glared at me and calmly, but angrily commented, "Maybe I'm not looking for a man, Artemis. Did you ever think of that?"

I hadn't actually, but I wasn't going to tell her that. I already felt like an insensitive jerk. She put her hand back on the steering wheel. "Now if you don't mind, I'd like to wait here quietly until Rosemar-"

For some reason, she stopped in mid-sentence and just started staring at something behind me with her eyes wide open and her jaw in her lap.

"What? What is it?" I asked as I turned around in my seat to look for myself.

And there she was, the new and damn sure improved, Marley Aprilson. Her normally frizzled hair had been perfectly straightened. It looked as if strands of chocolate silk were growing out of her scalp. Every ounce of makeup on her had been applied with great precision, from her glittery eye shadow to the fuchsia colored lip gloss shimmering on her lips. Her slender, six foot tall body had been decorated with a low-cut, jet black dress that was juuuust long enough to not get her detention for violating dress code; which was good because Marley had legs for days. Her feet were strutting in a pair of shiny, ruby heels that matched the color of the fashion belt on her dress. Now, my jaw was on the floor along with Lauralee's. Marley's normal appearance was very average and plain, but today she looked like a runway model. I noticed that Ophelia had a video camera in her hand while she was standing in the doorway watching Marley walk towards us. It was one of the few times I ever saw Marley and her mother getting along.

"Bye, honey! Have a good day at school! You look gorgeous!" Ophelia happily called as she got one last shot of Marley before ducking back inside the house.

Marley apparently wasn't all that moved by her mother's compliments. "Yeah, yeah. The only time the bitch cares is when I look the way she wants me to," Marley grumbled as she entered the car and fastened her seatbelt. Judging by the fragrance that filled the car upon her entrance, she had on the new Victoria's Secret perfume called "Secret Vixen."

"Whooo! Babe alert! What or WHO has gotten into you this morning, Rosemarley?" Lauralee playfully blurted out as she pulled off and began to drive.

Marley didn't answer. She just looked into a compact mirror she had in her snakeskin black and gold purse, which was replacing her dingy book bag today, and began to apply one last coat of her berry-scented lip gloss.

"Marley?" Lauralee called, glancing back at her for a second through the rearview mirror.

Marley stopped applying her lip gloss and whispered to herself, "Oh, right. You're talking to me."

I let out a laugh. "Well, yeah. You're the only one in this car with that name, silly."

Why was Marley acting as if she didn't recognize her own name when she heard it? Something was going on with her, and it astounded me that even I, her best friend, couldn't figure out what it was.

CHAPTER EIGHT

"You're no friend of mine."

Marley's sudden change in fashion caused the jaws of males and even females to drop onto the floor. Being the sudden center of attention for once obviously appeased Marley, as she was strutting and smiling all day long. Wasn't this the same girl who put her head down in embarrassment just because of a simple squeal I let out? Nonetheless, I was happy that Marley was finally feeling confident and looking gorgeous while feeling that way, but I barely recognized her now. The only traces of Marley that remained were her bright, pink braces, since she had left her glasses at home. She looked good, but she is terribly near sighted and need me to tell her what the questions said on the board during class. I guess Marley is letting her notes take a backseat today. At lunch, boys were so preoccupied with violating Marley with their eyes that they almost forgot to eat. Even Callista, being pregnant and greedy, was too shocked to eat her meal. Her jaw dropped and her eyes followed Marley until Lauralee, Marley, and I found a table to sit down at. Even Nate and Keegan Hunter were surprised when they came to our table to visit me.

"Hey, Minnie. Hey, Lauralee. Hey, Mar-" Nate would've finished his sentence, but he became mesmerized by Marley's new supermodel alter ego.

"Hi, Nate," She greeted in a sultry voice much different from her normal, humble tone.

"Uhhh, wow. You look...different today, Marzo. Not a bad different, a good different. Not that you don't normally look okay. I mean, this is certainly an improvement but-" Nate said, in a poor attempt to give Marley a compliment.

"You look really, really beautiful, Marley," Keegan interrupted, smiling charmingly at Marley. Ooooh, has someone been struck with Cupid's arrow?

Like Lauralee and I, Nate had this puzzled expression on his face as if he was trying to figure out why Marley was dressed like that in the first place. I mean, I didn't even think she could look that pretty....Man! Am I a bad person for thinking that? I guess Callista and her group were in a bitchy/troublemaking mood because out of the corner of my eye, I saw the three of them casually stroll up to our table. I'm really not in the mood for this today. Her normal crew consisted of the conceited-for-nothing slut, Rebecca Hardwick and the future criminal Jessica Ward, but since Rebbie had a doctor's appointment (probably to check for more sexually transmitted diseases) and Jess had another court date (some employee made her mad at McDonald's so she decided to trash the place), Callista was just hanging out with Sybil "The Wannabe" Florentine and Lauralee's sophomore cousin, Stephanie Giovanni, for today. Lauralee worries that Callista will be a bad influence on her cousin, since Steph's at that age where they are so obsessed with being "bad." However, Steph doesn't heed Lauralee's warning because she thinks Lauralee is, and I quote, a "lame goody-goody." Once they reached our table, she slammed both of her hands on our table, startling all of us a bit except for Marley. You'd think with her being a teen and pregnant, she wouldn't be spending money on Evanescence and Linkin Park merchandise and getting her nose pierced. Her brother, Michael, always said that Callista was bad at managing money. I know Callista won't be a bad mother, but if she doesn't grow up in the next month or so, she'll surely be a broke one.

"What's happenin', Nate?" Callista greeted sweetly as she smiled and batted her eyelashes quickly at him.

"Hey, Callista," Nate replied after taking a sip of his Dr. Pepper.

Her expression changed from flirtatiousness to mischievous once she focused her attention back on the rest of us. Actually, Callista's attention seemed to mostly be focused on Marley, probably because of her change in wardrobe. Sybil Florentine's leaf green eyes were focused on me. Her fake eyelashes, makeup, hair extensions, tan, push-up bra, fake nails, and face caked with makeup, along with her size is why I gave her the nickname "The Big-Boned Barbie." I'm surprised Piggy even hangs out with Callista considering what happened between the two of them back in eighth grade. She's probably just desperate to gain some popularity around here. She reeks of desperation and cheap, old lady perfume.

"You're hot stuff today, Marley," Callista complimented. She's never that nice to me anymore. "Do me a favor though, and take off all the makeup. Minnie's the one who needs it, not naturally pretty chicks like us."

No response from Marley. I don't know if she was simply ignoring Callista or forgetting her name again.

"Umm, HELLO!? Marley Aprilson, I know you heard her talking to you!" Stephanie scolded, now sitting on the edge of the table.

"Yeah, I know you're not deaf AND ugly," Sybil added.

"Watch your mouth, Florentine," Callista commanded sternly, defending Marley.

"You reeeally wanna talk about LOOKS, Piggy?" I snapped at her. Seeing that she had no possible way to win an argument against the two of us, she shut up like a good girl and looked down at the table, nibbling on her acrylic, white nails.

As I finished putting Sybil in her place, Callista made an attempt to fiddle with some of Marley's hair. Marley countered her attempt by quickly and firmly grabbing Callista's right wrist and twisting it. Callista winced and shrieked in pain and stood up in an attempt to escape from Marley's grasp, but all Marley did was stand up with her to ensure she wouldn't escape that easily. Marley's behavior was becoming odder by the minute. We all stood up and rushed to defuse the situation before Marley ended up breaking the wrist of a pregnant woman.

"Whoa! Marzo, relax! She's pregnant!" Nate shouted as he rushed to grab Callista. He almost slipped on the tile floor, desperately trying to reach her.

As Lauralee rushed to restrain Steph from jumping in and attacking Marley, Keegan and I grabbed onto Marley to try and pull her off of Callista.

"Let go of me, Marley!" Callista screamed as she made futile attempts to escape. "I wasn't gonna hurt you! I'm your friend, remember?"

"As long as he wants you, you're no friend of mine," Marley growled in a low, sinister voice. If I wasn't so close to her, I probably wouldn't have even heard it.

I've never seen Marley like this and honestly, it struck a touch of fear in my heart. Just when I thought Marley was surely going to snap Callista's wrist in two, something changed. Marley no longer seemed enraged, now she looked as if she had returned back to her normal self. Marley quickly released her grip of Callista's wrist and began to back away slowly, looking as if she was appalled with what she had done. Once Marley let go of Callista, we let go of Marley. Lauralee released Steph, and Nate let go of Callista, but still remained by her side. She began to rub her wrist to soothe some of the pain.

"Are you ok, Calli?" Steph and Nate asked simultaneously.

Callista quickly turned to face Steph. "Am I ok!? Stephanie, you idiot, look at my wrist! Does that big, red mark indicate that it's ok!?"

Steph looked confused. "Why are you yelling at HER? She's not the one who was trying to make a pretzel out of your wrist!" Lauralee defended.

"I haven't done anything to you, Callista," Steph timidly responded.

Callista stepped closer to Stephanie and yelled, "That's right! You didn't do a god dammed thing! You couldn't even pull your weak cousin off of you to help me! Steph, you're useless!"

As soon as she yelled the word "useless," she struck Stephanie across the left side of her face with her right hand. The blow was loud like thunder and echoed throughout the room since everyone was now quiet with their eyes on us. I heard a lot of people gasp though and one boy even muttered obscenities. I know Callista was angry and humiliated and just decided to unleash her fury on Stephanie, since she'd never do anything to her precious, I mean, MY precious Nate. Instead of retaliating and brawling it out with Callista like I thought she would, she did nothing. She held the left side of her face and she stared Callista deep in her eyes as they began to fill up with tears. Steph must've felt an unbearable amount of embarrassment and betrayal. It seems as if Calli can't help but to ruin friendships. Stephanie began to sprint far away from everyone who had their eyes on her long, mocha brown hair flowing wildly with every stride.

"Stephanie!" Lauralee called after her cousin, but Stephanie didn't even look back. Lauralee turned to Callista and growled, "You're so asinine. Let's see how you like it."

She returned the favor by slapping Callista hard across the right side of her face then running towards the exit to catch up to her upset cousin. I glanced around and Marley had disappeared as well. Since we didn't have last period together, I wouldn't see her or either of the Giovanni's until afterschool or maybe the next day. Knowing how much Angel City loves drama, this lunch period is surely going to be talked about for a while.

CHAPTER NINE

"A frantic 9-1-1 call is made from Angel City High School for a female student who is unresponsive after falling down a flight of stairs."

2:45 p.m.

I'm sitting in my Anatomy and Physiology class hoping and praying that time will somehow go by a little faster. I've never seen a clock tick-tock so damn slow. Just when I thought I was surely about to die of boredom, I receive a text from Keegan: "Hey, Minnie. I got sumthings 2 tell u. Meet me in hallway, K?"

I was baffled as to why Nate's best friend wanted to talk with me privately in a hallway, but as bored as I was in Ms. Delmore's class, I was ecstatic to finally have something interesting to do. I politely asked Ms. Delmore to use the restroom. After she gave her consent, I quickly exited the classroom.

2:47 p.m.

After searching for him, I find the hallway Keegan is waiting in. He doesn't look like his normal, charming, playful self. Instead, he looked as if something was weighing heavily on his mind at that moment.

"Keegan? What's the matter? You said you have some things to tell me."

He took a few glances around, as if he was making sure no one was lurking or eavesdropping nearby. When the coast was clear, he removed his hood. He fixed his reddish brown hair that hung just above those radiant, green eyes. I can really see why the girls in this school gave him the nickname of "The Irish Temptation." I know he's Nate's best friend, but he's sure made my body temperature rise a few times.

"Look, Minnie. I shouldn't even be telling you this. I am Nate's BEST friend, after all. However…you're a good girl, Minnie and my guilt, no, my conscience is telling me to do what's right." He mysteriously stated.

Before I could ask him what the hell he was talking about, he poured his heart out to me about everything. He told me about how Nate and Callista have been having a secret affair since the very beginning of our relationship. He told me how Nate would say that he only wanted me so that he could brag about he was the one to take my virginity, like my body was nothing more than some sort of challenge to be conquered, or a cheap trophy to be strutted around and showed off. Keegan told me that he didn't want that to happen because he knew it would ruin my reputation; and I knew girls around here are just dying for Minnie Carlisle to slip up. Lastly, he informed me about how Nate was never going to stop seeing Callista, as a matter of fact, they went on a date just a few days ago. After he was finished speaking, he took a step back and just stared at me with eyes full of sympathy.

"Are you….alright, Minnie?" He inquired softly.

Of course I wasn't alright. He had just confirmed my biggest nightmare. I was showing nothing on the outside, but inside, my heart was tearing apart piece by piece. My whole world came crashing down and I was too overwhelmed with shock and sorrow to move or speak at that particular moment. When Keegan attempted to reach out to hug and comfort me, I ran. I sprinted into the nearest ladies restroom, ran to the farthest stall, and broke down crying. I didn't care who heard me or saw me. I didn't care about much of anything at that moment; I just wanted a little privacy.

2:52 p.m.

I had enough of crying and feeling sorry for myself. I was not about to sit in this under-cleaned bathroom stall around these dirty walls and just play the victim. I was going to confront the "friend" that ruined my relationship. I wiped away my tears with my hand and whipped out my cell phone to text Callista. Believe me, I've deleted her number many times out of frustration, but I know her digits by heart. I can delete her from my phone, but not from my memory. I sent her a simple text; no need for explaining or yelling. I'd save THAT for later. "Meet me on the 3rd floor of the tech. bldg. Look, don't ask questions. Just do it." Then, I quickly pressed the send button. I slowly exited the stall and luckily, no one was in the bathroom at the moment to witness my moment of shame. I quickly fixed my hair, which had become a total a disaster from all the sprinting I had done, and began my walk across campus to the technology building. On my way there, I texted Marley and filled her in on what was happening with Nate and that I was on my way to confront Callista at that very moment. However, I was so concentrated on meeting Callista that I didn't even respond to the text she sent me as I entered the building and made my way up towards the third floor.

2:54 p.m.

After a minute or so of waiting, I finally heard some slow, somewhat quiet footsteps headed up towards my floor. I was actually relieved to see that it was Callista and not some bitter, underpaid teacher just waiting to give me a detention for even looking suspicious.

"You just love to see a chick suffer, don't you, Artemis?" Callista harshly blurted out as she began to catch her breath after reaching the top step. Walking up these stairs near the end of her pregnancy seemed to be absorbing every ounce of energy out of her.

"I know."

She jerked her head up and stared at me with a mixture of confusion and aggravation. She stood straight up and rubbed her temples with her index and middle fingers, as if I was causing her to get a migraine. Hell, she had been the cause of many migraines I've had over the years. "What the HELL are you blabbering about?" She blurted out again; even more agitated than the first time.

With my fists clenched, my arms crossed and my eyes darted straight into hers, I stepped closer to her and seethed, "I know. I know all about your little, slutty affair with Nate. I know that you've been sleeping around with MY boyfriend."

She paused and just stared at me with this blank expression on her face. Then, she closed her eyes, ran her fingers through her hair, and sighed deeply. She actually looked guilt-ridden. "Look, we didn't mean for you to find out this way. I never really wanted to hurt you. I-I didn't mean for this to go this far. I wasn't thinking things all the way through."

I didn't know if I wanted to punch her in the face or breakdown into tears. "How could you!? You were supposed to be my best friend…my sister."

"Someone killed that a while ago, Minnie. Babe, just let me explain-"

Without hesitation and without thinking, I quickly rushed up on her. Thank God she didn't instinctively take a step backwards because she was standing directly on the top step.

"What is this about, Callista!? Hmm? I've done NOTHING to you, except be like a sister to you since we were kids! How could you!?"

Her remorseful expression vanished and was replaced with shock. She looked at me as if I shouldn't even have the audacity to even ask that question. "How could I? Minnie, how could YOU!? You made Marley and me feel like straight garbage compared to you! Always bragging, always showboating, and always making other people feel low so you can feel above everybody else. If you were our so called "sister", you wouldn't have flaunted your looks and popularity in our faces constantly! You neeever take responsibility for the stuff you pull! Never!"

With my index finder pointed inches from her face, I growled, "I did NOT flaunt anything. If the two of you had low self-esteem, that was NOT my fault! We all have insecurities, Calli, but that is a lame excuse to stab your best friends in the back!"

I expected her to respond with anything that gave me further insight as to why our friendship fell apart or why she changed for the worst. Instead, she violently swatted my finger away as if it were a mosquito that had gotten on her nerve for the last time.

"Get your dirty finger out of my face. I just might fight you pregnant, Minnie, don't think that I won't." Callista always was quick to fight because she loved the adrenaline rush. I guess that's a side effect of growing up the youngest child and the only daughter out of five. Her rebellious attitude and quick temper used to get her into a lot of trouble in middle school. I see why Jess Ward and her are such good friends now.

I stepped backwards, shaking my head. "I'll never get through to you. I'm beginning to grow tired of talking to you."

As she began to quickly place her hair into a ponytail, she quickly responded, "So stop all the chit-chat and let your fists do the talking. That's obviously the only way I'm gonna get through to you. We're going to settle this one way or another."

For the next few minutes, I tried to be rational and talk things out with her, but she was just itching to fight me right there in that stairwell. After she had removed all of her jewelry and had kicked off the yellow and black Jordans she was wearing, I realized it was no use.

2:59 pm.

"Oh, come on, A.C. Don't tell me you're one of those cowardly, big mouth-having girls who can't back up what they say with their fists," Callista taunted.

I sighed deeply. "I'm NOT going to fight you, ok? It's pointless and besides, you're like 9 months pregnant. You look like you're about to pop."

She laughed. "Ha! Don't let my pregnancy fool you. This mama's a fighter. I can still beat your stinkin' ass. It'll be the fight of the year."

The last remaining item on her was her glittery, canary yellow cell phone which was sitting comfortably in her back pocket. She pulled it out and placed it gently on the ground along with the rest of her belongings. Once she was finished, she tied her maternity pants tighter with the drawstring and took two steps down.

"Come on, Minnie. Let's settle this once and for all. I'm sure lots of your "adoring fans" would love to see how this match would turn out." She sneered as a devious grin slithered across her pouty lips. She had her right arms extended with her hand open and pointed directly out towards the rest of the stairwell, as if she was inviting me to come down and join her there.

3:01 p.m.

The more she insisted on brawling with me, the more obvious it became to me that things between us weren't going to change. Maybe the damage was irreversible. I only met with Callista to confront her about what she had done and to perhaps call a truce with her, not to bash her brains out. I decided it was time to end this conversation and return to Ms. Delmore's class. I'd probably receive a nice, hot detention for staying out of class for so long.

"I'm not going to fight you. After all you've done, I still love you too much to ever lay a finger on you. I came here to make peace with you, but it's painfully obvious all you want to do is settle things the wrong way. As much as I still care for you, you've changed and I can't deny it any longer. Nate apparently meant more to you than me so you can have him. I guess it's time for you to go your way and I go mine. Goodbye, Callista.

3:04 p.m.

After we stared deeply into each other's eyes for a few quick, silent moments, I slowly turned around to take the long way back to class. Once I had begun to walk down the hallway, I heard Callista call out, "Moon Eyes, wait! Just let me explain!" Her voice was shaky and riddled with emotion, which was not like her at all.

It stunned me to hear Callista call me by the nickname she gave me years ago because of my big, grey eyes. However, what I heard next did much more than stun me. It made my heart drop and sent chills creeping carefully up my spine. I heard Callista scream for dear life at the top of her lungs, which was followed by a bunch of loud, odd noises. By the time teachers and students had poured out of their classrooms and into the hallway, I had already sprinted my way back to the top of the stairwell. What I saw will haunt my memories forever. I saw Callista laying still on her side at the bottom of the stairwell. Her hair was covering her face and her arms and legs were positioned motionless on the floor. She wasn't responding; and she wasn't moving. Then, I heard another odd set of noises, like a clicky-clacky sound that began to quickly fade off into the distance, but I was too preoccupied with Callista to really pay any more attention to it. I hurried down to tend to Callista. I got down on the ground and placed her head in my lap.

"I'm sorry! I didn't mean it! I don't really wanna say goodbye! Please, wake up. You're my Calli Doll, you can't just leave me like this! No! Wake up, Callista! Say something! Say anything…" I hysterically cried, my tears falling onto the ground and into her hair.

3:06 p.m.

A frantic 9-1-1 call is made from Angel City High School for a female student who is unresponsive after falling down a flight of stairs.

CHAPTER TEN

"Suddenly, the silence around us was shattered by a high-pitched scream followed by sounds of sobbing."

Despite all of the skeptical glances being constantly shot my way combined with the rumors and chaos circulating around me, the only thing on my mind was getting to the hospital as soon as possible. Once word had reached Apollo's ears, he scurried to me and we quickly headed for his car. While we were speeding our way to North Memorial Hospital, Apollo was trying his best to get me to open up and tell him what really happened, but I just couldn't talk about it right now. I guess it was shock. Although I was anxious to see Callista, the receptionist at the front desk informed us that we had to wait in the Waiting Room until the doctors come and inform us of her condition. However, we were not alone while in the waiting room. We were joined by Callista's older brothers--Michael, Raphael, Gabriel, and Uriel Arden. They didn't speak to us and we certainly returned the favor. I was in no mood for small talk anyway. Apollo was nice enough to let me lean on his shoulder for comfort.

"You don't think I did it, do you? I-I'm not a killer, Apollo. I'd never hurt her." I sniffled.

"I know you're not. It'll be ok, sis. Big Brother Apollo will take care of you," He whispered to me softly. Apollo always has been very protective over the four of us. Although I'm only like a year younger than him, he still looks at me like I'm the same little girl he used to push on the swings with the bright, periwinkle seats at the local playground. I loved for him to push me up so high that it felt like I would fly right into the sunset. I wish we could go back to those times now. Why doesn't life have a rewind button like my television set at home?

Unfortunately, Apollo just had to be the one to try and break the awkward silence. Sometimes, it's meant to be quiet. He cleared his throat and said, "I'm sorry about what happened to Calli. She was a apart of all of us and I hope we can all come together as one and-"

Michael, the oldest Arden, interrupted Apollo's kind gesture. "Look, I appreciate what you're trying to do, but it's been a really rough day and we're all upset so if you could just-"

"Keep the sorry pissy comments to yourself because we don't wanna hear that mess," 19 year old, Uriel blurted out. He's hot-tempered and blond, just like his baby sister.

"Uriel!" Rafe growled in an attempt to correct his younger brother's aggressive behavior.

Uriel shot Rafe and evil eye. "What? His sister put my sister, OUR sister, in a hospital bed and you want me to spare his feelings? To Hell with that!" Uriel responded before he slipped his head inside his hoodie and turned away from all of us, indicating that he no longer wanted to be bothered. Normally, Apollo is not the type to take any crap from anyone, but I know he was letting it all slide because of the circumstances. I'd be a little temperamental too if Athena or Dite was the one laying in the hospital bed and people were trying to give me small talk instead of leaving me alone. Just then, we saw Stella and Eric Arden, Callista's parents, rushing to the emergency room, hand in hand, escorted by a doctor. Following behind them were my parents, rushing towards Apollo and me.

"Apollo and Minnie, you two had me worried sick!" Mom dramatically exclaimed as she grabbed a hold of both of us and squeezed us tightly. Her long, blonde hair fell into both of our faces, tickling my nose and getting into Apollo's eyes. Now, I finally see Apollo gets his over-protectiveness and where Dite gets her dramatic side from.

"Are the both of you alright?" Daddy asked.

"Of course they are. They aren't the ones fighting for their lives," Uriel mumbled.

Gabe said nothing but the glare he shot at me and his mischievous smirk indicated he sided with his brother's statement. Mike and Rafe shot Uriel two pairs of evil eyes, although he didn't even take the time to turn around and acknowledge them. I was desperately hoping Callista and her baby would pull through this one. The longer we waited for the doctor, the tenser and emotional we all seemed to become. I imagined Apollo and Uriel would be tearing each other limb from limb in a few minutes. None of this should be happening; not our rivalry, not her accident, no waiting room, no hospital, NONE of this should be going on right now. Callista may have pushed my buttons, but I certainly didn't want her or her baby to die for it. I'd trade anything I have to be able to go back in time right now. Oh, God, please don't take her away. We waited there for what seemed like an eternity. I went back and forth from laying on Apollo's chest, to Daddy's chest, to Mom's shoulder, to getting up and pacing back and forth, fiddling with my fingers. This awkward, butterfly feeling in the bottom of my stomach caused by all this worry and anticipation is by far the worst feeling I've ever experienced. It was absolute torment. I kept replaying the last time I got to look in her eyes. I kept replaying our argument at school.

"What the hell is wrong with me!? Who invites someone pregnant to argue on top of a flight of steps!?" I angrily thought in my head, blaming myself for Callista's misfortune. Why didn't I at least try to hear her out? A high school relationship isn't worth my best friend's safety and well-being. However, it's sad that I'm just realizing it. Suddenly, the silence around us was shattered with a high-pitched scream followed by sounds of sobbing. We all quickly rose to our feet and turned around to see Mrs. Arden running from the emergency room, before she finally collapsed to her knees and began to cry and holler hysterically.

"NO!!!!! Not my baby! Not my little girl, Lord!" She shrilled.

Seconds later, Mr. Arden came running to comfort his hysterical wife although it seemed as if he was fighting back tears of his own.

"Come on, Stella. We have to be strong. She'd want us to be," Eric consoled.

My heart sank at that very moment. Of course, my common sense was telling me, "She's gone. I'll never get to see her again." However, my heart, or maybe my denial, was telling me, "No, the Calli Arden I knew could defeat anything; even death. She's alive...she has to be." As doctors swarmed to aid the Ardens off of the cold, tile floor, a nurse slowly strolled over to talk to us. She could hardly look us in our eyes.

"I-I'm sorry," was all she could bring forth to say as a single tear fell from her right eye.

All of us seemed to breakdown at the same time, as if it hit every single one of us at the exact same time. Michael punched the wall, while tears flowed from his eyes. The pain of his fist colliding with the cement didn't faze him nearly as much as the pain that was in his heart right now. Uriel had to be restrained by Gabe and Rafe, because he began to violently throw things around the waiting room. Apollo and I both started crying, I much, much more than him.

"Come here, baby. It's gonna be ok. She's in a better place now," Mom consoled as she pulled us both close to her and Daddy.

Callista had some minor bodily injuries but her cause of death was traumatic brain injuries and brain hemorrhaging caused from the impact of the fall. She shouldn't have had to suffer like that. No one deserves to leave this world in that way. I don't know whether this is a blessing or not, but since Callista was so close to her due date, her daughter was saved and was currently being tended to. Maybe it's God's will. Perhaps, for some unknown reason, He wanted her daughter to live on. Is it bad that a part of me would trade her daughter's life for Callista's?

Isobel Callista "Calli" Arden, my best friend, is gone forever. Time of death: 5:55 p.m.

CHAPTER ELEVEN:
"This is our daughter, Violet Juliette Jacobs."

There's only a few seconds of stillness and silence before things took yet another turn for the worst.

"Your sister is a damn KILLER!" Uriel yells, before he charges angrily at Apollo. With tears still on his face, Apollo pushes away from Mom and me and quickly steps aside to prepare for Uriel's attack.

"You're going to be lying in a hospital bed next, Carlisle!" Uriel threatens right before he reaches Apollo.

"Let's just see about that," is all Apollo growls before he casts one hard, left hook to the cheek of Uriel's face. Uriel is slowed down a bit, but it doesn't stop Uriel from tackling Apollo. Uriel's body weight causes them both to crash into the white painted walls. Now, doctors' and Uriel's brothers are swarming around trying to break up the two, as they are rolling around on the ground trading punches and insults. The enraged and upset Uriel is quickly gaining the upper hand on my brother. I expected my parents and Callista's parents to step in and act more mature than their sons, but all they did was add to the chaos by yelling and arguing with one another. This is NOT how Callista's death should be commiserated. I couldn't take any more of the chaos taking over the environment I was in so I decided to just get away from all of it. I sprinted around the corner and quickly hopped on the first elevator I saw. They probably didn't even notice I left. I decided to go to the nursery, I knew it would be quiet there and I wanted to get a peek at Callista's baby girl since she's the only piece of Callista left to love. The cheesy, elevator music helped to calm me somewhat. Once I reached the nursery, I quickly began to press myself up against the window as I began to closely examine each newborn to see if one had blonde hair like Calli or maybe her button nose and high cheekbones. I noticed that one baby was missing from its bed and disappointment rushed over me. I guess one of the nurses was caring for her at the moment. Before I turned around to leave, I was suddenly hit with this odd feeling; almost like the feeling you get when you somehow sense that someone is standing directly behind you. I took a deep breath as I turned slowly around to see. Nate standing there looking me dead in my eyes.

"Nate, you cheating bastard, what are YOU doing here!?" I hissed quietly, trying not to awaken the slumbering infants.

He looked downward, took a deep breath and whispered, "I'm here because she's the product of my affair with Callista, Minnie."

I took a step backward, accidentally bumping into the nursery window. "What did you just say?"

He slowly moved his head up and I could see that his eyes were red and beginning to water. He came a bit closer, pointed to one of the newborns and responded, "That's our daughter, Violet Juliette Jacobs."

CHAPTER TWELVE:

"I could cry a million tears, but Callista's body is still growing colder by the minute."

This has got to be the worst, most hellish day of my life. It just seems to be one bombshell of bad news after another. As I was silently processing what Nate just threw at me over and over again in my head, he spoke up to fill the quiet that had fallen between us.

"Uh, well, she has Calli's heart shaped face, don't you think? Her middle name is Juliette. Callista came up with that. I wanted to name her Isobel but Callista hardly liked that name. My mom came up with the name Violet c-cause it's her favorite color. You know Juliette was Callista's favorite name of all time and-"

I put my hand up to silence him just as Lauralee put her hand up to silence me earlier that day. I was not about to let him get out of talking about what he did by rambling on about Violet. My eyes began to water as I walked up to him. The difference was that his were watering out of sadness and guilt and mines were watering out of fury and hurt. I always knew Callista wanted to have a daughter named Juliette. I just didn't know the father would be my boyfriend. Crazy how life turns out, isn't it?

"So…THIS is how I have to find out who Violet Jacobs is?"

His facial expression reminded me of a child who knew they were about to get scolded for doing something wrong. He knew I was pissed with him, and I had absolutely no sympathy for him. He brought all of this on himself.

"I was going to tell you. I promise," He responded softly.

"You promise!? You can't even keep your hormones under control, you expect me to believe that you would've kept that promise? You are a dirty, lying, cheating DOG, and nothing more!" I've never been more grateful that I didn't go through with having sex with Nate. I feel disgusted for even lusting after him.

"I didn't mean for all of this to happen and I'm sorry, Minnie. Really, I am. I made a bad choice."

I rolled my eyes. "You made quite a few, Nathaniel," I growled.

"I did. It's just that…you weren't giving me what I needed and being with Callista felt right. She made me feel good and-"

Before he had the opportunity to throw anymore bullcrap at me, I struck him across the left side of his face with a slap so hard, it damn near echoed. I slapped some of the tears off of his face and onto the palm of my hand. Not only that, a bright, red imprint of my hand was beautifully displayed on his face now.

"I don't CARE how damn good it felt! Sticking your dick in my best friend was DEAD wrong and you know it! Goodbye, Nathaniel. You and I are over."

I grabbed the necklace he had given me for our three-month anniversary, ripped it from my neck, and threw it angrily at his feet. It bounced off of the top of his Nike's before it clanged as it hit the ground. I stared evilly at him, then without saying a word, I turned around and began to walk back towards the elevator. As I turned the corner, I could hear one of the infants slowly beginning to cry. It was the whimpers of Violet. Nate began talking to her gently and softly through the window to comfort her. I guess Violet didn't take to kindly to me putting my hands on her Daddy. Once I exited the hospital, I found my parents waiting in the car for me. Apollo's car was absent from the parking space he hurriedly occupied when we arrived. So, I guess he was already home, blowing off steam. The prideful ego of Apollo must have taken a huge blow since the outcome of the fight didn't look like it sided in his favor.

"Sorry about how we behaved, Minnie. We had no right to do that at a time like that." Daddy apologized as he checked for oncoming cars before he pulled off. Mom turned around in her seat so that she could face me before asking, "By the way, Minnie, where did you sneak off to?"

"The nursery," I quietly answered as I put on my seatbelt.

I assumed that by the way I answered combined with the way I looked her in her eyes, she knew I did not want to be badgered at the moment. She stared at me for a few more seconds with her "worried mother" look before she replied, "Ok, honey." I stared blankly out of the window, the blur of traffic, businesses, houses, and pedestrians whizzed by my eyes as Daddy drove. Once we arrived home, I quickly jolted past all four of my siblings and directly went into my room. I just wanted to slam the door and be alone. However, even after all of the crying, screaming, and punching my pillow until I grew weary, it changed nothing. I could cry a million tears, but Callista's body is still growing colder by the minute.

CHAPTER THIRTEEN:

"I put that heart there because hearts mean love and that's how I feel. I love you, Minnie."

After I had drained all of my energy releasing my anger, guilt, and grief, all I could do was lay across my bed with all of the lights off and dried up tears on my cheeks. I was suffering from a terrible headache, but I was in no mood to risk my family hovering over me since Mom keeps the Tylenol in the bathroom. I probably needed to eat; I hadn't eaten anything since lunch. I'm not leaving my room. I have some gummy worms and a bag of Hershey kisses in my drawer. That will just have to do for today. Suddenly, I hear my doorknob begin to turn and light slowly flood into my room from the hallway. I assumed that it was one of my parents coming to check on their "little girl" again so I turned over on my right side and slipped the covers over my body and face. It was hot under my heavy, blue blanket, but I'd just have to bear it until whoever it was got the hint that I wanted to be left alone. Instead of hearing the voices of my mother and father, I heard the gentle voice of a very special six year old.

"Minnie? Minnie, are you feeling better now?" Ares whispered.

I slowly sat up in my bed and pulled the covers from my face. I saw the face of Ares, along with Dite and Athena, standing directly behind him. Although I wasn't in the best of moods, I didn't have the heart to kick my baby siblings out my room when they obviously came because they cared enough about me.

"Hi, Minnie," Ares greeted. The look in those beautiful grey eyes of his were filled with worry. To me, his eyes were saying "I don't quite know what's going on but all I know is that my big sister needs me."

"Hey, buddy," I groggily responded, moving my hair from my face and tucking it behind my ears.

"I'm sorry about what happened to Callista. I made you a necklace today and Athena brought you some food 'cause Mom told us you might be hungry and Dite brought you your favorite CD so you could listen to some music. I hope it makes you feel better," He explained, with the hope that it really would cheer me up a bit.

"I, uhh, kinda took it out your room last week. Sorry," Dite humbly confessed.

Ares's necklace was made out of some kind of black wire and was decorated with all kinds of multi-colored charms and beads. In the center of those charms and beads hung a medium sized, gold heart. It was better than anything I could buy at Tiffany's. I could tell by the adorably, hopeful expression on his face that he wanted the gift to make all my tears go away and to make me act like his favorite big sister again. If only it could.

"I put that heart there because hearts mean love and that's how I feel," Ares explained, "I love you, Minnie."

Now that statement made me feel like the most beloved big sister in the world. The way he said it almost made me wanna cry, but this time, I'd be crying tears of joy.

"I love you, too, Ares," I replied, as I leaned over and embraced him in a warm hug. After he eagerly put the necklace around my neck, I whispered to him, "Ares, would you mind giving me, Athena, and Dite some privacy? There's some stuff I'd like to talk with them about."

Ares nodded his head and quickly scurried out of my room. After he was gone, I turned towards Dite and Athena, who looked confused as ever.

"What was that all about?" Athena asked as she cleaned her glasses with her oversized t-shirt.

"Yeah, Minnie. Did we do something or whatever?" Dite added.

Actually, neither of them had done anything wrong. I wasn't even mad at Dite for stealing my CD. I had grown used to her having sticky fingers around the house. I just felt the need to talk with them, to give them advice so that nothing wrong happens to them like it just happened to me today. With Athena being eleven and Dite being thirteen going on 25, I felt the time to talk with them was now. As we all know, the older you get, the LESS you want to listen to others.

"What happened between Callista and I was tragic and completely uncalled for. I had to sit and watch my relationship with someone I considered another sister crumble to pieces. I considered her one of my best friends and we sacrificed the bond we had over a stupid boy and a couple of misunderstandings. Before we even had the opportunity to salvage what we had, she was gone. Callista is dead and I will have to live with the fact that I never got the chance to tell her how I truly felt about her. I refuse to allow what happened to our relationship to happen to yours as well. Dite and Athena, the two of you are sisters and that means you were born to be the best of friends. Never ever let anything or anyone sever the bond that you have. You two have had eleven great years with each other. Continue to cherish every single day because you never know what life will throw at you. You don't know what I'd give to spend ten more minutes with Calli. I'd love to be able to take back every negative comment or thought I had towards her and to hug her one more time."

After my heartfelt speech, we all just sat there in silence. I was beginning to wonder if I would get a response from them at all or if they were just going to stand there and stare at me for the rest of the night. Suddenly, Dite started breathing rapidly, burst out into tears, and quickly embraced Athena in a tight hug. Athena, who was crying as well, embraced Dite just as tightly as they both began to repeatedly tell each other, "I love you." It felt good to know that I brought my sisters closer together. At least SOMETHING good had happened during the course of this terrible day.

CHAPTER FOURTEEN:

"Jess's angry words echoed in my head like a haunting melody."

As I expected, my parents allowed me to skip school the next day. With everyone gone off to work and school, I decided to take advantage of some of the privacy. I had to talk with Cassidy.

"Damn, I'm sorry that had to happen to the both of you. Sometimes, life is a real pain. I never expected something like that to happen to Callista, though. I always thought that a rebel could fight anything and win," Cassidy spoke. I smiled faintly. "Even death?"

"Yeah, even death," Cassidy somberly repeated. "I guess this is goodbye, old friend," he mumbled, talking to Callista.

I sighed deeply. "I know how you feel. I wish I could just hit rewind and go back in time to when Marley, Callista, and I were happy-go-lucky kids. You know, go back to when the only arguments we had were during a game of backyard tag."

"Ha, that's easy. Marley would always win. We were no match for those long arms and long legs. She could give you a twenty-second head start and could tag you before your feet even started hitting the ground good," Cassidy joked.

I chuckled. "Callista hated that. Since she was the shortest out of the four of us, it was harder for her to tag people cause of her tiny arms."

We both laughed. Reminiscing about the good old times made me miss her, but it also made me realize that everything between Callista, Marley, and I wasn't all bad. I needed to remember the good times I had with her and the things I loved about her. I remember one time we stole some of Ophelia's liquor and drank it in her room when we spent the night at Marley's house. Marley, being the goody-goody that she is, took ONE shot and repented for it the next day. I loved her fighting spirit. She was never the type to back down from a fight from anyone. I think she got that from her brother, Uriel. I loved her loyalty and her sarcastic humor. I loved how she proclaimed she was a rebel and tomboy, yet she would unleash a girly shriek like a hyperactive, six-year-old at Christmas upon spotting a great pair of sneakers at the mall. Yeah, THAT'S the Callista I needed to remember. "Ahh thanks, Cassie. I needed a big stress reliever."

"I got a big one for you, alright," He suggestively hinted.

I smiled again. Cassidy always had a hidden talent for making me laugh no matter how pissed off or upset I am. I'm thankful for that because I need as many chuckles and giggles as I can get right now. "Cassidy Paris, are you trying to make a sex joke?"

"Hehe, trying and succeeding, Babe. It's nice to hear you laugh again, Minnie."

I blushed. "Even though I don't have much to laugh at as of lately. You know, even though I knew Nate was pretty much the stereotypical jock, I was still surprised to find out he cheated. Who cheats on me?"

"A fool, that's who. I toooold you that douche was no good. Guys like him don't deserve girls like you and you damn sure didn't deserve what he did to you." Cassidy replied, some hostility in his tone. I paused for a second. "Then what do I deserve?"

He took a brief pause of his own before he calmly responded, "Someone who sees you for what and who you truly are. Someone who's going to treat you right."

"Ha!" I mocked, "Where on this planet am I going to find that guy, Cassie?"

"I don't knooow," He sang. "He could be closer than you thi-"

Cassidy's sentence was broken off by a sudden knock at the front door. Once Cassidy and I said our goodbyes, I got up off of the couch to answer the door. I tiptoed, careful of trying not to make the floor creak, to the peephole to see Marley and Lauralee on my front porch having a conversation. I was relieved that it wasn't Rebbie or Jess who had returned to torture me some more. They were here earlier, threatening me and yelling. Rebbie threw some pebbles at our front door and once she broke one of her precious nails, she got even angrier and kicked some dirt on my car. I was angry about my now dirty vehicle, but I'm no fool. Once I stepped outside, they'd both pounce on me like two hungry lions on the last piece of meat in the jungle. I was not about to take another trip to North Memorial Hospital anytime soon.

"You're gonna pay, Minnie Carlisle! Do you hear me!? Callista's death WON'T go unpunished, you bitch!" Jess's angry words echoed in my head like a haunting melody.

As I slowly opened the front door, I heard Lauralee whine, "When will it happen again? I'm tiiiired of waiting." Marley, realizing the door was opening, quickly and firmly answered, "We'll talk later."

"What was that all about?" I nosily inquired; my curiosity getting the best of me.

"You know what curiosity killed, Minnie." Lauralee happily exclaimed, as they both walked into my house. I quickly closed the door behind them. I wouldn't be surprised if Jess and Rebbie jumped out of the bushes and did a home invasion on me. Call me paranoid if you want to, but I'm not taking any chances.

"Aren't you two supposed to be in school?" I asked, "and why are you wearing matching outfits like some dorky, newlywed couple?"

Lauralee was wearing a long, canary colored dress with coffee brown, wedge heels. The color of the dress went great with her complexion and her hair, which had been curled and placed over her left shoulder. Her face was decorated with glittery lip gloss, gold eye shadow, and mascara and her body was adorned with fancy (probably overly expensive) gold, white and brown jewelry. Lauralee always followed a color scheme when she dressed. Marley, of course, was not as dolled up as Lauralee. She had her hair pinned up in a weird pony-tail/bun combination with just a few strands sticking out over her face. She was wearing a yellow top that cut right above her midriff and blue jean shorts with a few rips in them and brown flip-flops. The only makeup she did have on was some mascara and Chap Stick; and the only jewelry she was wearing was a pair of brown, feather earrings. Marley never fails to surprise me. One minute, she dresses like she doesn't have a care in the world and the next, she waltzes in my house with her legs and tummy exposed. Full of surprises, she is.

"I persuaded Rosemarley to dress in accordance with my outfit. I think we look adorable," Lauralee giddily explained. She's such a diva. "By the way, can you please put this flower in my hair for me, Marley?" Lauralee added as she dug in her brown and gold purse for a fake, yellow rose. Marley simply rolled her eyes and strolled over to her.

"Well, we would be in school, but Daddy's Girl here charmed her parents into letting her stay home, and my Mom let me stay home because of…well, you know." Marley explained as she finished pinning the flower.

"Thanks, Babe," Lauralee replied.

We spent our school free afternoon sitting on my living room rug having girlfriend time. We talked about the teachers who seemed to be determined to fail us, cute boys (of course), the losers, girls we couldn't wait to kick in the throat, and shopping. I told them about how Rebbie Hardwick threw dirt on my car and pebbles at my front door. I also told them how Jess Ward had threatened me during their visit earlier that day. Marley called me a punk for not fighting them and said that if it had been Callista or her sister, Rebbie and Jess would've been leaving in ambulances. It was nice. It was nice to have my friends around to distract my mind from everything else that was going on.

"Minnie, I got some bad news for you," Marley suddenly stated after she finished off her last sip of cranberry juice.

Lauralee and I stopped laughing and just stared at her. "I thought we were going to break it to her slowly, Rosemarley," Lauralee criticized.

"I'm too impatient for that crap. We'd all be five minutes from death before you got the nerve to tell her," Marley snapped.

"Tell me what!? What's going on?" I frantically shouted. Now, I was starting to panic.

"You're on the news and NOT in a good way," Marley answered.

"What!?" I shrieked as I rose to my feet.

"This IS Angel City, so don't act too surprised, Minnie," Lauralee reminded as she and Marley stood up as well.

Oh, yeah. How could I forget that I lived in the most drama-loving, scandal-obsessed city in the nation? Damn this place. Damn it all!

"They're calling it 'The Arden Incident'. They say it's one of the biggest scandals to hit here since the Angel City Murder-Suicide that happened eighteen years ago." Lauralee finished.

"Plus, they're kinda making YOU look like the number one suspect in Calli's murder," Marley added.

CHAPTER FIFTEEN:

"I could barely stand saying goodbye to her, so how would I EVER have gotten the courage to take her life!?"

My heart sank to the pit of my stomach and I felt like a wave of fear. Panic and confusion had overtaken me. A suspect? ME? How could they even think of pinning Callista's death on me? I could barely stand saying goodbye to her, so how would I have EVER gotten the courage to take her life!? None of this made sense to me. My life seems to be falling apart bit by bit; day by day.

"Why MEEEE? Why am I the main suspect?" I whined. I swear I was about to be on the verge of a mental breakdown. If I would've even gotten a broken a nail, I would've cried.

"Well, let's see. You had the most motive. Everyone knows you and Callista weren't so buddy-buddy anymore and she did get impregnated by your boyfriend," Marley responded as she filed her long, olive green nails.

"Nate and I broke up," I quickly corrected. I didn't want anyone to think I was still with him. Last thing I want to hear is someone still calling me, "Mrs. Nathaniel Evan Jacobs." Nooooo, thank you. I'll stick with being a Carlisle for now. She stopped filing her nails and raised an eyebrow. "Oh, really?"

I groaned in frustration. "I know there was some bad blood between us-"

"Psh, isn't THAT the understatement of the year?" Lauralee sarcastically mumbled.

I shot Lauralee an evil eye. "Anyways! I know Callista and I had our problems, but isn't that what all friends do? They butt heads. I mean, Lauralee gets on my nerves aaall the time, but I don't literally wanna kill her."

"I'll...take that as a compliment, I guess," Lauralee mumbled to herself.

"Still, your history with her makes you look like Callista's number one enemy," Marley reminded.

Deep down inside, I knew Marley was right. Every single thing Calli ever did to me—ruining our friendship, sleeping with Nate, getting pregnant by him, and torturing Marley and me has now become evidence against me. I knew the truth. I knew I hadn't done anything to cause Stella and Eric Arden to lose their baby girl, but I knew it sure didn't seem that way in the eyes of others and I'd have to work my rump off to prove it. I began to feel angry. I'm a lot of things, but I'm not crazy like one of those homicidal housewives you see on the cheesy Lifetime Movies. I just didn't think it was totally fair that I was automatically the prime suspect, so I did what anyone else would probably do…I attempted to shift the blame onto someone else.

"What about you and Stephanie, hmm? Maybe Steph decided to finally get even with Callista for slapping the taste out of her mouth. Or, maybe her older cousin decided to do it for her. You may act like a ditzy priss, but I know you got that Italian, mob-wife assassin temper inside of you."

"That 'Italian, mob-wife, assassin temper'!?" Are you SERIOUS!? Don't bring my entire ethnicity into this! Stephanie and I may not have approved of some of Callista's actions, but it was NOT enough of an excuse to commit murder and CERTAINLY not an excuse for you to demean an entire group of people, Artemis!" Lauralee furiously responded, arms crossed and lips pouted like an ill-tempered toddler.

"And what about YOU, Marley? The two of you have a heated argument. You damn near break Callista's wrist in front of everyone while she was pregnant. Then, you magically disappear until the next day. That's kind of suspicious, don't you think?"

Marley stepped closer to me; her right hand on hip and her left hand in my face. "Ok, first of all, she deserved it. Second, I "magically" disappeared because Marley got an early dismissal and Ophelia came to pick us up, kay?"

"Why are you speaking in third person?" Lauralee chimed in. Good question.

"Who cares!?" Marley roared, "That's not the damn point! The point is that this self-absorbed bitch is blaming US for something SHE did!"

We spent the next couple of minutes arguing, trading insults, yelling and getting in each other's faces. It's amazing how a vibe can change in just a matter of minutes. The tension rose to the point where Lauralee refused to hear any more from me. She shoved me out of her way, as she stormed out of my house, dragging an angry Marley along with her by the hand. Once Marley glared at me before violently slamming the front door so hard, one of the lamps on a nearby table shook. There was nothing left but me and silence. I knew what I said to them was dead wrong. I shouldn't have tried to cast the blame on them. I should be grateful to still have someone to call my best friend since Callista is now gone. It wasn't their fault I was the main suspect after all. However, my pride and my ego wouldn't let me follow them back to the Giovanni Mansion to apologize. Part of me just couldn't admit when I was wrong. I lit up when I heard my doorbell ring again; hoping it was Lauralee or Marley. I zoomed to the door, not even bothering to check the peephole, and quickly opened it. I did find two people standing on my porch, but they were two members of the ACPD.

CHAPTER SIXTEEN:

"However, instead of hearing cold, metal handcuffs clink around my tiny wrists, I hear laughter."

I had no idea who the brunette, female officer was, but I knew the other one very well. He's my Mom's younger brother and my uncle, Daniel Davidson.

"Uncle Danny?" I asked, "What are you doing here?"

He brought his fist up to his mouth and cleared his throat. "Is Patrick or Diana home?" He inquired, referring to my parents. He was acting so formal, I guess in an attempt to look "professional" in front of his partner.

"No, just me. Please, come on in."

I had watched enough movies to know what was about to happen next. They always arrest the prime suspect and drag her outside to the police car in slow motion with suspenseful music in the background. While she's bawling until her mascara is running hideously down her face and screaming until her voice gets raspy, all of her neighbors gather around looking afraid and shocked. Then, one aggressive and one "nice" officer interrogate her in some small, grey room with a light in her face that's so bright; it blinds her until she breaks down from all the pressure and confesses. That's the way the cookie always crumbles. After I closed the door, I stood behind them and stretched my arms out in front of me with my wrists side by side and my hands hanging downward.

"You mind telling us what it is that you're doing?" The female officer asked.

I took a deep breath and closed my eyes. "I know you're here to arrest me, Uncle D. Just go ahead and book me so we can get this over with."

I was feeling both brave and afraid after giving them permission to arrest me. There wasn't any sense in delaying the inevitable, so why sit around and play these mind games? However, instead of hearing cold, metal handcuffs clink around my tiny wrists, I heard laughter.

"Joyce, didn't I tell you my niece was a little bit of a drama queen? I swear, sometimes you are just like Diana when she was your age." Uncle D laughed, holding his stomach.

Quickly realizing that they weren't here to put me behind a jail cell, I placed my arms behind my back where I should've kept them in the first place. Instead of shaking with fear, I was now blushing with embarrassment. I was humiliated, but also relieved. At least I wouldn't be sent to jail to wear that awful prison uniform. Orange never was a good color on me.

"We're just here to ask you a few questions. No need for handcuffs today...Art-tie-mis?" Officer Joyce replied, mispronouncing my first name.

"Artemis," I corrected, "but everyone calls me Minnie."

So, the three of us sat on our wine colored couch and talked. They asked me just about everything that had to with Callista's death and our less-than-perfect friendship. With every answer I gave them, no matter how much I tried to sugarcoat it, I felt as if I began to look more and more guilty. Marley was right; everything that happened between us did make it seem as if I had the most reason to kill her. The only answer I gave that didn't that didn't make me worry was when they asked me to state my full name for their records. I tried not to sweat bullets or fiddle with my hair and fingers too much during their questioning. Just as we finished, my parents and all four of my siblings came through the door. I've never been so relieved to see them.

"Uncle Danny!" Ares and Athena squealed as they eagerly ran to hug him.

Were my brothers and sisters happy? Yes, because they saw Danny, their favorite uncle. Were my parents happy? Mmm, not so much because they saw Daniel Davidson; an ACPD member who could possibly arrest their baby girl.

"Danny, what are you doing here?" Daddy asked with a small, hint of worry in his voice.

"That's what I'd like to know, Daniel," Mom sassily added with her arms crossed. The temperamental side of her normally, sweet personality was coming to surface.

"Calm down, Diana. We just came here to question your daughter, that's all," Officer Joyce calmly answered.

My Mom quickly directed her attention to Joyce. "Sorry, but I don't even KNOW who you are, and I'm NOT in much of a good mood. So, I suggest you go munch on some Krispy Kreme's or something; and not tell me what to do in my own house."

My Mom can be a real firecracker, but sometimes, she needs to watch who she gets feisty with. I think everyone in that room was thankful that Joyce didn't lose her temper and beat my Mom down to our cherry wood floor. Instead, Officer Joyce gave my Uncle a "We'll talk about this later" look, and then turned to walk out of the front door. Since Mom, Dad, and Uncle Danny didn't want the "children" to hear what they were about to talk about, they decided to hurry into the guest room to finish their discussion. If I already know the discussion is going to be about me, why in the world can't I listen to it? I'll never understand parental logic. Ares went out to the backyard to play fetch with our Labrador, Rusty. He'd probably get more dirt on him than Rusty would; which drove my Mom crazy. Athena grabbed a juicy, green apple to snack on while she went into her room to finish up some homework, and Dite strolled into the kitchen to raid the fridge. She was probably searching for some Jell-O which has remained her favorite snack since she was old enough to chew it. Apollo and I decided to eavesdrop on their conversation. The younger siblings may not be wise enough to understand, but Apollo and I understood how serious this situation could become. Because the door was closed and they were speaking kind of low, we could only hear bits and pieces of what they were saying:

"Why are you here?...under arrest?"

"...Minnie in trouble?"

"No…just investigating…"

"Nothing to investigate…her death…an accident…not our daughter's fault."

"Relax…I'm just doing my job…she's still family."

"Go do it somewhere else.. Nothing is happening here. Minnie is innocent."

"…Something could happen…Things…could get worse."

After hearing Uncle Danny say that, I pulled away from the door, killing my ability to hear anything else they were saying. I don't even know if I really wanted to hear anything else to be honest. How in the world could things get any worse? Why me? I held my best friend in my arms less than 24 hours ago, as she was dying. Wasn't my life bad enough already?

"Minnie?" Dite softly called from behind us.

Apollo turned `around to face her. I remained facing the door, because I felt the urge to start crying. I didn't want Dite to see me in that sort of vulnerable state again. But, since she had called for me, I knew I had to be the one to answer. "Yes, Dite?" I mumbled.

The next thing I knew, she had quickly run up to me, embracing me in a hug from behind. "It'll be alright. You'll see. Things always work out for us Carlisles in the end."

"She's right," Apollo added, "You just gotta let nature take its course, Minnie."

I guess Dite was old enough to understand more serious matters now. I had underestimated her maturity, because of her goofy personality and diva ways. It felt nice to know I had people in my corner to support and love me unconditionally. As I ruffled her golden locks and hugged her back, I whispered, "Thanks, sis."

CHAPTER SEVENTEEN:

"I'm so glad that I won't have to see your face ever again, after they put you behind bars, Minnie Carlisle!"

As I expected, the drama and the rumors were flying full force at me when I returned to school. It's amazing how the stupidest, wildest rumors can be believed depending on the people involved and the circumstances. People who probably didn't even know me were spreading lies about my situation just for the hell of it. I heard things like:

"I knew she was just TOO perfect. I bet the little witch would've killed Nate if he were there."

"I heard Nate got her pregnant, too, and her hormones drove her to kill poor Callista."

"They should just go ahead and send her skanky behind to jail now. Everyone knows it's the pretty ones who turn out to have the most problems."

Some of the rumors and weird stares that came my way were from people that I thought were my friends. Grandma always said that you'd find out who your real friends are when you need them by your side the most. Hardly anyone talked to me; even my teachers avoided eye contact with me and calling on me in class. So, I didn't even bother to raise my hand to answer a question. I even heard that Jess Ward plans to "beat me 'till I'm black and blue" as soon as school ends. I think we're a little too old to still be arranging afterschool brawls. You would think that Jess would be on her best behavior on school property considering the fact that this is her last year of high school, and she's already been threatened with expulsion. But, Jess was never has been a rational thinker. She's exactly the type of girl who'd risk her diploma for something like this. I bet Callista had her hands full with Jess, when she was alive. I decided to talk to Rebbie. Not only was I hoping for her to talk Jess out of attempting to fight me, I was hoping to reach out to her. Callista was her best friend, too, and I was thinking that maybe we'd connect because of that. After searching intensely for her through the blue, grey, and white hallways of our school, I find Rebbie standing at her locker.

"Rebbie, can I talk to you?" I politely asked.

"I really don't have anything to say to you," Rebbie coldly responded as she brushed her wavy, strawberry blonde hair.

"Rebbie, pleeeease," I pleaded. "Just give me five minutes. If not for me, do it for Callista."

She exhaled deeply and turned to look at me in my eyes with a stern expression on her face. "What is it, Minnie?"

"I want you and Jess to know that I didn't kill Calli. I loved her, too. She was my best friend. I wouldn't lay a finger on her."

"Mmmhm. Whatever you say." Then, she redirected her attention back to her mirror hanging inside her locker. I see that she, too, was one of the many people who believed I was Callista's killer. I knew it wouldn't be easy.

"I know that you and Jess are hurting. I'm hurting too, Rebbie."

Rebbie laughed. "HA! Not as much as you're gonna be hurting later on today." I knew she was referring to Jess wanting to fight me.

"I'm not going to fight Jess. I refuse to."

"Yeah, just like you refuse to admit you killed her friend, huh?" She responded as she began to apply an ugly shade of reddish-orange lipstick.

"Can you just talk to her? You know, calm her down a bit, because-" I started.

"Noooow we're getting somewhere," Rebbie interrupted, turning away from the mirror to look at me. "You're only trying to save your own skin. You don't want my friend to scar that pretty face of yours, huh? You're a killer AND a coward."

I was beginning to reach my breaking point. I know I was the one begging for Rebbie and Jess to forgive me, but I wasn't going to stand here and let her drag my dignity through the mud.

"I'm only trying to talk things out with the two of you. I'm not trying to start any argument or start any trouble, ok?" I sassed.

She adjusted her blue jean miniskirt before replying, "You started trouble the moment you pushed Callista down those stairs. You've always been a self-centered, mean girl. You try to act like you're so perfect, but you're really just a bitch. No wonder Callista left you and that loser nerd to become friends with us. No wonder Nate cheated on you. You deserve to be alone; and to be betrayed; and to be thrown in jail. Like I said, you're a killer and coward. I'm not stupid. I see exactly what you're trying to do."

That's it! That did it! She wants to resort to personal attacks? She wants to get her hands dirty? This reject video vixen thinks she's big and bad? Okay, I'll play your game, Rebecca Hardwick.

"No, Rebbie. You ARE stupid. You are, by far, the dumbest slut to ever grace the halls of this school. You think you're the bomb.com, because you have guys who are always trying to have sex with you? They don't want you because you're irresistible; they want you because you won't resist them. You're EASY, Rebbie. That's all you're good for. Your only talent is opening your legs as wide as you open that big mouth of yours. There's nothing else special about you. You have a plain face; and there's nothing remotely sexy about your body; no matter how much of it you try to expose. You have a pudgy stomach, stick thin legs, no hips, and a flat butt. You THINK you're gorgeous because you have porn-star sized boobs and long hair? You're pathetic. YOU'RE really the one who's going to be alone. No wonder no guy talks to you the moment he leaves out of your bed. Know your place, Rebecca. I didn't' take that crap from Phyllis James, and I won't take it from you or anyone else, either."

I may have gotten way too harsh with Rebbie, but I had to stand up for myself sooner or later. I bet no one has been this mean to Rebbie, since Sophia Carlos, also known as "Lazy Eyed Sophie." She splashed some vodka all over Rebbie at her house party last year, for catching Rebbie with a mouthful of her boyfriend a few days before. Then, everyone got hyped up and joined in. Rebbie was soaked in alcohol, food, and tears by the end of that night. Ooooh, Jess and Calli were ready to rip Sophia to shreds that night. I'm sure they would've come for me if they had found out I tripped Rebbie, while she was trying to frantically run out of the door. She fell hard against Sophia's hardwood floor, causing more laughter to erupt from the house. She didn't even take the time to look back and see who tripped her. Sophia almost transferred to a new school after Callista keyed her ugly, brown Toyota. Well, she accused her; but she was never proven guilty. I expected Rebbie to make a scene, argue back with me, or even try to punch me dead in my face. Instead, she just stood there without moving and without speaking. Sybil Florentine, who I had seen walking up from behind Rebbie had finally reached us and when she saw Rebbie was distressed, she asked her what was wrong. Rebbie didn't reply. She just continued to stare into the mirror she was using to apply her make up. She turned to me, with her fists balled, and eyes watering and hollered, "I'm so glad that I won't have to look at your face ever again, after they put you behind bars, Minnie Carlisle!" She sprinted off, wailing, crying with her hair flying all over the place. Everyone in the surrounding area just stared at me, whispering and pointing. I had officially made things worse for myself. Still angry, I seethed to Sybil, "What are you looking at? Shouldn't you be off somewhere trying to make friends with a treadmill, Piggy?"

Sybil glared at me, jaw tense and shaking her head. "Minnie Carlisle strikes again," She grumbles. She stood there, angrily glaring at me, before she went off to find Rebbie. There was no one on my side this time. It's a weird and empty feeling, being all alone. You think it's no big deal, and you think you can handle it, until it actually happens to you. The only people who didn't treat me like an outcasted killer were Marley and Apollo; who were also getting the cold shoulders from their friends, as well. Although Marley and Lauralee forgave me after I begged them to, Lorenzo and Darla Giovanni still didn't want Lauralee and Stephanie to hang around with a "suspect." So, they aren't allowed socialize with me, until I'm cleared of all charges. To make sure of this, Darla took Lauralee's beloved Hummer and is forcing her and Steph to be driven to and from school by a personal chauffeur. As badly as I wanted to go, and as badly as I want to say goodbye to Callista one last time before they buried her, my family and I were forbidden from attending her funeral. The Ardens made it crystal clear that if any of us attended, the cops would be immediately called on us. Part of me understood. What parents would want to attend their baby girl's funeral and see the woman who may have killed her sitting right beside them? I guess visiting Callista at Resting Angels Cemetery would have to suffice. I feel like I'm just a skip away from reaching my breaking point. I've been shunned, talked about, threatened (mainly by Jess and Rebbie), and some have even gone as far as to harass me and leave cruel messages at our doorstep. Even my family is suffering. Mom and Dad no longer go out as frequently with friends as they used to. No one wants to associate with two people who raised an alleged maniac. Apollo and Ares have gotten into heated verbal confrontations at school, trying to defend my honor. Apollo ended up losing his temper and taking his anger out on some jerk who decided to get bold and come to our house disrespecting me to the verge of tears. He never did that again, but it didn't help our family's image. Now, it just looks like the Carlisle's raised TWO bad seeds. Fortunately, Dite and Athena have not gotten into any fights.

But, the way their so called "friends" treat them is absolutely heartbreaking, especially for Athena. Athena is not as outspoken and feisty as Dite is; so this teasing hits her harder. Athena cries almost every single day now. I just want this nightmare to end. This sudden isolation and constant anxiety is beginning to overtake my mind. I'm used to being the social butterfly that everyone constantly flocked to. I went from being the biggest star to biggest target in a blur of seconds. Other than my family, Lauralee and Marley, I felt like no one was on my side. School campus had now become a battleground; and I fight to cling onto the remaining ounces of sanity I have. Graduation spells freedom for me. Free from this school, these people, and this town. While standing friendless at my locker, as usual, I was more than thrown off guard when a gentle hand landed on my back and a suave voice greeted, "Hey, Minnie."

I jumped, dropping the algebra book and notebook I had in my hands to the floor. The voice belonged to Damian Abernathy, a recently transferred, very handsome senior. His chiseled face is a welcomed surprise.

"Hi, Damian," I humbly greet back. I could still feel my startled heart pounding through my chest.

He ruffled his fingers through his curly, dark brown hair. "I didn't mean to scare you."

God, he's beautiful with that flawless dark skin and that radiant white smile. I knew my face was probably as scarlet as a summer strawberry from being so flustered around him. "I-it's okay, Damian."

He slid his hands in the pockets of his denim jeans. "I was wondering if you'd like to come to a party I'm having at my house tonight. You know, drink, let loose, and have fun for a change."

I quickly glanced over at him, staring him deep into his honey colored eyes. I hadn't been invited to anywhere in ages. I must've looked like a total creeper staring him dead in the eyes without uttering a word.

"Are you gonna give me an answer, or just stand there and have a staring contest with me all day long?" He joked, flashing a beautiful smile through those seductive lips.

"Why?"

Damian tilts his head slightly right. A confused expression overtakes his face. "Huh?"

"Why would you invite ME of all people to a party? I mean, haven't you seen the news lately?" No sense in getting my hopes all up. I know he was new to Angel City High, but surely someone had told him about Minnie "Killer" Carlisle. He's far too handsome to live under a rock.

"I don't believe everything I hear in the streets or see on the television, Minnie. I'm inviting you because I want you to be there. You're a beautiful girl and honestly, now that Nate is out of the picture, I'd like the chance to…get to know you a little better. So what do ya say?"

This could be one of many first steps to regaining a normal life again. First, partying, then maybe dating. I couldn't think of a more handsome rebound boy than Damian Abernathy. There was only one thing to say to Damian's partying proposal…

"Can I bring a friend?"

I couldn't drive home fast enough once school ended. I called Marley first to invite her to come with me, but she declined. She said she'd rather enjoy a quiet evening in her room studying for an upcoming test. So I invited Lauralee, who was more than happy to tag along. Since Apollo had already made plans to attend Damian's party, we just decided to take his car there. My parents weren't too thrilled about me going out. With all the bad publicity I was receiving, they were worried someone might try to "do something" to me. They were slightly relieved once they knew Apollo and Lauralee were going to be there with me, but I could tell they were still uneasy about the idea. They'll get over it. I have a social life to get back to! I adorned my body with my light blue, denim shorts, a tight, white shirt, red heels, and my favorite Victoria's Secret push up bra. I applied my red lipstick and mascara with surgical precision and wore my hair in the most beautiful, baby doll curls ever. I look gorgeous every night, but I just haaad to look absolutely flawless tonight. I just had to. I yelled goodbye to everyone in the house before rushing outside to Apollo's car, where he was impatiently awaiting for me to join him.

"You look like a hooker," Apollo bluntly stated. "You don't have any jeans or a jacket you could put on instead?"

I rolled my eyes. Apollo sometimes forgets that his name is not Patrick Carlisle, and therefore, he is not my father. "I'm not changing Apollo. You might as well go ahead and drive, because you're wasting all your gas."

He growled before shifting the car into drive and pulling out of the driveway. I was excited and anxious the entire seven minutes it took us to get to the Abernathy household. I had butterflies raging in the pit of my stomach.

"This is it," I thought. "My life is finally going to go back to normal." Maybe if I remind my peers of how fun and energetic I was at parties, maybe they'd finally come back to my side. I mean, everyone knew Minnie and Apollo Carlisle as being the life of the party. They'd see I wasn't a killer; but that I was just a party-loving teenager who was at the wrong place at the wrong time.

"We're heeeere." Apollo announced as he parked his car on the curb. The Abernathys lived in a beautiful, two-story brick home. It looked like one of those houses from out of a magazine. The house's elegance was accentuated even more with lights and the big, lovely moon shining above it. There was no one outside, but plenty of cars parked all around. I couldn't wait to get inside and join the party…and to see Damian, of course.

"Isn't that your friend?" Apollo asks as we exit his vehicle and he presses the lock button.

I glance to our left to see Lauralee cautiously sprinting towards us in her Christian Louboutin's and a giddy smile. "Click Clack!" was the sound her heels made as they were hitting the pavement. For a second, it brought me back to the moment I heard that sound after Callista's fall. Click….clack....

"Hey, Apollo! Hey, Minnie!" She exclaims, waving her arm as if we don't already notice she's running towards us. Her speaking snapped me out of my daze and back into reality. "It took you guys forever to get here!"

Apollo checked his Rolex. "It's only 8:37. We're only seven minutes late."

Lauralee shrugged her shoulders. "Better late than never, I guess."

Arm in arm with Lauralee, the three of us made our way up the driveway to the front door. Apollo casually rang the doorbell. Diiing dooong! I bet the tune echoed in a house as big as this one. I could already hear music and people chit chatting inside. I was gonna explode with excitement in a few seconds, I could feel it. Damian answered the door, looking devilishly handsome in a plaid, blue shirt. He smiled at us.

"What's up, guys? Welcome to the party," He greeted.

"Thanks," Apollo replied.

Damian opened the door and the three of us walked in. I imagined people laughing, socializing, and dancing, but instead, we saw everyone crowded around staring at us with bags in each hand. The bags were dark grey, so I couldn't tell what was inside of them. The music stopped once Damian slammed the front door. My excitement faded and fear for my safety began to take over.

"W-what's going on here?" I uneasily asked.

Damian walked over and stood in front of us. He lifted his head and bellowed, "The Carlisles are here!"

A few seconds later, Jess Ward appeared from out of the kitchen. She stood in the doorway with her long, kinky blonde hair draped over her right shoulder, arms crossed, eyes glaring dead at me with a smug grin on her face, before she began to walk towards us.

"Well, well, well. It's about time you suckers showed up," She said as finished making her way through the crowd to stand beside Damian. I'm not lying when I say I saw nothing but evil in Jess's dark brown eyes that night. Everyone had gathered around us. I felt like some defenseless animal about to face its doom. Lauralee gripped my arm tighter, as if she was looking to me for protection. Hell, I was hoping Apollo would protect the both of us.

"What the hell is going on here?!" Apollo angrily questioned. He was shifting into big brother mode.

"I'll tell you what's going on here. Your sister is gonna get what she deserves. I told you, Callista's death wouldn't go unpunished. Thanks, D. I couldn't have done this without your help in seducing this dumb ho."

"Damian…why are you helping her?" I could feel myself about to cry already.

Damian draped his left arm around Jess' shoulders and smiled mischievously at us. "I don't owe you an explanation."

"No, but I owe you an ass whooping!" Apollo growled.

As soon as Apollo took one step towards Damian, everyone reached into their bags and started throwing rotten food at us. Lauralee and I both screamed and covered our faces. I felt consistent pain as vegetables and fruit struck my body and head. Something hit Lauralee in the gut so hard it caused her to bellow out and double over at the waist in pain. My temple was hit and I felt dazed for a second. Apollo grabbed both of us by our shoulders and rushed us out of the house.

"You're not getting away that easily!" A voice yelled out once we were attempting to make our way across the lawn.

Suddenly, we were sprayed full blast with a water hose. The blast hit Apollo in the back, causing him and us to fall over. I glanced over to see that it was Rebbie who was behind the water attack.

"I'm gonna kill you, bitch!" Jess shrieked as she rushed out of the house. She immediately charged towards me and roughly tackled me into the dirty, soaked lawn. Once Rebbie saw that Apollo was coming to break up the fight, she sprayed him, and then rushed over to help Jess attack me. There was no way I could fight both of them simultaneously. All I could do was attempt to stop them from seriously injuring me by blocking some hits with my arms covering my face. I felt knuckles thrashing against my head and nails digging into my legs. My hair felt as if it was being ripped from my scalp; and the weight of Jess sitting atop my stomach only made it more difficult for me to breathe.

"Get off her!" Lauralee commanded, as she grabbed Jess by the waist in an attempt to break up the brawl.

"You get off Jess!" Rebbie yelled. She stopped scratching and pulling my hair and ran over to Lauralee. I felt the klutz almost trip off my leg as she rushed up to Lauralee and pulled her off Jess by her long, brown hair. Hands full of Lauralee's precious locks, she slung her a few feet away from her onto the lawn. Now they were tussling around in the dirt. With Rebbie gone, I could handle Jess a little better. With one good punch to the center of her abdomen, I winded her and I used that window of opportunity to push her off of me. I rushed to my feet. I ran over to Rebbie and violently dragged her by her hair to free Lauralee. Rebbie will surely have whiplash tomorrow from the way I snatched her.

"Apollo!" I screamed. I frantically surveyed the scene and noticed he was in the street fighting Damian against someone's dark green truck. I admit, Damian can hold his own but no man on this Earth can best a big brother defending his little sister.

"We can't wait on him!" Lauralee yelled to me. She grabbed my hand and began to run to her truck.

"Get back here!" Jess shrieked from the distance.

If she didn't trip and fall over the curb, she would've caught us before we made it safely into Lauralee's Hummer. Lauralee loudly honked the horn twice, getting Apollo's attention. He kneed Damian in the gut one last time, knocking the wind out of him just as I did Jess, then ran to his own car. We both cranked up and sped off. Shock and adrenaline were running rampant through my system. I was hyperventilating and couldn't speak. My mind raced, disabling me from thinking clearly. Tears ran down Lauralee's cheeks and she was practically shaking as she sped through the streets. Lauralee is not a fighter, not even in the slightest, so she must be traumatized after what just happened. It was Lauralee's idea to go to Marley's house as a hideout. When Marley opened the door, her face damn near went pale.

"What happened!?" She shrieked in concern. "Come in, come in!"

Marley let each of us shower and gave us each a change of clothes. While Apollo was taking his shower, Lauralee and I talked in Marley's room.

"Tell me exactly what happened tonight," She ordered.

"All we wanted to do was to go to Damian Abernathy's party..." Lauralee started.

"But, it turned into a complete disaster," I finished.

We informed her about how they pelted us with rotten food. How they just stood there and laughed as they continued to strike us as if we were less than human. How Rebbie sprayed us with the water hose when we tried to escape. We told her about Jess and Rebbie jumping me. Lauralee broke down into a fit of tears, while telling Marley how Rebbie attacked her when she tried to assist me. Nobody came to our aid. Nobody was on our side tonight. They didn't care how much it hurt when the food pelted my body. They didn't care about how the blast of cold water would almost make us freeze to death since it was already a brisk night. They didn't care when Jess and Rebbie were attacking us. No, they just stood there and laughed and recorded it. Lauralee and I would be an Internet sensation by tomorrow afternoon. The thing that hurt the most was to feel that betrayed and humiliated by people who I thought were my friends. I had invited some of those same people to my house for parties. Some of them I went to elementary school with. People are backstabbing and cruel, and they make sure you won't forget it. Wow, this is what it must feel like...to be the loser. I had made fun of them for years, and now I finally feel just a sliver of what they've always felt.

"Did you say Damian Abernathy?" Marley questioned.

Lauralee and I glanced over at each other then back to Marley. We figured she'd be more concerned with our well-being than who was hosting the "party."

"Yeah, I said Damian Abernathy. What about him?" Lauralee answered.

"You mean, you don't know? Nobody's told you?"

"Told her what?" Apollo asked as he stepped shirtless into the room, drying his hair with a slightly ragged, green towel. That's just what we wanted to know.

Marley and Lauralee were both distracted momentarily by my brother's half-nakedness, but Marley managed to get her libido under control and continue with her story. "W-Well, Damian is the son of Edwin and Gabrielle Abernathy. Gabrielle has a younger sister named Tracey. I'm pretty sure you know Tracey Ward's daughter...Jessica."

All of our jaws dropped in surprise at once. So, that's why Damian agreed to help Jess! Jess is his cousin, and, of course, he would help his own flesh and blood! I'm so stupid! I shouldn't have been that gullible! If I would've done my research instead of being smitten, I would've saved the three of us a lot of heartache.

"I'm gonna kill him!" Apollo growled, throwing his towel angrily at the floor.

"No, Apollo," I urged.

"No, if he thinks he's gonna get away with some bullcrap like this, he's got another thing coming!" He began to pace back and forth as he hurriedly put on a yellow polo shirt.

"Apollo, you'll just make things worse. It's best if we just keep this between you and me. Mom and Dad don't have to know. We all need to just let this pass."

I didn't want more chaos and drama engulfing my life. I didn't need Mom and Dad to take my affairs into their own hands. I didn't want some never-ending war between Jess and I or between Damian and Apollo. I wanted peace. I just wanted peace…

Apollo stopped pacing the floor and looked me in my eyes. "Minnie, please, just let me do this for you."

"If you want to do something for me, let it go. Please, Apollo. I don't need things to get worse."

We stared at each other for a few silent seconds before he closed his eyes, exhaled, and growled, "Fiiiine, sis." I smiled and happily ruffled his hair. "Thanks, big brother."

Once we all had eaten and showered, we decided it was time to get out of Marley's hair. We placed our dirty, foul-smelling clothes into grocery bags and prepared to get on our way. It was only 10:30, so it wasn't late enough for Mom and Dad to start worrying where we were.

"Thanks for everything," We both whispered to Marley as we hugged her by her teeny waist.

"Anytime," She casually replied. Apollo reached out and hugged her, as well. "Thanks, Marley." Marley grinned as she returned his hug and patted him on his back. "You're welcome, Apollo."

Lauralee blew a kiss and I waved goodbye to Marley before we began to walk towards our cars. I'll be so glad when I'm safe at home and this night would finally be over.

"Call me if you need me!" She called to us.

"We will!" Lauralee and I answered back.

Apollo listened to angry music the entire ride home. He sped and cursed under his breath at every red light. I know he's trying to protect me, but all I need from my brother and Lauralee was to forget this night ever happened. Apollo used his keys and we entered the house.

"How was the party?" Dad asked once we shut the door.

Apollo glared at me with his jaw clenched and barged off to his room without a word. The typical maternal, concerned expression came over Mom's face.

"What's the matter with him?'

Time to think of a lie and quick! "Umm, he's just upset about some guy who made him mad while we there."

"Ha! What else is new? Apollo does have your temper, Patrick," Mom joked as she poured herself a glass of lemonade. Dad chuckled. "My temper? No, he is definitely his mother's son."

Just as I thought I was in the clear, Dite nosily blurted out, "Why do you have on different clothes than from before?"

Curse that blonde haired brat! I'd worry about strangling her later, now I had to think of another lie. "Well, that's actually what Apollo is angry about. You see, some dumb guy tripped and spilled his food and stuff all over us. It was all in my hair and on his favorite shoes and everything. It was a real mess."

Athena giggled. "He sounds like a real klutz."

"You mean like you?" Dite quipped with her eyebrow raised.

"Shut up, Dite!" Athena barked.

As Mom and Dad turned their attention towards my younger, bickering sisters, I snuck off to my room. Now, I was in the clear. As I undressed and went to lie down, my mind began to replay the disastrous events that occurred tonight. For as long as we lived, Apollo, Lauralee, and I would never forget this night. The anger and betrayal would stick with us like glue for the rest of our lives. Today was a nightmare. I kept blaming myself, although it was unreasonable for anyone to expect me to know the family tree of everyone who lived in Angel City.

"I should've said no. I should've said no." I kept repeating in my head until I dozed off.

CHAPTER EIGHTEEN:
"The looming accusations of murder won't ever pass."

The police and the media are determined to prove me guilty. I'm constantly being brought in for questioning and the scandal-loving reports just twist all of my words around no matter what I say or how I say it. It's like living in a hell I can't escape. My family and I just keep praying that this ordeal will end sooner than later. It's late April now and I just wonder how much longer this can drag on. Fortunately, the events that occurred at Damian's "party" months ago have somewhat passed. I'm thankful Lauralee didn't tell her father about what happened. Lauralee said that "her Dad would've declared World Wars 3-5 on the Abernathys; and she didn't want anything embarrassing tainting their family's image anyways." Damian's surely gotten over it. Lately, he's been bragging about some tall, hot brunette who "was surprisingly wild in the sheets." The anger and embarrassment will always be there but at least people aren't talking about it as much now. However, the looming accusations of murder won't ever pass. Sometimes, I felt like I was in a permanent slump. However, having someone who knew Callista for as long as I did, like Marley, made grieving a little easier. We would talk on the phone about our feelings. We both shared the same main feeling. Some days we could think of Callista and still function. We could still go to school or go grocery shopping as if nothing ever happened. But some days, her memory crippled us. Marley said she cried for over an hour on her bedroom floor yesterday. I'd cried so much I thought my eyes would forever remain bloodshot by now and that my nose would almost run dry. When we were lonely and wanting someone to reach out to, we called each other. Lauralee didn't know her and love her like we did, so she wouldn't be much help in grieving her death, especially after what went down between her, Stephanie, and Callista. Not to say Lauralee wouldn't care that a 17-year-old pregnant woman was murdered. But, when you don't know the victim personally, your ability to empathize with their pain is diminished. Marley terrified me when she confessed that "Ophelia's bottles of liquid joy were starting to look better and better." Marley knows that her father's death persuaded Ophelia to turn to alcohol to soothe her pain, so why would she even consider following in her mother's footsteps?

That's what scared me the most; Marley becoming the second alcoholic in her family. Callista, nor Donald, would want that for her. I persuaded the grieving and confused Marley out of sipping out her mother's vodka bottles. Once she regained her composure, she promised me she'd never go down her mother's drunken path. I couldn't have been more relieved. This is what best friends are for. Not just for shopping and telling silly stories, but uplifting each other when we hit our lowest points. I was also beginning to worry about Marley's home life. When I saw her the other day, she had two, fresh wounds on the top left side of her forehead. It looked like someone scratched her or maybe hit her with something. She says she has no idea where they came from and that she just woke up and realized they were there. But, I don't believe that. Makes me wonder if she and Ophelia maybe had a "physical disagreement" sometime recently, but I'll trust Marley to tell me the truth when she's ready. I'm sure that even when I'm proven innocent, people will still call me Artemis "Killer" Carlisle. Once ignorant people have an opinion of you, you stay in that light no matter what happens. The truth is too boring for some. Like I said before, some Angeleans practically feed off drama and scandal and I know I'm providing a hearty meal for a lot of ignorant Angeleans right about now. At least it's Thursday and almost the end of the week. Saturday and Sunday are the only times I get a break from Angel City High so I greatly look forward to them now. Normally, I try to be the very first person in every class. Early means I get to choose my favorite seat in the farthest, coldest corner of the room. Early means I have less of a chance of anyone doing anything or trying anything with me in class because I'd be so quiet, they'd quickly forget I was in the room. Thanks to my bladder going into overdrive at the very last minute, I was now officially late to my Algebra 3 class. Great, my day is already getting off to a bad start. I zip through the hall, sassily muttering, "Excuse me" as I fight to get through the last remaining swarm of tardy students blocking my way to Mrs. Patton's classroom. I finally arrive in front of Mrs. Patton's room. I pause a moment before opening door, taking a second to catch my breath and prepare for a bunch of glares and awkward silence upon my entrance. I open the door and before I even step both feet into the classroom, the spotlight is unfortunately on me. Mrs. Patton stops teaching and she and the other 20 students have their full, undivided attention on me. I gulp and close the door behind me. My heart begins to beat slightly faster.

"You're late, Miss Carlisle," is all Mrs. Patton says to acknowledge my presence, as if I wasn't already aware that I had arrived late. I simply apologize and stare down at my nails as I make my way to a desk, far away from most of my peers.

Mrs. Patton resumes her lecture. A few students glance my way, snicker, and whisper to their friends as she teaches. A small, silver object is suddenly flicked at me and hits me on the apple of my left cheek. I look down to see that it is a crumpled up, bubble gum wrapper. I look over to my left to see that it was projected from the lovely Jess Ward, who smirks and throws up two middle fingers in my direction.

"Jessica, do you know the answer to number eighteen?" Mrs. Patton asks. Jess quickly puts her birds away and directs her attention back to the front of the class. "Uhh, is it 20?" She hurriedly answers. Her tone indicates that she has no absolute clue what Mrs. Patton is talking about.

"Wrong answer, idiot," I snide happily in my head. Carmella Carson, who is sitting 4 seats up from Jess, giggles at Jess's stupidity.

Mrs. Patton sighs. "No, Jessica. The final step to finishing this equation was to solve four to the fifth power which is 1,024. You gave me 4 times 5. Maybe if you'd pay attention instead of badgering your classmates, you would've gotten it right."

I smirk, Carmella giggles again and Jess looks completely embarrassed and frustrated at the same time. After about fifteen more minutes, Mrs. Patton gives us some busy work while she steps out to go to the teacher's lounge. Of course, as soon as the door slams shut behind her, everyone either whips out their phone or turns around to talk to their friends.

"You found something funny, Carson?" Jess blurts out, capturing the attention of everyone in the class. Carmella stops choosing a song on her iPod and her Barbie blonde bob whips as she turns around in her seat to look Jess in the eyes. "What are you talking about?"

"What the hell were you laughing about earlier when Mrs. Patton called on me, hmm? Something got you tickled pink over there?" Jess growls.

Carmella places her iPod and neon orange earphones on her desk. "Yeah, I found something hilarious. You're an idiot, that's what funny, Jess. You wanna get mad at me because your dumb noggin doesn't know how to use exponents? Are you mad because the only A's you'll ever have in life are in your bra? Sit your stupid, wannabe hardcore ass down."

The class erupts with laughter and Carmella sits back in her seat with a pleased grin plastered on her face. I place my hand over my mouth as I laugh. Knowing Jess, if she hears me laughing at her expense, she'll probably re-direct her attention back onto me. Jess shoots up out of her seat like a rocket. "I'll slap you off that high horse you're on! You think you're something because of your GPA, bitch? Yeah, it's 4.0, the same as the number of different guys you've slept with every week since the school year started. No, honey, I think you're mad because your body will be worn out quicker than those cheap highlights."

The class erupts with laughter again. I don't know who should be more offended because both of them are telling the truth. Jess is an idiot and Carmella is a whore albeit an intelligent one. Tehe, this is getting good. Carmella angrily stands back up, hands placed firmly on her hips.

"Uuugh!" She groans. Her face is hideously contorted from aggravation. "I'm already pissed about some other stuff, in addition to my newly broken nail, and I'm NOT about to deal with your bull today, Jessica! You didn't have to go there!"

"I'm not about to deal with your bull today, Jessica. You didn't have to go there!" Jess mocks in a nasally voice.

"You're so damn childish and annoying and just ugh! I swear, you're just like Cal-"

She stops her sentence short before things get too far, but she has already crossed the line. The class, which was once overflowing with laughter, grows nearly silent, with the exception of a few gasps. Jess and I exchange looks with one another and for once, I think we're on the same side.

"Say what you have to say, Carmella! Say her name, I DARE you to!" Jess warns as she begins to quickly remove her student I.D. and multicolored bangles.

Carmella begins to step backwards, back towards her seat. She's worried now. She knows she's messed up; and you can tell it by the look of fear in her eyes.

"How dare you talk about Callista like that! Don't you have any respect for the dead!?" I yell at her.

Defensive, she angrily retorts, "What does it matter to you!? You killed her! Now that baby's got nobody because she had friends like YOU!" She points at both Jess and me.

"I didn't kill anyone!" I shout back at her. There are tears flowing from my eyes because I'm so angry. I'm squeezing my fists so tightly, it almost hurts.

"That's it!" Jess screams as she attempts to charge at Carmella, but a couple of other students restrain her. I'm so worked up that my ability to think rationally has flown completely out the window, and I charge at her, as well. I push and shove desks out of the way and they make loud, thundering sounds as they fall against the checkered floor.

"Get her good, Minnie!" Jess shouts.

All I can concentrate on is wrapping my fingers around that tiny neck of Carmella's. All I can think about is ripping out her artificially blonde hair. All I can do is buck and kick and scream as I am held back by Jonas DiCamillo and some other student before I can even reach Carmella's body. Summoned by the noises in the classroom, Mrs. Patton and two other teachers rush into the chaos. I'm desperately trying to get free of the hold my classmates have on me, but the two of them easily overpower me. Jess is bucking so hard to loosen the grip her restrainers have on her that they fall onto the cold, tile floor. The room is drowning in absolute chaos. Jess frantically gets to her feet and steps toward Carmella, but she is restrained again around her waist by one of the male teachers. By this time, Carmella is escorted out of the room by Mrs. Patton. She glances over at Jess, who is still kicking nearby desks and screaming obscenities. Then, she glances over at me, eyes green and full of regret. The fact that she gets to walk away freely after speaking about Callista like that set my blood aflame. I lose control again and begin screaming, "Let me get her! Let me get her!" as I make more futile attempts to get away. I'm enraged! I'm infuriated! I'm PISSED OFF! Even though people already think I murdered Callista, I've never wanted to hurt someone so badly until Carmella pissed me off today…and I pray to God, that I don't feel like this ever again.

CHAPTER NINETEEN

"He gave me a false hope."

After order was regained, Jess and I had the pleasure of getting a stern talking-to by the principal. Luckily, we weren't expelled, but we were sentenced to some in-school suspension for the next week. Our mothers were not happy, not even in the slightest.

"Why are you always getting yourself in trouble, Jessica? Hmm? You think I like working 10 hour shifts for a daughter who loves to raise Hell? First, you wanted a tattoo. Then, you snuck and got your nose pierced. Then, you decided to dye your hair that ridiculous color; and now you're just getting out of hand! You just wait until I call up your father when we get home. Oooh, Malcolm is NOT gonna be happy with his little girl, y'know," Tracey lectured.

"Moooooom," Jess groaned. "You don't have to call Daddy."

"Afraid he's gonna chew your ear off for this? It's a little too late for that now, Jess. Just because he lives in Manhattan now does not mean you get to be spared from his wrath, too," Tracey finished as she opened the office door and she and Jess exited. I could hear the sound of Tracey's voice and sneakers squeaking taper off as they continued down the hall.

Mom was pretty sullen when we left the office. There was not a peep out of either of my parents until we got into the car actually. Dad was doing most of the lecturing, Mom would just chime in here and there to give her two cents. I don't know if she was more pissed or disappointed. As Dad was pulling up in the driveway, we noticed a mysterious, black Dodge Charger parked in front of our house.

"You expecting company, Diana?" Dad inquired as we exited our car.

"No…and I know Minnie better not have any company coming over, right?" Mom hinted, staring dead at me.

"N-no," I stammer. God, Mom can be intimating when she wants to be. A man steps out of the Charger and we see that it is Chief Marshall Carson, Head of the ACPD. Aww, hell. Haven't I had enough of a rotten day already?

"Chief Carson!" My Dad greets, waving his hand in the air. "How are ya?"

"Patriiick!" Mom hisses. She, like me, is wondering why Dad is being so hospitable to the chief of police when I'm up for murder charges.

"What!? If we act jumpy and defensive every time a cop strolls by, it'll make Minnie look guiltier. We just gotta play it cool." Dad whispers to us and Chief Carson walks towards us.

"Is there something we can help you with?" Mom sternly inquired. She was having none of this "play it cool" stuff Dad was talking about. Dad shoots a look at Mom, who raises an eyebrow right back at him.

"I just wanted to talk with Minnie for a while. Is that okay with the both of you?"

"Talk?" Mom asks.

"Just a few questions. I'll be out of her hair before your wife can get dinner on the table," He jokes, but I don't find it funny. I don't want him in my hair at all. Why me, Lord? Why me? Dad looks over at Mom who looks back at him then they both look at me. I guess they were letting me decide on this one.

"It's okay. I'll talk to him…but, just for a little while," I answer. They both sigh and begin to walk towards the front door.

"Good to see you, Chief," Dad remarks as he locks the car.

"We'll talk later, Minnie," Mom warns.

After Mom's warning, they both enter the house arm in arm. At first, we are silent. There's some kids laughing a few houses down the street. I hear gravel being crushed and rocks being scattered as a car drives past us. I see two squirrels chasing each other up a large tree in our yard. This silence is just too much for me.

"You wanted something, Chief Carson?" I ask, growing bored with the non-talking.

"Yes, I do want something," He replies mysteriously. He fixes his shirt collar and then continues, "but please, call me Marshall."

Under this sunlight, I never realized how much Carmella's dad looked like a younger George Clooney. "Ok, Marshall?"

"Brenda told me about your little spat with our daughter today," He informs, referring to Carmella's mother. "Our daughter always has been a drama queen. She overreacts to everything like women always do. Sometimes, I think if Brenda had given me a boy, we wouldn't have nearly as much trouble out of her."

I glare at him like the misogynist he is. He quickly changes the topic.

"This, on top of your charges do not lean in your favor, Artimy."

Artimy? What the hell is that, a village in France or something? "It's Artemis," I correct.

"Artemis…that's a pretty name," He compliments.

Ignoring his compliment, I reply, "I know all about my reputation in this town, Marshall." It feels so weird calling him by his first name.

"You're suspected of first degree murder. The murder of your friend-turned-enemy who stole your boyfriend and got pregnant by him."

I roll my eyes and stick out my hip slightly. He looks downward as I do so. "It's not that simple. She was my best friend. I'd never hurt her." I'm getting sick of singing this same tune.

"How old are you, Minnie?"

"Eighteen."

"Hmmm," he retorts. "Only eighteen and suspected of a crime that could get you sent to jail for a looooot of years. Maybe, I could help you."

I dart my head from staring at the ants troop by on the ground to Chief Carson's dark green eyes. My eyes widened with the hope that I may have found a way to get out of this mess. "Help? How?"

He gave a mischievous smile, as if he were up to something. "I was just thinking that you should use your assets to their full potential. You have so many assets that could prove valuable to help you, Minnie."

I grinned from ear to ear as I eagerly fiddled with my hair. "You mean it, Chief Carson- I mean, Marshall? That's great! Just tell me what I need to do to get out of this mess and I'll do it!"

He stepped closer to me, hands in his pockets. "That's good to hear, Minnie."

"Well?" I start.

"Well, what?"

"What do you need me to do?"

He laughed nervously a little to himself as he took one hand out of his pocket and smoothed his hair from front to back. "Umm…how do you feel about fellatio, Minnie?"

My happiness is momentarily subsided by my confusion. "Fellatio? What's that?"

"It's the only job a woman was put on this Earth to do, Minnie. Think over it for a few days, and then call me when you've made a decision," He smiles charmingly as he hands me a small, white card. I glance down at it.

"Marshall: 737-8378,"it reads. There's even a small, smiley face in the lower left corner written in black Sharpie.

"I'll get back to you as soon as possible!" I happily exclaim. This is the start of me being able to clear my good name. Finally, someone was on my side.

"That's good to know," Marshall responds. "I'll…see you later then, Minnie. Enjoy the rest of your evening."

We both turn around and part ways. I practically run to my house, clutching Marshall's card to my chest as if it were my newborn child. I rush into the house and Dad momentarily stops me by announcing, "Dinner's ready." I'm hungry, no doubt, but I ignore his announcement and continue speeding into my room, almost knocking over Dite in the process. Once in my room, I quickly grab my laptop, open it and power it on. First things first, I need to know what this word "fellatio" means or else I'm gonna be walking into this plan dumb and blind. I assumed it was a cop term or legal technicality or something. Next, I'd call Marshall and let him know that I'm in. I unlock my laptop and scurry to the Internet. I type in the word in the Google search bar and in a matter of milliseconds, search results pop up. My hope and happiness is immediately murdered.

"Fellatio (noun): The act of stimulating the male sex organ with the mouth for sexual pleasure," my screen defines.

I was just solicited by my enemy's father for oral sex. I'm practically mortified. The grin was immediately erased from my face upon reading the definition. I read the definition like 3 more times, as if it would change somehow. This is the guy who everyone in this city admires. Chief Marshall is like a hero, everyone likes him. Now, he's just our friendly, neighborhood pervert.

"Minnie Carlisle, why the hell are you looking up that kind of stuff!" a voice hisses from behind me.

I jump in my bed. My laptop falls off my lap. It's my Mom, who's managed to sneak up from behind me, probably came in to remind me about dinner.

"Mom, I can explain-" I start.

"Don't you know there are KIDS in this house!? This is a home, not a pornography studio!"

Before I can even try to explain again, she yells, "Patriiiick!" After a few seconds, Daddy comes into the room.

"What's going on?" He casually asks.

"Your daughter is in here looking up fellatio, that's what's going on," Mom snitches.

Dad's eyebrows come inward, indicating that he's about to get pissed off. "What the hell for!?"

"Because Chief Marshall told me to!" I blurted out. Their expressions soften a bit, going from angry to skeptical.

"The chief of police…told you to come home…and Google sex terms?" Mom responded, her left eyebrow raised in disbelief.

So I began to explain to them all about the conversation I had with Chief Marshall after they left us alone and went into the house and left me with a George Clooney impersonator who was looking to get his rocks off.

"And that's why I rushed into the house like that…I thought it was a plan to help me. I thought he was trying to help me with my charges," I began to cry as soon as I finished my sentence. I felt like an idiot for being so gullible. I felt like a pawn in his sexually twisted game. I felt disappointed because for a brief moment, I really believed he was on my side. I really believed in him. He gave me a false hope. Mom walked over and held me warmly in her arms in comfort. She reached over on my nightstand and grabbed some tissues to wipe my eyes. Dad was silent.

"I'm going…to kiiill him," is all he seethes before attempting to storm out of the room.

"No, Patrick. You can't do that and you know it," Mom warns. Dad turns around. I've never seen Daddy look so angry. Mom has always been the feistier and outspoken one out of my parents. Anger is simply out of my Dad's usual character so we all know if he's the one upset, something serious must be going on and to just stay out of his way.

"Then WHAT am I supposed to do, Diana!? He solicited my little girl and I'm supposed to just be happy with it!? No, Diana, I'm not just going to do nothing!"

"And I won't allow you to get sent to jail for that scumbag, Patrick! If you put your hands on the chief of police, you're gonna be the one to suffer the consequences! Violence is only going to make this worse, Patrick," Mom advises.

Dad closes his eyes and inhales, deeply then exhales slowly, as a means of attempting to calm himself down. "I want him dead, Diana," he growls.

"I know you do," Mom responds, taking Dad's hands gently in her own. "We'll report him. We'll get 'em fired so he can't try this stunt on nobody else's daughter. Don't allow him to drag you down with him."

Mom and Dad decided to leave Apollo and me in charge of Dite, Athena, and Ares while they go run "errands." I turn the television on a family friendly comedy, as Apollo fixes everyone's plate of the deliciously cheesy, lasagna Daddy made. It's his specialty. As my siblings go back and forth between engaging each other in conversation and bursting at the seams with laughter because of the movie, I zone out. Fiddling with my food, I can't help but to wonder, "How many other girls has he tried this on and gotten away with it?" He seemed so confident, as if he knew from experience that I was going to say yes. Is it bad that despite our argument, I felt sort of bad for Carmella? I even kind of worried about her for a bit. Her mother is a subservient doormat, she just lets her husband walk all over her, and her father is a misogynist pervert. It causes me to wonder if he's pulling stuff like this in the streets. What the hell is he doing or saying in the privacy of the Carson home?

"You okay, sis?" Apollo whispers to me after he takes a sip of his soda.

I step back into reality. "Uh, yeah. I'm fine." Apollo knows me better than that, he can tell when something's bothering me. Instead of digging deeper, he just stares at me before responding, "If you say so," then returning his attention back towards the television set.

CHAPTER TWENTY:

"Killers shouldn't be allowed to wine and dine like kings, Minnie Carlisle."

Dad, in an attempt to lift the spirits of everyone in the house, decided we all have dinner as a family at the local restaurant, O'Charley's. Mom has a different set of plans though. She has already started baking brownies and preparing extra buttery popcorn in hopes of having a quiet, family movie night. She says she just wants to spend some quality time at home with all of us, but Dad and I know it's because she doesn't want to run the risk of someone saying or doing something hurtful to any of us again. I'm torn between both of my parents' ideas. Part of me just wants to play it cool and stay in the nice, safe haven I call home forever. The other part of me is going stir-crazy. I feel like a prisoner sometimes, being forced to stay within the walls of our home. I'm sitting in the kitchen playing a game on my cellphone though I've already beaten this level a thousand different ways. Ares is practically drooling at the oven door, as he intently watches Mom's fudge brownies bake to perfection. The sweet, alluring smell of the brownies along with the tantalizing, buttery scent of the popcorn is making my stomach growl. Athena is peacefully reading a book on Dad's favorite recliner; and Dite and Apollo are arguing over what genre of movie to watch. After my parents close their bedroom door to continue their "discussion" (they're still weary of using the word argument around Athena and Ares.), I sneak carefully on tiptoe behind them to listen at their door.

"Diana, we can't stay in this house forever," Dad starts.

"I pay half the bills in this house. Me and my babies can stay in it if we want to," Mom childishly reasoned.

"Diiiaaaaanaa," Dad groaned.

"Paaaatriiick," Mom mocked.

Just as I leaned in closer to hear Dad's next response more clearly, my cellphone dropped out of my bra and fell loudly against the door and carpet.

I curse in my head as I carefully placed my phone into my pocket.

"I don't know which one of you is there, but you'd better get away from that door!" Mom warned from the other side of the bedroom door.

I took Mom's warning to heart and headed back into the kitchen to rejoin the rest of my siblings. I decided to sit down with Athena and read her favorite book "Huckleberry Finn," with her on Dad's recliner. As soon as I started getting into it, we heard a door suddenly open, and then Mom stormed out of the hallway. She was obviously on a warpath. The first thing Hurricane Diana did was turn off our big screen television.

"Heyyy!" Apollo and Dite protested.

Next, she turned off the oven, ceasing Ares from enjoying baking of the brownies.

"Come on, kids. We're going OUT to eat." She seethed as she stormed past Daddy without making eye contact with him. The five of us just glanced around at one another without a word and then went into our rooms to get dressed.

Mom was silent on the way to O'Charley's at first, but Daddy worked his Carlisle charm and managed to calm Hurricane Diana down. They were disgustingly lovey-dovey with one another the whole way there. I think they might make another Carlisle tonight. I don't know what freaked me out more; the thought of my parents being sexual or having a fifth sibling. Once we entered the restaurant, the waitress kindly showed us to our table. While walking to our table, I noticed a boy and a girl I presume to be his sister staring at Athena. She stopped happily discussing her favorite chapter in her book with me upon noticing them looking in her direction. She moved closer to me, as if she was looking for me to protect/comfort her. I gently placed my hand atop her hair, stroking it in an effort to calm her nerves. Dite, in an effort to get Athena's attention, poked her in the side near her rib, but apparently Dite doesn't know her own strength and ended up hurting her.

"Ow! What do you want, Dite!?" Athena hissed, glaring at Dite.

"Who are those kids staring at you, Athena?" I whispered.

"That's Nicholas Quentin and his older sister, Tessa. Dite deals with Tessa all the time in class, but Nicholas has been bothering me ever since…"

She tapered off. From there, I automatically knew why the Quentins were badgering my sisters. It's because they're related to the girl who kills pregnant women and gets everyone's favorite police chief in a heap of legal trouble. How dare them! Using someone's death as a scapegoat to taunt someone. Kids can be just as cruel as adults, don't let anyone tell you otherwise. My jaw clenched in anger. The pure frustration of not being able to intervene was maddening. Now I really know how Apollo felt when I told him not to do anything in return for what Damian and Jess did to us at their setup party.

"You want me to make them cry, Athena? Hmm? Come on, I can take 'em. All I have to do is call him "Fat Nikki" one good time and he'll have tears rolling down BOTH of his chins like a poor sap sucker," Dite eagerly offered, looking ready to pounce on the opportunity to make Nicholas suffer. I was glad that Dite was willing to stand up and defend her younger sister when she needed her; but violence will only beget more violence. It was time to stop trying to fight fire with fire; and time to start turning the other cheek…no matter how hard it may be.

"No. Just leave it alone, Dite," Athena humbly mumbled as we got to our seats. From there, we all grabbed plates and proceeded to choose our meal from the buffet lines. I chose broccoli and cheese pasta, garlic bread, and string beans. Weird, I know, but I had a craving for it like none other. Back at the table, Mom and Dad were sharing a bottle of red wine with their meal and holding hands. Apollo was having an eating contest with Ares, and Dite was telling one of her many, corny jokes to Athena. Maybe it's her way of cheering her up. The punchlines are horribly obvious; but they are hilarious to her. Whatever floats her boat, I guess. She was regaining her composure and was in the midst of starting another joke.

"Okay, okay, okay. I got another one," Dite laughed. "What kind of music do mummies listen to?"

Athena and I smirked as we shrugged our shoulders. Just as Dite was about to hit us with the big punchline, a voice from behind us answered, "Wrap music, duh." We turned in our seats to see Aunt Liz, Uncle Danny, and our cousins, 18-year-old, Tony and 14-year-old, Christian. The mood lightened even more upon them joining our family get-together.

"Sorry, we're late! The traffic out there always gets bad around this time, I swear." Aunt Liz commented as she and Uncle D took a seat close to our parents. Tony sat in-between Apollo and Ares and Christian, who was the one who ruined Dite's joke, sat to the right of Dite.

"You ruined my joke, Christian!" Dite lamented, pretending to be upset.

"Who cares? It was going to be lame anyways," Christian joked as began to eat his macaroni and marinara sauce.

This is exactly what I needed. Getting out of the house and being surrounded by good food and great people was like medicine to my tortured soul. The parents were sitting at the head of the table, chatting and getting a little tipsy off the champagne. How selfish. I'm sure Tony, Apollo, and I, especially, would love some alcohol in our system. Since when does being underage matter anymore? Speaking of Tony, he had now engaged in the testosterone-induced, food eating contest with Apollo. Ares was happily cheering, although he was torn between rooting for his favorite and only brother and his favorite cousin. As Dite watched the contest, her prankster cousin slipped some salt into her pink lemonade. Athena, Christian, and I all burst out with laughter as Dite's face cringed upon sipping the tainted drink. Nothing is more healing than just being yourself with the ones you love. Maybe Daddy's idea wasn't such a bad one after all.

"Killers shouldn't be allowed to wine and dine like kings, Minnie Carlisle," A voice growled from behind us.

I turned in my seat again to see an infuriated, Stella Arden with Eric standing behind her. She looked locked, loaded, and ready to cause a scene. Well, so much for our peaceful family time.

CHAPTER TWENTY-ONE:
"It's sad it had to come to this."

The reason behind Stella's more aggressive than normal anger hits me with the force of a speeding freight train.

"Today is Stella Arden's birthday. This would be her first birthday without all five of her children here to celebrate it with her." Remembering what today means for her makes me sympathize with her, however, Stella looks to be quite unsympathetic tonight.

"Come on, Stella. Let's just go back to our table. The boys are waiting for us," Eric calmly reminds her as he attempts to lead her back to their side of the restaurant by her hand. She quickly yanks away from his grip. He exhales deeply; obviously frustrated with his wife's stubbornness.

"Did you hear what you just said, Eric!? The boys are waiting for us! We used to have a girl but thanks to Killer Carlisle here, that's been taken away from us!"

I noticed the Arden boys rushing over from wherever their table was to stand by their parents' side. Uncle D stood up. "I think it's time you leave, Stella. Let's not cause a scene," He suggested. Uriel decided to join in on the attack. "Oh, what are you going to do, arrest her? You need to be arresting your niece for the murder of my sister!"

"Don't talk to my Dad like that!" Tony threatened as he put his glass of Pepsi down and rose to his feet. Normally, Tony is very level-headed and introverted, but he won't allow anyone to disrespect his family, especially in front of his face. Apollo soon followed suit, looking ready to redeem himself after losing his last physical encounter with Uriel. Uh oh. There's no way this is going to end well. See? We should've just stayed home and ate those brownies.

Gabe stepped in, defending his younger brother. "Don't come at my brother like that! You'd better sit down."

"Make me," Apollo and Tony challenged, harmonizing with one another. Mom shot Dad and Uncle D a look that said "Get your sons under control, now!" The Carlisle/Davidson and Arden families were about to raise absolute Hell. So much for a family-friendly eating establishment.

"Stella, there's no need for you and your boys to make a scene," Aunt

Liz proclaimed.

"There's no need for you to jump in business that isn't yours, ELIZA! Stay out of this!" Stella barked.

"Now you just wait a minute!" Aunt Liz started.

We were now encircled in a mass chaos of insults, threats, and yelling. All eyes were on us. The spotlight was shining its negative light on us again. All these emotions running rampant were almost too much to handle and get under control. Dad's idea for a serene, Thursday night dinner is turning into a battleground. Suddenly, Athena screamed, "STOP!! Just STOP!!!!"

Athena's wails seemed to pierce through the chaos for a moment. It might as well have stopped time. Everyone stopped yelling and acting like animals and just paused to stare at Athena, who was now being coddled by Dite and Christian.

"Athena, baby. It's okay. Mommy's here." Mom consoled as she and Dad walked over to her to comfort her. Dite and Christian moved so that Athena could now be comforted by our parents. Just when I thought the madness had come to a halt, Stella remarked, "See, what you've done, Minnie? Why don't you just confess? You're dragging your whole family down."

Mom began to look irritated. "Stella, Minnie didn't upset Athena. YOU did. You don't even know who killed Callista so don't go around pointing your fingers at my daughter."

Stella rushed over to my mother. They were now face to face; glaring each other deep in the blues of each other's eyes. They were probably close enough to hear each other's heartbeat.

"I didn't kill Callista, Mrs. Arden," I mumbled. I was almost begging for her to believe me.

She turned to me. "Yeah, sure you didn't. I wonder if you love lying as much as you love pushing pregnant women down flights of concrete steps."

My Mom shoved her by her shoulders, apparently forgetting that her brother is a cop and is standing right across the table from her. "That's enough, Stella! You clearly don't know what you're talking about!"

Stella faked laughed loudly, completely unbothered by my mother's attack. "Oh, I don't know what I'm talking about? I know the justice system is failing to keep narcissistic psychopaths like her off the streets. I know your daughter is a killer who deserves to either rot in prison or in a mental hospital. I know your daughter has always been a jealous, conniving brat ever since she was young, and the apple apparently doesn't fall too far from the tree! I don't know why you're so against the idea of Minnie being thrown behind a filthy cell. It's not like you don't have two other girls. You'll never even miss her."

Mom was clearly taken aback by Stella's offensive, ruthless remarks. Her demeanor softened a bit. "It doesn't matter if I have 2 other daughters or 12 other daughters, Minnie is irreplaceable. As a mother, I'd think you'd understand that perfectly."

Stella moved her blonde tresses out of her face then crossed her arms and raised an eyebrow. She wasn't backing down. "Irreplaceable? Please, anybody can find a common trash psychopath from any back alley gutter with no morals. You've let your daughter get away with murder since she was a kid, now you're LITERALLY letting her get away with it. Your daughter-"

My mother interrupted Stella's bombarding insults by thrashing both of her fists on the table. Glasses and plates clanged loudly from the impact. She screams, "My daughter this and my daughter that! What is it, Stella!? Are you jealous that you don't have one anymore!?"

The restaurant fell into a short period of undisturbed silence and minimal movement. I think I had forgotten to breathe for a moment. Granted, Mom's last words were harsh but Stella had pushed her over the edge of thinking rationally by insulting the thing that mattered most to her, her kids. Dad placed a hand on Mom's shoulder and judging by Mom's facial expression, she was immediately and deeply regretting what she had said. She looked guilty, sad, and speechless. There's nothing one could say in this moment to make up for a statement like that. Stella just continued to stand there and stare at Mom for a few more seconds. She didn't move or speak. I don't think she even blinked for a while. With her fists clenched, jaw tense, and eyes beginning to water, she abruptly turned in the opposite direction and frantically ran towards the nearest exit. Uriel glared at Apollo and hissed, "This isn't over," before he and the rest of his brothers chased after their mother who had now exited the restaurant. Eric takes one step, looks at all of us and simply mutters, "It's sad it had to come to this." Then, he follows his sons and wife out of the door. I'd never seen him look so worn out, like he was ready for all of this to be over.

It's beyond sad. It's a low that I'd never thought our families or I would reach. This whole ordeal is tearing our family apart. My Mom and Stella were once good friends before Callista's death and now look at them. Callista's death seemed to make Stella grow a little colder, little less compassionate, whereas, it's had the opposite effect on Eric. He's not nearly as much of the "macho man" Callista used to love to brag about and I can see it in those sad, brown eyes of his. Maybe Stella's right. Maybe I should just confess and let us move on with our lives. I could picture it now. Mom happily living with Apollo, Dite, Athena, and Ares…forgetting she and Daddy ever even had me. Stella's words were starting to get to me, and it was driving me up a wall.

"This is all my fault! I'm dragging you all down and it's not fair to any of you!" I cry as I abruptly rush to my feet and toward the exit on the other side of the establishment. My family calls after me, but of course, I don't stop running. I wait for them beside my parents' car. Without making any form of eye contact, we all pile in. No one dares to talk to me. They're probably afraid to even look at me, unsure of how I'd react in my current, unstable, emotional state. Upon entering our humble abode at last, I sprinted to find solitude in my bedroom. I just wanted to lay in my little dark corner of the room and remain unbothered. I fell asleep soon after throwing myself onto my unmade bed.

Later, I was awakened by the sound of my door opening, then closing, and the near-blinding lights flickering on inside my bedroom. Who the hell has the gall to disturb me after I think I made it clear I wanted to be alone?

"Minnie? Wake up, sweetie," My mother's voice breaks the silence in the room.

I growl and rustle around in my bed a little, but I do not actually sit up to greet her eye to eye.

"What? You didn't hear your mother? Get up, Artemis." My father sternly commands. He feels sorry for me, yes, but won't tolerate blatant disobedience. How typical.

I roll my eyes in protest under the covers before I sit up in my bed. My hair is all over the place and I have to squint my eyes to numb the burn from the bright, bedroom light overhead. My mother sits on the edge of the bed next to me and Daddy stands directly beside her.

"W-what's going on?" I groggily inquire as I wipe my eyes with my bare hand.

Mom reaches out and gently holds on to both of my hands. "I am soo sorry, Minnie. I shouldn't have let things escalate that far with Stella in front of everyone like that." Dad runs his fingers through his red hair. "No, Diana. It's my fault. I should've just stayed in the damn house. I should've listened to you."

"It's not either of your faults," I spoke. "Whoever killed Callista...it's their fault. When we find him or her, I'll be sure to let them know repeatedly."

"Your graduation is just around the corner. You shouldn't be dealing with this for your last year of high school," Mom pointed out.

"I shouldn't be dealing with it at all, Mom," I responded. I placed my face within the palms of my hands and groaned. "Argh, I just want to escape, to be honest."

"What if we told you that we've found a place for you to escape to?" Dad remarks.

I put my hands back down on my legs and glance up at him. "What? Are you sending me to an orphanage?"

Mom smiled faintly and tucked my hair behind my ears. "I wouldn't dream of it. No, we made a few phone calls and asked for some favors and we've decided to let you take a trip to Fola. We wanted to tell you at dinner, but certain circumstances distracted us."

I knew Fola was the name of the more rural town that Cassidy and my grandparents lived in. It was by no coincidence that they chose that particular place to send me to. Why do I feel like they had some kind of ulterior motive to sending me to Fola?

"Are you tired of dealing with me?" I whined.

"No, of course not, Minnie. We love you," Daddy reassured.

"We'd never leave you behind just because things got tough. We just thought it would be good for you to leave for a few days. Just for the weekend, though. Think of it as a mini vacation."

To a lot of people, this "vacation" to Fola will be an admission of guilt. The criminal attempting to flee the scene now that the walls are starting to close in on her. I don't want to run away from my problems, but I think it's best for my sanity if I just take my parents offer and spend the weekend in Fola. Who knows? Maybe Cassidy can help me forget my problems, even if it's just for 48 hours. There was nothing left for me to do but smile and ask, "When do I leave?"

"Tomorrow. Your aunt is going to Fola to take care of some errands for her business, and she'll be here at 9 a.m. to take you with her."

CHAPTER TWENTY-TWO:

"It was a major relief to know that he had forgiven me. I'm sure Calli is somewhere smiling at us."

I decided to spend the time I had left with Marley and Lauralee. I texted them both and let them know that I wanted to meet them at Marley's house in five minutes. I hopped in my car; still happy as can be. Normally, it would take about three-five minutes to reach Marley's house, but there was some road work being done, so I had to take a detour located near Callista's house. As I approached her two story home, I slowly started to get goosebumps. However, before I could pass it, I noticed Eric Arden sitting on his porch reading a newspaper. When he recognized my car, it seemed as if he was trying to flag me down. I stopped and slowly pulled into their driveway.

"Is there something I can help you with, Mr. Arden?" I unsurely asked as I exited my car.

"Yeah, I was wondering if you had the time to come in and talk to me. I've been meaning to talk with you for a while, but could never find a good enough time. You don't have to worry; Stella went off shopping with coworkers, and the boys are doing some fishing today."

I felt uncomfortable and tense being around Eric. I mean, this was the man who I imagined was supposed to despise me most in this world. What could be urgent enough for him to want to talk with me so desperately? Well, I guess I should be thankful that someone besides my family still wishes to talk to me. I slowly closed my car door, locked it, and followed him into the house. He led me past the large living room and the kitchen, up the stairs, and down the dimly lit hall to the last room on the left, which I knew was Callista's room. Once I entered, I was in complete awe. Her room still looked exactly the same. Being surrounded by so many of Callista's personal things made me feel like I got to be with her again. It felt as if her spirit was somehow connected to her room still. The color scheme of the room was eggshell and canary yellow, which were Calli's favorite colors. Everything in that room seemed to have some sort of memory embedded in it. We'd pretend we were famous ballerinas and dance to the tune of the silver music box sitting on the dresser that her grandparents gave her for her sixth birthday. There was the giant Tweety

Bird that Marley won for Callista at the State Fair lying on her bed. Sometimes, Calli would use the lava lamp Rafe brought her, wrap a towel around her hair, and pretend she was a fortuneteller and tell us our future. It may sound silly or lame, but I wouldn't trade these memories for anything in the world. I looked up to see the diamond and platinum "B" necklace that was hanging above Callista's mirror. Marley and I have matching necklaces with the letter "F." The idea to get those BFF necklaces was mine. After all the years that has passed by and after everything that happened between the three of us, I'm surprised she still had it. Pictures of Callista with her family and friends reminded me of the best friend I missed so damn much. Eric walked over to the dresser, reached into it, and pulled out a black notebook with big, yellow stars on it. He held it close to his chest, as if he were hugging it.

"Did you know my girl had a secret love of poetry, Minnie?" He inquired.

I was shocked. A rebel who loved poetry? That's like discovering Shakespeare spent his late nights jamming to rock and roll while playing his air guitar. "No, I hadn't actually."

"I came up here one day and found an entire book of poems that she had bought from the bookstore. Stella says some of them are, and I quote, "the most exquisite pieces of work she's ever read." Apparently, our daughter loved poetry so much that she wanted to give it a try."

I raised an eyebrow in slight disbelief. "Calli wrote poems?"

"Well, she doesn't have enough to fill a book, but she did write four. I've read them already, and they are good. They have such meaning to them," He smiled faintly, showing that death cannot even stop a parent from being proud of his child. Now, that is a father-daughter bond that can't be broken. "I want you to have them, Minnie. Callista would've liked that."

I slowly walked up to him and he handed me the notebook. Why did he feel I even deserved this? "Why are you giving me this? Don't you hate me, Mr. Arden?"

Mr. Arden wiped his eye. "I did. I was furious with you, but I was grieving the death of my only daughter. She was our princess, Minnie. Me and Stella's smart-mouthed, hard headed princess," he jokes with a radiant smile and teary eyes. "At that time, I hated everyone. After a while, I realized that you obviously cared for Callista as much as I do. You considered her your best friend and throughout all the changes and all the stuff she did to you, you remained loyal to her. That's a true friend, Minnie. That doesn't sound like someone who would be cold-hearted and cruel enough to murder a pregnant woman. It's going to take some time for Stella and our sons to forgive you, but I already have. If I ever did or said anything to you or your family that was offensive, I sincerely apologize."

He reached out and we embraced in a hug; both of us crying as we squeezed each other. No, these were not tears of sadness; they were tears of joy and relief. It was a major relief to know he had forgiven me. I'm sure Calli is somewhere smiling at us.

"You should go before my wife returns. Before you do, take these."

He handed me a small photo of Callista, Marley, and I when we were at Callista's fifth birthday party and her "B" necklace. I can't even begin to tell you how much it meant to me to have these in my possession.

"I'm sure they mean much more to you than they do to me," He said with a radiant smile on his face. "Go now. Stella might be home soon. Also, do me a favor. Don't read all the poems at once. Read them one at a time, when the moment's just right."

I agreed and hugged him one more time before I rushed out of the house, hopped back into my car, and sped to Marley's house.

CHAPTER TWENTY-THREE:
"Never to return to the pearly gates, I hang my head in silent shame."

"Artemis Wilhelmina Carlisle, where were you!?" Lauralee scolded with her hands on her narrow hips. She reminded me of someone's angry grandmother. "You know I'm still not allowed to see you. So, when I finally get the chance to sneak and see you, you drive me crazy by waiting!"

"The news I have to tell you is worth the wait, Little Lee." I replied as I stepped into the house.

"Did something happen?" Marley asked as she turned the television off. I see she was back to her normal, glasses-wearing, frizzled-hair, soft-spoken self that I loved. I went over to the kitchen, sat on one their stools that squeaked every time you turned in it, and blurted out, "I'm going to Fola tomorrow morning."

"Fola? Isn't that a little, rural town like three-and-a-half hours from here?" Lauralee inquired.

"It's also where Caaaaassidy lives," Marley sang out with a sly smile upon her face.

"Aprilson, get your mind out of the gutter," I responded, sending a smile right back at her.

"Wait a second! So, you're leaving us to get jiggy with Cassidy Paris right before Prom? Wilhelmina, you horny devil," Lauralee teased, making Marley and I both chuckle.

"No, silly. I think the two of you are thinking about "getting' jiggy" with Cassidy more than I am. My parents are sending me up there for a few days to take a breather from Angel City," I explained.

"That's great! You need one," Marley agreed.

After we finished talking about my Angel City free trip to Fola, Cassidy (again), and everything my family and I were going through, I decided to tell them about my visit with Stella Arden.

"Babes?" I called, referring to both of them. They both directed their attention away from their cellphones to me.

"The reason I took a little bit longer to get here is because I went to talk with Eric Arden."

Lauralee's jaw almost dropped into the lap of her apricot skirt and

Marley's green eyes nearly bulged out of the lens of her glasses. I knew it would come as a surprise to them.

"W-why? Doesn't he hate you?" Lauralee spoke.

"How did it go?" Marley added.

"Well, it turns out that he doesn't hate me. At least, not anymore. We went up to Callista's room and we talked. He gave me Callista's 'B' necklace, an old picture of us, and…some poems that she wrote." I explained, putting the necklace around my neck. Marley stared at it with a faint smile on her face, as if she was recalling a pleasant memory. She was probably thinking of the day we went to buy the necklaces with our parents' money, of course. It was as if Marley was stuck in a trance, but at least it seemed to be a happy one.

Lauralee gave a small, fake laugh. "Ha, poems? Callista Isobel Arden wrote poetry?"

"No, you have it backwards. It's Isobel Callista Arden," Marley corrected. I was satisfied with Marley correcting Ms. Know-It-All. I don't know why Lauralee laughed like she was some hot-shot intellectual and was surprised that someone like Callista was even interested in poetry. My best friend was probably bad at writing poetry. Meanwhile, Miss Priss over here struggles with basic algebra and the spelling of the word, "indecisive." Oh, the irony.

"Whateves," Lauralee growled in response. Score 1 for Aprilson, nada for Giovanni.

I know Eric told me to read her poems when the moment's right, but I'm sure one wouldn't hurt. I was just too eager to wait and see what Callista had to say.

"Ok, I'll read ONE," I announced as I flipped to the first page of her black and yellow notebook. The first poem was titled "I Am."

"I am Isobel C. Arden
With age, I became beautiful, but also became a nightmare that disrupted my Heaven.
How did I become my own nightmare?
Now I'm not sure if I belong in the Heavens.
Never to return to the pearly gates,
I hang my head in silent shame.
They have stripped me of wings slowly and with regret
But I have broken their hearts oh so quickly.

Redemption seems impossible.

Perhaps in death, Isobel C. Arden, will be forgiven."

Once I was finished reading, no one said anything. We all just sat there, blinking and pondering. Who knew Callista had such a way with words?

"Wow, that's so…deep," Lauralee finally spoke, breaking the silence.

"No kidding," Marley added. "It's like it has some deeper meaning to it that only she would be able to understand. What do you think it means, Minnie?"

I shook my head. "I have no clue, but I wish I could tell her how I feel in person." After a few seconds of silence, Lauralee's, along with my cell phone began to ring. My Dad was calling me to tell me that I should come home, because dinner is almost ready. He also reminded me that I needed to pack for the trip. I was so into Callista's poem that I almost forgot I was leaving tomorrow.

"I gotta go," I informed them once I hung up the phone.

"Me too! That was my Daddy, my Mom is in labor!" Lauralee exclaimed as she rushed to get her things and sprint out of the house. She blew us kisses goodbye before rushing out of the front door. I hugged Marley goodbye as I, too, hurried to get home.

CHAPTER TWENTY-FOUR:

"It was as if I had suddenly rewound time and went back to when things were perfect and good."

I have never, in my eighteen years of life, been so excited to wake up at eight o'clock in the morning. I jumped out of bed the second I heard my alarm ring off and immediately began to get ready. I'm sure my family wasn't too thrilled that my early morning ruckus prematurely awoke them, but, oh well. My siblings all hugged me and said their goodbyes on their way out the door to school. Apollo told me to behave since us Carlisles have a tendency to find trouble. Aphrodite told me NOT to behave.

"There's no point of going on a parent-free, work-free vacation, if all you're gonna do is sit at home and watch the walls collect dust," Dite reasoned. I see that girl getting into a lot of trouble when she hits sixteen. All Athena asked me to do was bring her a souvenir; and Ares told me not to forget him…like I ever could. Mom and Dad, of course, told me that they loved me and to be careful. I hugged them then proceed to thank them one last time before Aunt Liz's Ford Explorer pulled into our driveway. I waved to my family from the passenger window until they were out of sight. I talked with Aunt Liz for about an hour during the drive, but the early morning activities combined with staying up until one in the morning eventually caught up to me and I fell asleep with my head rested on the window beside me. What a great way to pass the time. I awoke around one–thirty, but I was no longer in the passenger seat of Aunt Liz's beige SUV, I was in a bed. I turned around to see the most handsome, blond haired boy standing over the computer waiting for some files to download with his hands in the pockets of his dark blue jeans. My yawning alerted him, and he turned his head to face me.

"Hark! Sleeping Beauty has awoken," Cassidy teases.

I slowly started to smile. Seeing Cassidy after all the chaos I had going on back home just made me practically burst with joy. I felt like a puppy who hadn't seen her owner in days. I quickly jolted out of the bed and leaped into his arms, wrapping my arms around his neck as I hugged him tightly. Thankfully, he was strong enough to hold me up while he hugged me back.

"Cassidy Paris, is it really you!?" I happily squealed.

"In the flesh," He answered as he gently placed me on the ground.

I still couldn't believe I was standing face to face with Cassie again. It's been so long that I hardly recognized him. I stepped backwards, with my hands on my hips, and began to analyze him.

"My, my, my. You have grown. I see you've finally grown some muscles."

"I see you've finally grown some hips," He laughed, tickling me under my chin with his left index finger playfully.

"You're a douche!" I laughed as I quickly threw a pillow at his midsection. Cassidy and I are so childish when we are together.

"Come on, they are waiting for you downstairs." Cassidy informed as he took me by the hand and began to lead me downstairs.

Once we were downstairs, I saw Grandma, Grandpop, and Benjamin Paris talking amongst each other in the living room. They all smiled and their faces lit up when they saw me.

"Heeey, Princess! Come give your Papa a hug," Grandpop happily exclaimed as he held his arms out. I rushed over to hug him with an eager smile. He always smelled like cologne and traces of Newport cigarettes, which Dad always scolded him for smoking.

"It's so nice to see you again, Minnie," Grandma rejoiced as I hugged her, as well. "Ooh, look at all this long, red hair! You have your Daddy's eyes and that pretty smile! You've gotten so beautiful, Minnie! Hasn't she, Monty?" She complimented.

"Yeah, she's a beauty. Just like her Granddaddy," He joked.

Like any other grandmother, Grandma had baked some of her famous double fudge nut cookies in preparation for my arrival. It's a part of one of her many top secret recipes. Even my Mom and Aunt Liz are dying to learn how to make them. I loved visiting my grandparents. Everything about their house was just comforting to me. There was the sunflower colored kitchen that Grandma would let Dite, Athena, and I help her bake goodies; my favorite being her raspberry cheesecake. There was a blue, red, and grey plaid couch that Grandpop would tell us his hilarious, and supposedly, true childhood stories. From the tree swing that Grandpop built on the oak tree in the backyard to picking fragrant flowers from Grandma's garden, I felt surrounded my positive energy and love. Even the scent of oregano that wafted through the house was relaxing to me. After my grandparents finished asking me just about every single detail of my life back in Angel City, Cassidy decided to take me out and give me a little tour of Fola. He knows I've been to Fola a thousand times, but I think he just wanted to get out of the house. We drove past Fola High School and it was then that Cassidy rubbed it in my face that there was not nearly as much drama there as it is at Angel City High. He's such a show off. Next, we passed by the mall. Here, I got revenge by bragging about the size of our mall which had to be like two times bigger than the munchkin mall that was here. Luckily, we found a parking space close to the mall's entrance. Cassidy complained that except for the food, there was rarely anything worth buying from their mall as we strolled leisurely past stores. In the midst of Cassidy telling me a funny story, we passed this store called "DollHouse." In the window, there was a toddler sized, Huckleberry Finn doll. He was dressed in a red and white plaid shirt, blue kapris, and a straw hat. He was holding a long stick and a small, brown basket and an adorable grin was plastered on his face. I gasped with excitement.

"Athena would looove this!" I exclaimed as I dragged him inside the store by his wrist.

"Athena likes Huckleberry Finn?" Cassidy questioned. "Wouldn't you rather get her an Easy Bake Oven or whatever else girls play with?"

As the cashier was ringing up the overly priced, $25 doll, I shot Cassidy a pretend death glare. "You sexist pig," I joked. He smiled and backed away towards the exit with his hands up. "I'm sorry for offending you, Madam." After I purchased Athena's souvenir, we left the mall; and just for old time's sake, we stopped at Pete's Ice Cream Shoppe to catch up and talk a bit. The bell on the door rung loudly as we both entered.

"Wooow, this place still looks the same." I mumbled in amazement to myself. The large walls of the store were painted indigo with a white and black tile floor. Pete always swore that his floors were so clean that you could eat off of them. The booths consisted of a white table with black, cushy seats. There were bright, multicolored menus hanging above the shiny, silver counter and Pete's name written on a neon, sky blue sign beside a small television that nobody hardly watched. Whenever I came to visit, Benjamin would bring Cassie and me here all the time. After we were hyped up off ice cream, he'd take us to the park nearby where we'd enjoy playing hide and seek, playing tag, or climbing a tree, despite Benjamin's warnings. Pete's Ice Cream Shoppe became our favorite place as kids and we'd faithfully order the same thing every single time...

"One large banana split with caramel, chocolate syrup, nuts, sprinkles, and extra cherries," Cassidy ordered.

"I cannot believe you still remember that." I remarked as I playfully nudged him.

He grinned slightly and nudged me back. "How could I forget? You used to whine for an eternity if Pete forgot the extra cherries or the caramel."

Cassidy paid for the ice cream and I fetched two spoons before we took a seat in one of the booths. Our booth had a large window by it. The rays from the setting sun outside warmly kissed my cheek. We sat there and we talked, laughed, and ate our special banana split. I don't even know how long we were there, but I was enjoying every single minute of it. I felt like I was reliving a flashback. It was as if I had suddenly rewound time and went back to when things were perfect and good. Cassidy was making it very hard for me to want to leave Fola. Then again, that's probably what he wanted.

"Hey, you want this last scoop? It's got too many cherries on it for my tastes," Cassidy offered.

I answered his offer with an offer of my own. "Only if you'll take this last scoop. I know you looove it when the bananas get drowned in chocolate syrup."

I was simply going to turn the bowl around and let him spoon it out for himself, but he decided to go the extra mile and wanted me to feed it to him while he fed me. What did he think this was, our wedding? I decided to go along with Cassie's antics and I ended up with vanilla ice cream on my nose, and he had chocolate syrup drizzled on his left hand.

"How romantic of you," I giggled as I got napkins for the both of us.

After wiping the syrup off of his hand, he paused silently for a few seconds, then cleared his throat and said, "Speaking of romance, Fola High's Senior Prom is tomorrow night."

"Aww, and does wittle Cassie have a giiirlfwiend to take?" I replied, teasing him in my kiddie voice.

"Actually," He started to answer as he looked down at the bowl and toy with his spoon, "I was hoping you would come with me."

I was taken aback by that. I was silent for the next few seconds and just stared at him, which probably drove him crazy with anticipation. "Cassie? I don't know if you remember, but I have had OTHER things on my mind besides Prom dress shopping." Hell, I hadn't even been to the mall to even buy a pair of shoes in months. Rebbie works at my favorite store in the mall; and I'll be damned if I'm getting my hair ripped out over a pair of $15 boots. Nooooo, thank you.

"That's all been taken care of. Your Mom, Dad, and grandparents all helped to pay for a dress, shoes, and jewelry, before you were even sent here."

Those sneaky devils! I will never complain about washing dishes or babysitting Ares again! Ok, maybe I will, but that's not the point! All senior year, I've been talking about Prom and waiting for the day I could finally go. However, with all the drama happening around me, I never thought I'd be able to go and now, my loved ones were making it possible for me. Now I understand why they waited until this exact time to get me to come to Fola. There was only one thing left to say now…

"Cassidy Paris, I'd loooove to go to Prom with you!" I happily sang out. He smiled from ear to ear as he took a deep sigh of relief and replied, "That's great, Minnie!"

I got up, walked over to his side of the booth, and hugged him to death. I couldn't have been any happier. I was in absolute bliss. What a great end to a perfect day. Too bad it was interrupted by a, "Over my dead body! Did I just hear that yooou were going to Prom with Cassidy Paris?"

CHAPTER TWENTY-FIVE:

"If that deranged bitch wants to start drama with me, I damn well hope she's ready for me to finish it."

I released my hold on Cassidy's body and turned around to see a girl, about seventeen or eighteen, standing beside our table. Not to sound weird or anything, but this girl was undoubtedly gorgeous, as if she had just catwalked out of a Victoria's Secret commercial. She had flawless, milk chocolate skin that glowed as she stood in the sunlight. Her silky, raven hair gently waterfalled into waves and curls down past to her shoulders and to her mid-back. Her pretty face, with her pouty lips and high cheekbones, had become tense and her almond-shaped, light brown eyes were practically engorged with anger as she glared at Cassidy and me. Cassidy let out an irritated groan before saying, "Minnie, this is Nahaali Amard. Nahaali, meet Minnie Carlisle."

"Don't you mean Nahaali PARIS, Cassidy?" She giddily corrected.

"No," Cassidy quickly growled.

She smiled and batted her long eyelashes at him. "Oh, you're such a kidder."

"I'm NOT kidding. I never am with you."

Her flirtatious smile vanished once she redirected her attention to me. I haven't even been in Fola for one single day and I already have someone who dislikes me. Lucky, lucky me. Apollo was right, we Carlisles do have a tendency to find trouble. Next time, Cassidy and I will take our ice cream to go if I have to deal with all of this.

"Minnie…That's sort of a childish name, don't you think?" She sneered.

Really? We're taking it back to elementary school and making fun of people's names? Is that the best she's got? At least people could easily spell and pronounce my name. You ever had someone do or say something so childish or petty to you that you couldn't even get mad? You're just shocked that they're that stupid. Yeah, that's how I felt at this exact moment. "Well, it's short for Wilhelmina, actually."

She crossed her arms. "Hmph. I still don't like it. What's your relationship with my Cassidy?"

Excuse me? Since when does she own him? This girl was definitely off her rocker. "Well, he's a great friend of mine. I've known him since we were kids."

That answer seemed to make her unhappier with my presence. I'm starting to think she's just out to start trouble for the Hell of it because there's no way a girl can be this delusional and mentally off her rocker...right?

"Well, Mickie, Minnie, or whatever the Hell you said your name was, I suggest you find yourself a friend that's FAAAR away from Fola, because Cassidy Xavier Paris is m-i-n-e! You hear me? MINE! We are practically destined to be soul mates and no big nosed bimbo like you is going to intervene with my happiness! Let this be a warning to you, Mickie Carlton!"

After she finished her pleasant announcement, she stormed off towards the exit of the store; her hair swinging wildly behind her. One the way home, Cassidy explained everything about Nahaali "Nutcase" Amard. Nahaali's Jamaican father, Sean, divorced her Indian mother, Neha, when Nahaali had just begun preschool. Since Sean left Neha for another, younger woman and moved back to Kingston, Nahaali grew up watching her mother (who was disowned by her family for moving out of the home and marrying outside of the race without their consent) obsessively pine after her dad; who clearly didn't want to be with her anymore. The sad part is, Neha poisoned Nahaali's mind to be emotionally dependent on a man and to be obsessive and aggressive when it comes to finding love. Nahaali's craziest moment was when she attempted to sneak into the boy's locker room naked when her "target" was alone after a workout. I guess she thought he'd become so overwhelmed with desire that he would HAVE to take her right then and there. Unfortunately for Nahaali, all she found was her target's girlfriend, Aaliyah Johnson, awaiting her in the shower instead, dripping wet but blazing with fury. After receiving a busted lip, she never messed with him again and moved onto her next target. Knowing the full background story about Nahaali made me understand and pity her just a little bit. From the outside looking in, I saw her as a victim of her mother's shortcomings. However, I came to Fola to temporarily escape the drama that stalked me in Angel City; not to have even more of it slapped in my face. I'm normally not a confrontational person, but if that deranged bitch wants to start drama with me, I damn well hope she's ready for me to finish it.

CHAPTER TWENTY-SIX:
"A forbidden love seduced me into poisoning our friendship."

The entire next day was dedicated to getting me prepared for the Prom that night. My Grandma rushed me into a nail salon early that morning to receive my manicure and pedicure and then to get my eyebrows arched. Grandpop decided to contribute by paying for my hair appointment. In the midst of all the Prom chaos, Marley and Lauralee called to inform me of what was going on with them back at home. Darla Giovanni had given birth to an eight pound, two ounce, baby boy that Lauralee and Steph named Deangelo Joseph "D.J." Giovanni. Being the proud sister and cousin that they are, they are posting pictures all over social media sites of the new addition to their family. Marley informed me that the missing member of her family, Lydia, has popped up for a surprise visit from college. She seemed happy to have the opportunity to reconnect with her sister again. I was just thankful that they had some good news to tell me. Apollo called as well, with slurred and groggy speech as he was recovering from a night on the town he had the night before. I don't know if he forgot he was talking to his little sister but he started to go into details about some blonde, blue eyed "babe" he hooked up with last night. Disgusted at the mere thought of my brother penetrating anyone, I told Apollo to drink some coffee, get some rest, and call me when he's in a better state of mind. Big brothers, I tell you. The day slipped by faster than I anticipated and before I knew it, the time had come for me to start getting dressed. Upstairs, in my grandparents' closest, the most beautiful Prom dress was awaiting me. It was a strapless, mermaid-style dress that was the most gorgeous shade of deep turquoise you've ever seen. There was a black sash that wrapped around my waist and tied in the back as a bow. The heels that went along with it were sexy, black and decorated with tiny, sparkly rhinestones. They were a tad too high, but I didn't really care as long as I could decently strut in them. Once I had finished putting on my jewelry and adding some finishing touches to my elegant up-do, my Grandma came upstairs to my room to add one last, personal touch. She gave me my mother's platinum tiara that she had worn to her senior Prom.

"You look nothing short of beautiful, honey," Grandma complimented as she placed a warm, gentle kiss on my left cheek. "Whenever you're ready, Cassidy is downstairs waiting for you." She smiled lovingly at me, before she closed the door. My phone beeped as I received a picture message. It was a photo of Lauralee, in a short, fire engine red dress and matching lipstick; and Marley in a long, tourmaline pink gown, hugging each other and smiling. Lauralee chose to alter her appearance a bit and don a jet black wig cut into a bob with a swoop over her left eye. She looked like a little vixen ready to get into something. Marley shockingly got a ponytail extension that stretched down to her mid-back and even let Lauralee's stylist do her makeup. In the text, Lauralee explained that she persuaded Marley to go to Prom with her, since neither had a date. I know it took a lot of begging on Lee's part to make someone as shy as Marley go to Prom, especially wearing heels, hair extensions, and makeup. I hope they have tons of fun like I planned to have with Cassidy (get your mind out of the gutter). I'm sure if Callista were alive, she'd be dazzling us with a sexy, scandalous dress that would be no other color than her favorite, canary yellow. While Callista was on my mind, I decided to take this time I had to myself to read another one of her poems. I walked over to my luggage, took Callista's notebook out of one of the suitcases, plopped down on my bed, and flipped to the second page. This poem shocked me because it was titled, "Artemis."

"I know a gorgeous girl named Artemis.
She has hair like fire and eyes as grey as the moon in the night sky.
I admired her, but also turned on her
Though I find it hard to tell her why.
A forbidden love seduced me into poisoning our friendship.
I feel so foolish and immature.
It hurts me greatly to know I've hurt her.
She's hurting now, I'm sure.
Before I part with her forever,
I wish to leave her with these words from me:
Moon Eyes, from the very bottom of my heart,
Your Calli Doll, is truly sorry."

I almost started to get upset and cry, but I fought the tears because I didn't want to ruin my makeup. However, a few single tears escaped my eyes and ran down my cheeks. Oh, Calli. I wish you were here so I could tell you in person that I accept your apology. I yearned to hug her one last time. With a slightly teary eye and a smile, I placed her notebook back into my suitcase, and took one final glance at myself before I headed downstairs to meet Cassidy.

CHAPTER TWENTY-SEVEN:
"You don't have to fight me, Minnie."

Have you ever seen those sappy, super-predictable romance movies where the girl descends slowly and gracefully from the top of staircase looking absolutely gorgeous, and her man is waiting at the bottom, practically mesmerized by her beauty? Yeah, that's exactly how my entrance was. Super cliché, but I loved every single second of it. My grandfather was proudly snapping pictures on his camera every seven seconds, and Grandma was fighting her happy tears as she kept blabbering on about how beautiful I looked and how much I reminded her of Mom when she went to her senior Prom. After all of the pictures, kisses, and hugs, Cassidy and I finally made it out of the door and to his car. We arrived at Fola Conference Center about ten minutes later. Upon exiting the car, Cassidy gently took my left hand and looked at me with those charming blue eyes of his.

"This is it," He commented, as he smiled down at me. "Are you ready?" I returned his smile. "Ready? I'm more than ready. I'm damn excited!"

He unleashed a soft laugh and we began to walk towards the entrance. From the very second we waltzed in, hand in hand, my breath was immediately taken away. The lighting basked us in dark and mysterious, yet soothing ambiance. On the western half of the room, there were a multitude of small, round tables covered with decorate white tablecloths and black chairs. In the center of every table stood a clear, curvy vase that held delicate lilacs. To add an elegant appeal, some of the lilac pedals were scattered in a circle around the bottom of vase. On the eastern half of the room, there was a large dance floor with bright, colorful neon lights hanging overhead. Before the entering the main room, there was a large hallway where drinks could be found and a large display with fruits, marshmallows, chocolate and other delicacies for us to snack on during the course of the night. Being able to attend my senior prom with Cassidy was like stepping into a fantasy. Cassidy and I decided to go ahead and get our formal pictures taken before we did anything else, which was a smart plan because my Mom and Grandma would absolutely murder me if I didn't bring home pictures of this Kodak moment. After we were finished, we ran into some friends of Cassidy's.

"Hey! It's Cassidy!" The boy shouted.

"Hey, man," Cassidy casually responded, as they greeted each other with some sort special handshake of theirs.

"Who's your pretty lady-friend?" The girl in the silver and black cocktail dress beside him asked with abounding curiosity.

Cassidy stepped back and proudly wrapped his right arm around my shoulder

"Minnie, this is my best friend, Aaron Johnson."

"Oh, your BEEST friend, huh?" I joked, pretending to be hurt.

"Well, besides you, of course. This is Aaron's twin, Aaliyah. Guys, this is Minnie Carlisle."

Their faces lit up in delight. "So you're Minnie? Cassidy's told us so much about you!" Aaliyah squealed as she reached out to unexpectedly hug me. I felt flattered that Cassie thought enough of me to talk about me to some of his closest friends.

"It's good to finally meet you, Minnie Paris, I mean, Carlisle." Aaron slyly greeted. He darted his brown eyes at Cassidy with a sneaky grin on his face; and Cassidy jokingly nudged him in return.

I raised an eyebrow in suspicion. Was he insinuating that Cassidy and I were a couple? No, no, no. Cassie is just my very best friend. I didn't need to add romantic confusion to my list of many problems.

"So, have you met Nutcase Amard yet?" Aaron and Aaliyah asked simultaneously. Twin moments will never not be cute.

I wanted to blurt out, "Hell yeah I've met that crazy girl!" However, I didn't want it to get back to Nahaali's ears, giving her more of a reason to agitate me during my visit. So, I politely responded, "Yes, I met her yesterday."

Aaron and Aaliyah paused for a second, glanced at each other, then exploded with laughter. Must be one of those psychic moments twins have from time to time.

"Girl, you don't have to pretend that you like her! No one else around here does." Aaliyah laughed.

So Nahaali has no father, no man, and no friends. That might explain why she acts as insanely as she does.

"She was just as obsessed with me a few months ago. Then, Cassidy helped her open her locker one day and she's been scribbling X's and O's in her notebook ever since," Aaron explained.

Really!? Nahaali fell in "love" with Cassidy because he helped with her locker? I have to deal with this crazy girl just because Cassidy decided to be a gentleman? Why couldn't he have been an ass like Nate? Oh, how pathetic can one girl be? She reminded me of one those looney, lonely women who star in Lifetime movies. Nahaali was obviously in denial of reality. Life is NOT a movie and every love story can't and won't be like Cinderella's.

"Alright, I've had enough talk of HER," Cassidy blurted out. He grabbed my left hand with his right and said, "Why don't we get started on enjoying our Prom, hmm?" I smiled and responded, "Lead the way."

That night, Cassidy and I let loose and had a blast. I was finally able to leave my problems in the past for once and just have a great time with someone I loved. We played around, we joked, we laughed, and we danced (horribly) to every song. I truly didn't EVER want to go back home. I wish I could feel this sort of freedom and happiness for the rest of my life. Then, the part of Prom that every dateless girl dreaded inevitably snuck its way in. It was now time for the slow dance. Most of the dance floor cleared, but there was still a good number of couples still dancing, including Cassidy and me. I thought back to Aunt Liz's and Uncle Danny's wedding when Cassidy and I were dancing just like this and he was holding me the exact same way he is now. He had his left arm around my waist, my right arm resting on his right shoulder, and him holding my left hand slightly in the air with his. The difference between then and now is that then was eleven years ago. We are all grown up now and a different set of rules and feelings now come into play. Our talking had ceased and we were now smiling and just staring deeply into each other's eyes. My grey staring into his blue, like how the moon stares into the ocean on a serene, Summer night. He gripped my left hand slightly tighter and slowly pulled me closer to him. My heart began to beat faster, an anxious/butterfly feeling had now invaded the pit of my stomach, and I noticed his breathing became slower and deeper.

"Cassidy?" I called, hoping he would stop before things got too far.

"Artemis," He whispered back as he began to close his eyes, tilted his head, and inched closer towards my face.

"Oh my God. He's gonna kiss me. Cassidy Paris is going to kiss me." I frantically thought. As right as this felt, I just couldn't let it happen. I panicked and abruptly pulled myself away from him. I attempted to walk way, but he just wouldn't release his hold on my right hand.

"Minnie? What's wrong?" His eyes were pleading with me not to leave him.

I love Cassidy. He's been my very best friend since our days in the sandbox, but I can't drag him into the Hell I was experiencing back home; and I was still healing from Nate's stupid mistakes. Frankly, I was afraid of being hurt again, although I knew Nathaniel Jacobs and Cassidy Paris had personalities as different as night and day. Maybe if I begged and pleaded with him enough, he'd realize that this shouldn't happen between us and let me go.

"Cassie, thiiis can't happen. I just got out of a bad relationship and I don't fully know if I'm ready to get serious with anyone again. I already have to fight back home and…I think it's best if I fight you, too."

He paused for just a split second. "You don't have to fight me, Minnie," He seductively whispered as he quickly began to return my body back to his like a powerful magnet. Before I had the opportunity to tell him to stop, he embraced me with a sweet, juicy kiss. I thought kissing my best friend would be super awkward, but it actually felt too good to stop. I totally forgot about everyone else in the room at the moment. As far as I was concerned, they were irrelevant. Our simple, innocent kiss became more X-rated the more we got into it. It morphed into a heated, passionate make out session as his tongue smoothly entered my mouth and our hands began to explore each other's bodies. Let's just put it this way and say that Cassidy definitely grew since I last seen him. I started to become very into it...and very horny. No wonder Nate always said I was driving him crazy. Hell, I'd go crazy too if I felt like this constantly and had no way to solve it. Suddenly, Cassidy pulled away. While breathing heavily, he stated, "My Dad's going to be gone until tomorrow afternoon. You want to go to my place?" I know that normally, Cassidy would be too shy to ask so bluntly, but I think his teenage boy hormones were kicking into overdrive at the moment.

"Yes, Cassidy. Yes, yes, yeeeees." I responded as I grabbed him and planted another kiss on his lips.

At that point, we raced each other out of the building to Cassidy's car; and despite wearing high heels, I almost beat him there.

CHAPTER TWENTY-EIGHT:
"Always and forever, Babe."

Lauralee and Marley are going to go ballistic when I tell them I lost my virginity to Cassidy--especially Marley, since she insisted something was going to happen between us sooner or later. I can't wait to see their reaction. Lauralee's probably going to ask for every single detail and I do mean EVERY detail of what happened. My head was surely going to be in the clouds all day. I'd be reminiscing about Cassidy grinding his chiseled, sweaty body into me, me digging my nails into his back, and moaning with satisfaction. I was smiling just thinking about it. So this is what bliss really feels like. This is what it feels like…when it's meant to be. Being with Cassidy was like a perfect blend of domination and passion; aggressiveness and tenderness. Everything we had on for Prom, from my Mom's tiara to Cassidy's size ten-and-half shoes, had become nothing but a huge puddle on his bedroom floor. Sleeping peacefully on the left side of Cassidy's bed, I was awakened by the sound of robins chirping and the sun gleaming warmly in my face. I opened my eyes slowly then rose out of the bed to stretch a little. I looked over my shoulder to find Cassidy, resting his head on his left hand with his arm propped up for support. He had the most adorable smile on his face.

"Good morning, Minnie," He greeted. "You look like Hell." He grinned at me so sexually, yet so devilishly. I chuckled amusingly and simply replied, "Still a jackass, I see."

I thought about springing up out of bed, rushing to get dressed, and then returning to my grandparents' house. But after seeing Cassidy smile at me as if I was the best thing to happen to him since the invention of the television, I didn't want to go anywhere anymore. All I wanted to do was to lie back down and let the sun gently shine on us as he held me in his arms. As he played in my hair, I softly remarked, "So, where do we go from here, Cassie?"

"Wherever you want to go, I'll follow. It's your call."

I loved how he wasn't putting any pressure on me. Being with Nate was being hounded with constant pressure, mostly about sex. I realize that Cassidy has always been there to bring me joy at the time when I needed it the most. He was right; I shouldn't be trying to fight someone who has done nothing but make me smile and forget my problems each and every time I talked to him. So why not allow Cupid to do his job and see what this could become? You'll never know if you don't take the risk right? Life's all about taking chances.

"I think we should take things slow." I responded as I turned around to see him face to face. "I'm not going to fight you anymore."

He grinned as he delicately tucked my hair behind my ear as he asked, "Will you be mine always?"

"Always and forever, Babe." Then, I planted another one of those succulent kisses on his lips.

We laid there, with my head on his chest and his arm around me, and talked. We talked about everything imaginable and it felt wonderful to connect to someone on a real level again. Nate and I never connected like this. I guess just because you like someone and try hard to make the relationship work, doesn't mean that it's meant to be. Some people, like Nate and me, are doomed from the beginning. His arms were so comforting, his chest was soft and warm, and something about his heartbeat was so soothing and hypnotic that it began to lull me to sleep. Just as I was about to fall into a deep sleep, Cassidy spoke and I noticed that his tone unexpectedly switched from happiness to serious and solemn.

"Minnie…there's one last thing I need to show you before you return to Angel City," He apathetically declared.

"What is it, Cassie?" I responded. I was beginning to grow worried; I had never seen him so gloomy-looking.

"I'd rather show you. I'll take you home to let you change then we'll go." He answered as he got up and out of the bed without a stitch of clothing on.

I was worried and curious, but I decided to leave my trust in Cassidy and just wait and see what was up his sleeve. Once we put some clothes back on our bare bodies, we were ready to head out of the house. Benjamin, who must've got in late last night, was so deep into sleep that he didn't even wake up as we were leaving. I had taken off my noisy heels just in case they would disturb him from his slumber. We hopped into Cassidy's cream-colored Camry and drove off to my Grandparents' home. I slowly unlocked the front door and began my stealth mission up to my room. Every creak of the floorboards made my heart flutter just a tiny bit faster. By the time I had made it up to my room, I thought I was going to have a heart attack for sure. Callista would surely have a few not so nice names to call me for being such a drama queen. I set my Prom attire aside and changed into a pair of high waisted beige shorts, a white, short-sleeved shirt, and white flip-flops with silver earrings shaped like angel wings. I decided to wear something cute, comfy, and casual. I was lucky that my Grandparents were also heavy sleepers. If I had tried this with my Mom, she would've skipped sleep altogether. Mom would've been hyped up on Starbucks and fury to ensure she stayed awake to bust me the second I walked in. I managed to sneak out undetected and back outside to Cassidy. He still wouldn't tell me where he was taking me or even give me a damn hint. He's always been stubborn. After driving for about fifteen minutes, Cassidy made a right turn, and I could now see that were slowly driving into Fola Memorial Gardens. Why is he taking me to a cemetery?

CHAPTER TWENTY-NINE:
"Minnie…babe, I-I'd like you to finally meet my mom and sister."

We slowly drove past numerous graves, decorated with beautiful flowers placed there by the grieving loved ones that they left behind. The car slowly came to a smooth stop, then Cassidy turned the car off and began to unbuckle his seatbelt. Without making eye contact with me, he said, "Come on. Follow me." As I cautiously exited the car and slammed the door behind me, I noticed that Cassidy didn't even bother to wait on me. Instead, he stopped about thirty or so steps straight ahead of where he parked and seemed to be examining two of the tombstones. This was all just too damn creepy for my tastes. Being around so many graves and corpses just spooked the hell out of me and I've always hated walking in cemeteries. Stepping all over someone's final resting place is absolutely disrespectful to me. Once I had made my way up to where Cassidy was standing, all he did was look up at me, then look back down at the tombstone. I assumed he was hinting for me to look at them, too.

"Arella Rosalba Paris: July 19, 1956 - December 27th, 1997." The grave to the left of that one read, "Erica Christine Paris: October 31, 1979 - December 27, 1997. Gone too soon. We will always love you."

Upon reading their names, I immediately realized that these were the graves of Cassidy's mother and older sister. They weren't even my relatives; and I wanted to start crying. Losing my best friend broke my heart, but I'm sure no tragedy compares to losing your Mom and only sibling, especially on the same damn day. He basically lost half his family within 24 hours. No wonder why he always refused to talk about them and always changed the subject.

Cassidy wiped his eyes with his sleeve and mumbled, "Minnie…babe, I-I'd like you to finally meet my mom and sister."

CHAPTER THIRTY:

"We stood there and just held each other. The more Cassidy cried, the tighter his arms wrapped around me."

There were just too many things wrong with this. Not only was Erica my age when she died; they both died four months after Cassidy's and my birth. No wonder why I've never got to meet them and why the adults would never answer my questions when I was a kid. Poor Benjamin. I can't fathom what life is like to come home and find the love of your life and your only daughter both dead, and then having to raise your newborn son single-handedly. Not many men would be mentally strong enough to handle a crisis like that. I have 10 times more respect towards Benjamin now.

"Cassidy, how did this…what happened?" I really didn't know what to say, and even if I did, I wouldn't know how to say it. He cleared his throat. "You ever heard of the 'Angel City Murder-Suicide' that happened back in 97?"

Of course, I have. Anyone from Angel City knew about that. It practically turned our city upside down. It involved a mother and daughter who wound up with fatal gunshot wounds after a verbal and physical confrontation...oh my God.

"Judging by your facial expression, I can tell you've connected the dots."

This is one game of connect the dots I never want to play again. "I-I don't know what to say." I whispered to myself.

"It started with my mother, Arella. After I was born, life just got worse for her."

I could tell it hurt him to utter those words. I bet his Dad had to take an eternity to get him to stop blaming himself for this tragedy. It's funny how as kids, we blame ourselves when bad things happen; but as adults, we never want to take responsibility for anything. Cassidy was just a newborn when his mother died, yet he seemed so intent on blaming his mother's insanity on himself. Arella's job was to be his mother, caregiver, and guardian. It's not Cassidy's fault that she couldn't live up to that.

Cassidy continued, "Her job was becoming more demanding; hospital bills were climbing upon the other bills of the house; Dad was working late nights to make some extra money (which made Mom suspicious of infidelity and left her to take care of the house and a newborn); along with a teen daughter who went from being "Little Miss Perfect" to partying, drinking, and misbehaving. To escape the stress in her life, my Mom started using cocaine. Yeah, she just skipped alcohol or weed and went straight to the hard stuff. She started using it almost every single day and on December 27th, it contributed to her death. December 27th was just another late night. My Mom had put me down for bed, Dad was working, and Erica decide to leave and have a wild, party night without the consent of Mom, of course. What exactly happened will never be known, but it's suspected that my Mom went into some kind of 'drug-induced rage," once Erica came home. From neighbor's testimony, they heard screaming and yelling from our home. The police believed the confrontation reached a climax and Mom pulled a gun on her and pulled the trigger. Realizing what she had done, she then pulled the gun herself. To protect our family, my father decided to keep the names of my mother and Chrissie anonymous, which is why you never knew."

That had to be the most tragic, heartbreaking story I have ever heard in my entire life. If I was Cassidy or Benjamin, I wouldn't want to repeat it ever again. Repeating it is just like reliving it. I see why Arella's tombstone didn't have any loving words on it like Erica's. She didn't deserve any. I see why Benjamin moved Cassidy out to Fola. It was to escape the publicity, pain, and pity.

"You wanna know the punch line in all this? My Mom was accusing my Dad of cheating, but she was the one who had an affair with Lorenzo Giovanni around the time of Chrissie's conception. A paternity test proved that she's the sister Lauralee and I will never have the pleasure of meeting."

So that's the main reason why Governor Giovanni was so determined to keep this scandal under wraps. It was so he could continue his obsession with having a "perfect" city and save his own hide, of course. Lauralee's never talked about this to me before; and always referred to herself as being an only child before D.J.'s birth so I assume she doesn't know either. I glanced over and I could see that Cassidy was about to break down into a fit of tears.

"Cassidy...babe, please don't cry." I pleaded. It hurts me to see anyone cry, especially someone I love. If he started crying, my waterworks would kick in, too. I stepped towards him, with my arms opened wide, and he quickly embraced me in a hug. We stood there and just held each other. The more Cassidy cried, the tighter his arms wrapped around me. He must've gotten to the point where he just could not hold back the pain, and he let it all free at once.

"S-sorry. I'm sorry, Minnie." He blurted out in between tears.

"Cassidy, you don't have to apologize for being human," I consoled. I pulled my head back and stared deep into his eyes, running my slender fingers through his field of blond hair in an attempt to calm his troubled mind. "I love you, Cassie."

His crying ceased, although, I could still see a layer of water over his eyes. When he blinked, twin tears cascaded from each eye down his cheeks. His button-nose sniffled before he responded, "I love you too, Minnie."

He smiled faintly at me, before I pulled him closer for an intimate kiss.

CHAPTER THIRTY-ONE:
"Artemis Carlisle: The Bitch Unleashed."

As we were exiting the cemetery, Cassidy received a text from Aaron inviting the both of us to attend a pool party that he and Aaliyah were hosting (in their strict parents' absence, of course). I think we both needed a pleasant distraction from today's gloom, so he happily and quickly accepted.

"I wish I had brought a swimsuit. I love to swim," I whined once we arrived at the Johnson's home.

Cassidy freed a smile from his lips and responded, "Maybe you won't need it. I personally wouldn't mind seeing those curves without a bikini as you exit a pool dripping wet in slow motion...like in the movies."

I laughed. "Cassidy Paris, you naughty boy. Save that for some other time."

"Mmmm," He mumbled as he grabbed a handful of my softness and passionately kissed me. We got so into sucking each other's faces off, we didn't even notice Aaliyah open the door.

"Hey, hey, hey! The party's inside, y'know," she joked. Her dark chocolate skin shined beautifully like bronze under the sun's rays. Cassidy pulled away. "Hmm, says who?"

Aaliyah playfully slapped Cassidy on the arm, then led us through her beautiful house and to the backdoor, which I assumed is where the rest of the party was. However, instead of proceeding through the door, she stopped and turned around to face us.

"There's something I gotta warn you about, Minnie."

"What…is the pool water too cold or something?" I sarcastically responded. She exhaled deeply, then answered, "…Nahaali's here."

Great! My last day in Fola with Cassidy, away from all my drama back home, and I have to spend it around that pathetic lunatic.

Teeeeeeeeeeeriffic.

"Uuugh, why is SHE here?" I groaned.

Aaliyah simply raised her left eyebrow and glanced over in Cassidy's direction. She didn't even have to speak it. I already figured out the answer. She wouldn't dare miss the opportunity to strut her body around in a bikini in front of him.

"Ugh, of course. Why else would she be here?"

Cassidy wrapped his right arm around me. "Just be the bigger person. I know she's difficult, but try to ignore her. Don't let her ruin our day."

So I took Cassidy's advice, which was actually easier than I thought it would be. I managed to ignore Nahaali's "intimidating" glares and her snarky, under the breath comments, and had a blast. Besides, I had grown used to envious girls staring at me. Dancing, socializing, meeting more of Cassidy's friends and then getting my boobs fondled by Cassidy in a corner of the pool…good times, great stuff. As Cassidy and I were splitting a plate of food, Nahaali called Cassidy over to her, which wasn't very far from us, of course. I should rip that multicolored, a tad-too-small bikini top off her, and choke her with it. Yeah, that would alleviate my stress for sure. As they began talking, it was obvious that Nahaali was painfully aggravating Cassie. Cassidy must've reached his boiling point because he aggressively yanked away from the grip she had on his muscular bicep and began to walk back over towards me. Unfortunately, he only walked a few inches before she grabbed a hold of him again. This is what reeeeeally got to me. She shot me this smug, devious look before she got on her tiptoes and planted a greatly unwanted, severely unappreciated kiss on Cassidy's lips. Now my parents taught me how to be a lady and to turn the other cheek and be the bigger person and all that other irrelevant crap. I've dealt with Nahaali's insanity and her pettiness since I first arrived here and I'm already sick of her. That kiss was just blatant disrespect and was the straw that broke the camel's back. I'm sick of playing nice. Artemis Carlisle: The Bitch Unleashed.

CHAPTER THIRTY-TWO:
"I've never seen someone so alone."

I angrily dropped the red, plastic cup of spiked fruit punch I had in my left hand and began to speed walk towards her. My legs couldn't get to her fast enough, I tell you. Nahaali gave me another smugly deviously look as I began to close the distance between us. Apollo once said, "Some people are just too damn stupid to get out of the way."

"Look who's a jealous. Aww, how cute," She commented in a sardonic tone of voice. "Just what are YOU going to do about it, Minnie?"

Once she was within arm's reach, I began to show that lunatic just what I was going to do about it. I grabbed a fistful of all that pretty, black hair with my left hand, wrapping it securely around my hand as if I were a boxer wrapping his fists before a fight and my right fist landed on Nahaali's face like a missile impacting directly on its target. I hit her with such a force that she fell off her four inch heels. I've never felt like this before. It was as if rage and adrenaline were crashing upon me like a wave against a sandy shore. The grip I had on her hair tightened and my punches to her face and head came faster and faster. With this being my first real fight, of course, not all of my punches landed but Nahaali was doing far worse than I was. Sure, she tried to fight back, but since she had her head down and eyes sealed shut, her aiming skills were horrendous. Most of her cotton-soft strikes hit my shoulders or my arms. One hit my ear, knocking my pearl earring to the ground. She made a drastic attempt to escape her fistful of karma by quickly backing away, but all I did was follow her as she bumped roughly into a table which threw me off balance slightly. Then, she grabbed both of my shoulders and began to push. Once I realized she was attempting to shove me into the pool, I stopped punching, and grabbed her arms firmly. If I go down, she does too. As we both descended into the pool, I heard Cassidy bellow out, "Minnie, wait!" I couldn't see much, once I was submerged except a blurry Nahaali furiously kicking her legs. As I surfaced back to the top, Nahaali began to quickly grab onto my body. The extra weight was dragging me back down under the water. She had already gotten beat so now she was gonna try to DROWN me? I don't think so. I caught her hard in the cheek with my elbow and as I saw her grip on me becoming weaker, I kicked her in the lower abdomen with my right foot to finally get her away. Once she had no part of my body to cling onto, she sank like cement on a cloud. I'm sure Callista is somewhere in Heaven, where God can't hear her, cheering loudly and bouncing up and down with pride and devilish delight as she watches me fight. Before Nahaali could sink to the bottom, Cassidy, for some unknown reason, became her knight in shining armor and came to her rescue. Being a gentleman is what got him in this trouble in the first place. As I exited the pool, I was confused and certainly pissed off. I am his girlfriend, I am his date, so logically, I should be his top priority. Once Cassidy resurfaced with Nahaali, who was quickly gasping for air and desperately clinging onto Cassidy, I came to a shocking conclusion. Not only could Nahaali not fight, she couldn't swim. Now I see why she was trying to desperately to cling to me. I guess she was holding onto me in hopes that I would somehow save her. All I did was force her back down into the pool. I could've killed her. Upon realizing that the state of North Carolina would've deemed me responsible for the deaths of two people, my anger and narcissistic jealousy subsided.

"Are you alright, Nahaali?" Cassidy asked as he gently patted her back.

Nahaali, who was bent over with her hands resting on her knees and her soaking wet hair completely covering her face like a sloppy mop head, coughed and raspily mumbled, "I'm okay."

She slowly rose back to a normal standing position and cleared her black hair from her face by tucking it behind both of her ears. Then, she quickly turned around and threw her skinny arms around Cassidy's neck, embracing him in a damp, unwanted hug.

"Oh, thank you, Cassidy!" She loudly rejoiced like the dramatic, damsel in distress that she is. Cassidy sighed and mumbled, "Don't mention it. Really."

He pried her off of him and began to walk back over to me, by MY side where he belonged. Seeing her beloved savior return to the arms of her competition must've set a fire to her emotionally unstable candle because the expression on her face changed from peaceful to fury.

"Why do YOU get to have him!?" She angrily shrilled as she charged at me with her arms fully extended and her hands reaching towards me like claws with manicured talons. I backed up and prepared myself, ready to thrash her again, but all I could manage was to lay a light slap upon her temple before Cassidy and Aaron immediately broke it up.

"You've already gotten beat up, Nahaali! Stop embarrassing yourself!" Aaliyah loudly announced from somewhere within the crowd.

Nahaali didn't even bother to respond to Aaliyah's factual taunt. She looked around, staring into the eyes of all her peers. Peers that she managed to make into enemies and who were overwhelmed with joy that the infamous Nahaali "Nutcase" Amard got what she so desperately deserved. No one was on her side. She didn't have a brother to stand and defend her honor, or a sister to fight for or with her. Her father wasn't there to protect her from making humiliating mistakes; for he was probably enjoying his new family somewhere in Jamaica. The only parent she had was her mother; and she wouldn't be able to heal her baby's wounds. No, Neha was too busy obsessing over fairytale love and men to properly raise the daughter she brought into this world. Nahaali didn't even have friends. She had not ONE single friend to lean on in times of need or even a nice, young man to show her true affection. I've never seen someone so alone. When Nahaali stared into my eyes, my heart broke just a little. I never thought I'd feel so much sympathy for someone who caused me so much trouble. Her eyes began to water and instead of letting a crowd full of enemies see her at her weakest, she quickly and frantically sprinted out of the pool area and back into the Johnson's home. It was at this time, around one o'clock, that my Aunt Liz texted me to let me know she was on her way to my grandparents' house to pick me up so that we could head back into town. I informed Cassidy, who didn't look too ecstatic about me leaving when things were just starting to get good.

"You have to leave already?" He somberly stated, wrapping his arms around me.

I intertwined my fingers with his. "Unfortunately, yes. We should get going. I don't wanna keep Aunt Liz waiting for too long."

Aaron gave me my first goodbye hug. "You take care of yourself, ok? Don't hesitate to call me if Cassidy here not treatin' you right."

"Oh, come on. You know me. Minnie's a queen and I'll treat her as such," Cassidy lightheartedly responded as he and Aaron once again performed their secret handshake. While they were occupied with that, Aaliyah reached out and embraced me in part two of my goodbye hugs.

"It was nice meeting you, Minnie. It's about time someone put Nahaali in her place again. You got some fire in you, girl," Aaliyah joked. With a smile, I replied, "Thanks, Aaliyah."

The journey back to my Grandparents' home was pretty much silent. Cassidy wouldn't even look at me and I just stared out of the passenger side window. While soaking in every piece of Fola's scenery, I realized how serene and quiet Fola really is. Perhaps as a child, I never appreciated the beauty that this town has to offer. Now that I must return to the chaos known as Angel City, it makes me truly not want to leave this place. Fola's become my rural sanctuary. Cassidy and I finally pulled up into Grandma's and Pop's driveway way to find them, Uncle Ben, and Aunt Liz awaiting our arrival.

"Well, it's about time you two got here!" Aunt Liz exclaimed. "Go upstairs and get your things. I'll wait for you in the car."

"Ooookay," I sadly responded.

With my head down and my hands resting in my pockets, I began to slowly walk towards the front door and entered the house.

"I'll help you, Minnie. I wouldn't want you to do all of that carrying by yourself." Cassidy suddenly called after me.

Once we were inside, I turned to Cassidy and stated, "You just couldn't stay away, could you?" I was glad he decided to come and "help" me with my luggage. It would give us one short moment of privacy before I had to leave. Cassidy swooped me up in his arms and responds, "Nope. You're like candy to me, babe."

We share a kiss as he carried me up the stairs to my room. We laughed, talked, and played around as we placed all of my belongings back into my suitcases. Playing around and laughing with Cassidy like this is like living in a flashback. I remember the Cassie who would squeeze my hand when the roller coasters at Carowinds got too scary. I remember the Cassie who would eat Oreo's and peanut butter with a glass of milk, while we were watching cartoons after school. That gap-toothed, blue eyed goofball Cassie is now a romantic, loveable sweetheart who does nothing but put a smile on my face. I see that he's nothing I need to fight. Cassidy is a welcome, much needed change into my life. I believe this was destined to be.

"Well," I said as I zipped the last suitcase shut and placed the Huckleberry Finn doll on top of my suitcases, "that's everything."

Cassidy fiddled with my hair. His lips were all pouty and voice all soft and solemn. "I'm gonna miss you, Minnie."

I slowly put my head on his chest. God, I loved the smell of his cologne and I swear could listen to his heart beating all day long. "I'll miss you more."

We slipped in a long, lingering smooch, before my Aunt Liz began to impatiently honk her truck's horn. Cassidy and I quickly grabbed my bags, rushed downstairs, and out the front door. As Cassidy put my things into the trunk, I gave my grandparents and Ben quick, goodbye hugs. I got one kiss on the cheek from Cassidy which was accompanied by an "I really don't want you to go" look. I hopped in the passenger seat and as my Aunt began to drive off, I looked back and waved to the ones I was leaving behind. They all appeared sad, like they didn't want me to leave, but seeing that expression on Cassie's face for the second time made my eyes start to tear up. I really didn't want to say goodbye. I stopped waving and turned back around in my seat and turned my head to hide the tears from Aunt Liz. Thirty minutes into the drive back home and I was already feeling drowsy. I should've expected it though. Long car rides have always made me sleepy. I'm sure Aunt Liz wanted me to tell her all the details about my visit and Prom once she got off the phone with Uncle Danny. But, at that moment, I just wanted to drift off into a deep sleep.

CHAPTER THIRTY-THREE:

"A poison is more than a lethal liquid."

I suddenly open my eyes to find that I am laying in a small, brown bed with eggshell white sheets and brown and white pillows. For a minute, I have no clue where I am or how I managed to get there, but once I take a lingering glance around and notice the powder pink, chocolate and white color scheme of the bedroom and the portrait of the Aprilson family on the medium-sized, brown dresser, I realize that I'm in Marley's bedroom. Compared to the rest of the home, Marley's room was always the best kept with the exception of all the dirt and debris on her pink rug and beige carpet. This is no surprise to me. Marley always despised sweeping. She complained that she could never get the stubborn or hidden pieces of dirt off the floor. Frustrated, she'd throw the broom and dustpan on the floor only to make more dirt splatter on the floor. Callista and I would crack up laughing seeing someone become so irate over such a simple chore. There's a small television that sits in the left corner of the room, a hand-me-down from Marley's uncle, Albert. Ophelia always promised to get it fixed and working, but never did. I get up off the bed to explore a little bit more. On Marley's dresser were rows of nice jewelry and other fabulous accessories. Lydia and her grandmother gave her most of it, but I guess it was too fancy and flashy for Marley's humble tastes. She ended up giving some of it to me, Callista, and Lauralee, and, of course, Ophelia would "borrow" a pair of earrings here and there when she had a hot date. I turned to open Marley's closet door, which no longer had a doorknob. Marley says it was broken off one night when one of Ophelia's many boyfriends was throwing a temper tantrum.

"Hmm, Marley has more clothes than I thought," I thought to myself.

Her wardrobe looked like it belonged to an America's Next Top Model, even though the vast majority of the items were given to her by family members. I even brought her a skirt here and there and I spotted a pair of lavender, high heeled booties Lauralee bought her sophomore year. She never wore them or the skirt. There were trendy skirts, cute jeans, fancy shirts, and...dresses! I didn't even know she liked dresses like that. I swear I've only seen Marley wear a dress like twice every school year. She was always so uncomfortable with wearing dresses. Lauralee and I would have to pull teeth to get her to wear them sometimes. With all of these nice clothes and accessories, I'll never ever understand why she chooses to stick with wrinkled old t-shirts and jeans with holes in the knees.

"You knoooow, it's not polite to snoop, Artemis." A gentle, feminine voice declared from behind me.

I expected to see Marley, maybe even Ophelia or Lydia, but I turned to see a pretty, sandy brown haired woman looking and smirking at me in the doorway. Her smile reeked of mischief. Her eyes are almond shaped and blue. They were a pretty, somehow familiar blue; so familiar, as if I'm staring into the eyes of someone I already knew.

"W-who are you?" I asked.

"Well, Mama named me Erica Christine. Call me Chrissie if you want to."

No wonder those eyes felt so familiar. She's Cassidy's older sister and now I know that she's Lauralee's sister, too. She smiled once she saw I realized who she was.

"Erica? Is it really you?" I questioned in disbelief.

"The one, dead, and only," She so casually responded.

"Why are you here?"

"Why are you snooping through Marley's things?"

I peered down at the red, lace blouse I was holding in my hands and I quickly tossed it back into the closet. "Umm, no reason."

"You always were a nosey one. It's unfortunate that you weren't nosey when it came to certain things…" Erica mysteriously noted.

I raised an eyebrow and tilted my head slightly in confusion. "What do you mean?"

"A poison is more than a lethal liquid. A poison can be the toxic, flawed part of your character that ends up destroying some or all of the happiness and stability in your life. Sometimes, we don't see or accept our flaws until it's too late to reverse any damage that's occurred. I had many poisons, Minnie. I was hard-headed, rebellious, reckless, irresponsible, and cruel. My actions practically drove a wedge between my parents' marriage and deteriorated what was left of my mother's sanity-"

"Erica," I sympathetically interrupted, "You can't possibly blame yourself for what Arella did." Seems like she share that trait with her brother.

She looked over at me with eyes full of tears and guilt. Even death couldn't stop Erica from the guilt that was tearing her apart. "That's one poison we have in common, Minnie. We never own up to how our actions contribute to what happens around us. We lack responsibility. I didn't put the gun in her hand, but I guess I might as well have."

"It wasn't your fault," I responded.

"You know, that's what I always told myself. It wasn't MY fault. NOTHING was ever Chrissie's fault. I treated my mother horribly! She was dealing with some serious issues and instead of simply LISTENING to her when she tried to reach out to me, I rejected her. I was beyond a rebellious teen. I was cold-hearted. Even in death, I can't apologize."

I paused to think for a second. "Well, maybe you can. Arella's up there with you…right?"

Erica wiped a wayward tear from her left eye before tonelessly answering, "No." Damn, I really wasn't expecting that. Erica dried the rest of her tears with a tissue she pulled from her pocket. Once she had regained composure, she walked over to a pink, polka-dotted box resting on the left corner of Marley's dresser.

"Sorry. I didn't mean to digress like that. I'm not here to throw a pity fiesta. I'm here to deliver an important message to you."

She opened the box and in it was a white and gold diary with a tiny, golden lock.

"Marley's diary?" I asked in a mocking tone, "That's the message?"

Erica shook her head. "You know, you're really way too stupid to always try and be a smart mouth."

I was actually offended by that remark. Who knew Cassidy's sister was such a firecracker? I'd better behave before she'd turn around and haunt me or something.

"This diary is the voice of truth. It serves a bittersweet purpose. It will bring freedom and demise to two people in Angel City. You do have a good heart, Artemis. I can see why my siblings love you, but you also have a poisoned character. Your recklessness, insensitivity, and egocentrism have already caused problems in your life that you have yet to see. Maybe you're in denial or maybe you're just plain clueless. Your life is going to have some drastic changes thrown in it; and not all of them will be for the better."

Utter confusion and curiosity were running rapidly through my mind. I was about to open my mouth and ask her more about what she meant.

But, before I had the chance, she blurted out, “Think fast!” and lunged the diary towards me; the lock striking me upon my left temple.

CHAPTER THIRTY-FOUR:

"No WHORE is going to stop Nate and I from being together!"

4:25 p.m.

I awaken with a headache the size of Alaska, but at least I'm home now. My family rushes outside in happiness and excitement to welcome me back from Fola. My parents hug and kiss me like they haven't seen me in three years instead of three days; then proceed to talk with Aunt Liz as they help to carry my bags inside.

"Welcome back, kiddo." Apollo lovingly greeted, wrapping his long arms around my shoulders and ruffling my hair. I see he's much more sober than he was when I last talked to him. Thank God.

Once inside, everyone was practically swarming around me, awaiting the details about my mini vacation. Ares, who probably missed me the most out of everyone, was pretty much glued to my hip. Athena, as expected, went bonkers when I gave her the gift I brought for her. I've never seen her so giddy. Of course while telling them about my trip, I had to leave out my night of passion with Cassidy. Hehe, that's for my girl talk with Lauralee and Marley. Although I'm going to miss Fola terribly, it does feel good to be back. "There's no place like home"…isn't that what Dorothy always said?

4:45 p.m.

I would love to stay up and talk more with my family, but this headache is absolutely killing me. I eat a bologna sandwich, take a Tylenol from Dad's medicine cabinet, and go to take a much needed nap in my big, comfy bed.

5:00 p.m.

My beauty rest is disrupted when Dite and Athena barge into my room uninvited as usual. Apparently, they are suffering from household boredom. Mom is upstairs working on important documents for her job, Dad went to run a few errands and Apollo took Ares to the park to play baseball. So now, they have come to the conclusion that big sister, Artie, must entertain them. I'm a little groggy, but at least my headache is gone. Hmm, I wonder what Marley's up to.

"Hey, you guys. How's about a trip to Marley's house?" I yawn. Athena shrugs her shoulders and answers, "Sure."

"But Lauralee lives in a MANSION. Can't we go there?" Dite whines. I'm glad Athena isn't as picky as she is. Of course Dite would love to go to Lauralee's house because everything there is 15% bigger than the average person's house. I swear, the Hulk could fit inside of their fridge comfortably.

I slowly get out of bed. "Would you rather stay here?" Athena is, by far, easier to satisfy than Dite. Dite's future husband is going to need a lot of prayer and painkillers to handle her. Dite's blue eyes dart up to the ceiling as she ponders for a few, quick seconds. "Never mind, I'll go." After the three of us are ready to go, I text Mom to tell her we are planning to leave the house. Once she responds, we proceed out of the front door.

5:08 p.m.

We arrive at the Aprilson's front door, and Athena does the honor of ringing the out of tune doorbell. We hear footsteps coming towards the door then it suddenly swings open. There, looking me straight in the eyes is Marley's older sister and the girl Apollo had the hugest crush on, Lydia; five-feet and ten inches of stunning beauty. Her long hair cascaded into waves of jet black down her right shoulder and over her right breast. This new color of hair makes her look even fiercer than she usually does with her naturally sandy blonde hair. Her feminine, voluptuous figure stood poised in the doorway. She looked like a fierce, beautiful Amazon. Thank God looks can't kill because the way Lydia was looking at me…

"Hey!" Dite exclaimed. "You're Marley's sister!"

Her expression went from serious to giddy. "Yep, that's me. You two must be Dite and Athena. You're practically all grown up since the last time I've seen you. Come on in."

Dite and Athena rushed inside the house, but Lydia stopped me at the door.

"Well, well, well. Big Bad Artemis is all grown up." She was circling me like a vulture circles its next meal. "I'll never understand what my sister sees in you."

I forgot how intimidating Lydia could be. Her aggressive personality is a stark difference than that of her sister's. In fact, you'd never think someone like Lydia is the daughter of someone who was as gentle as

Donald. Those sharp, blue eyes and that mysterious smile of hers have two purposes: mesmerize you with her beauty, or scare you into a freakin' heart attack.

"Look," I start, hoping to reason with her, "I don't want to cause any trouble.'

"HA!" Lydia mockingly laughed. "It's a little too late for that." She then takes her hands off her wide hips and extends her left hand to me, perhaps, as a sign of a truce. I extend my left hand to her in return. At first she shook it, and then she squeezed the hell out of it. All those sports Lydia played made her athletic and strong. No wonder she won all of her fights when she lived here, earning her the nickname of "Lethal Lefty." She smiles mischievously, and then I follow her into the house.

"Oh, heh-wo, Minnie!" Ophelia announced with a mouth full of ice cream. She was apparently spending the rest of her day laid back on the couch in her lavender robe with large, green curlers in her hair and watching soap operas. "Will…you be a dear and chweck on your shisters? They're upsturs."

I was more than glad to do anything to get away from the hellish glares of Lydia. I quickly walked up the stairs, some of them letting out a small creak as I stepped on them. I expected to find them in the restroom, posing like divas for cell phone pictures but instead, I find them in Marley's room, ogling her accessories and clothes.

"You little snoops," I hissed, startling them, "What are you doing in here?"

"Umm, we were totally bored," Dite humbly answered before turning her attention back to the jewelry. She picks out a pair of skull and crossbones shaped earrings painted a metallic grey with amber gemstones in the eyes. Callista gave those to her, but Marley never wore them, stating that they were "too grim." "These earrings are so bomb, aren't they Minnie?"

I sucked my teeth. "Come on. Let's go before you destroy something I don't wanna pay for."

Athena unwillingly puts away the red, lace blouse she had her greedy paws on and then began to walk away from Marley's dresser, but not before she accidentally knocked over a pink, polka-dotted box on it. The impact from the fall opened the top of the box and an eerily familiar, gold and white diary appeared.

"The voice of truth." Erica's words echoed through my mind like the lyrics to a song you can't shake out of your head. It sent a shudder through my body.

"Let's read it!" Dite eagerly and nosily exclaimed, immediately picking up the golden key next to it.

By the time I tried to gently tackle her (I can't really tackle my baby sister, after all. My Mom would have a natural fit.), she had already opened the diary. While I had my hands full with the nosey blonde, Athena slowly picked the diary up off the floor and flipped through some of the pages.

"Minnie, who's Jezebel?" She softly inquired with her blue eyes focused on the page.

Upon hearing that name again, I gasped in shock and released the hold I had on Dite. Jezebel...that's the name Marley mentioned without any explanation. I walked over to Athena, with my arm extended towards her.

"Let me see that," I ordered.

Once she handed over Marley's diary, I began to read it for myself. One entry particularly caught my eye. It was written on the day of Callista's accident.

"Who does that little bitch think she is!? No WHORE is going to stop Nate and I from being together! Ha, I guess she can't stop me now, considering the fact that she's probably gonna die any moment now. I'm glad I pulled her down those damn steps. No one wants her here anyways. I did the world a favor by getting rid of Callista Arden. If Callista's bastard dies, I'm sure Nate will get over it eventually. I'll be more than happy to bear him more and better children. With Callista out of the way, all that's left is Minnie. She'll get what's coming to her soon. Everything is going according to my plan.

-Jezebel Jacobs."

CHAPTER THIRTY-FIVE:

"My adrenaline is pumping, my hair is whipping me in my face, and the setting sun is mildly blinding my eyes."

5:15 p.m.

I think I almost sprained my ankle running down those creaky steps so fast.

"Jezebel!" I yelled, flailing the diary around. I'm sure I probably looked like a maniac from their point of view, but at that moment, I wasn't the type to care.

"What the hell are you talking about now!?" Lydia barked as she shot up out of her seat. Ophelia has now muted the television and has walked over to stand beside Lydia. There was no time for dramatic explanations.

"Read this!" I commanded as I quickly handed Lydia the diary. They take about twenty quick seconds to read it then slowly look up at one another in astonishment. Lydia backs slowly away and Ophelia covers her mouth, as if she had just read the most horrid thing in her life.

"Who is Jezebel?" I finally asked. I was desperately in need of an answer.

"Jezebel...is Marley," Lydia quietly responds, staring down at the floor as she toys with her lip piercing with her tongue. It's the most demure I'd ever seen Lydia behave.

"BullSHIT!" I angrily snapped. My fists were balled and my jaw was clenched. If Jezebel confessed to killing Callista and Jezebel and Marley are the same person, then that means...no, it just couldn't be. This type of stuff only happens in movies. This kind of stuff doesn't happen to me. This was all too surreal.

"No, Minnie. Lydia's telling the truth," Ophelia interjects. She wipes a tear away then continues. "Marley was diagnosed with Dissociative Identity Disorder a few years ago. It's more commonly known as Multiple Personality Disorder. I knew Jezebel could be a lot to handle. But, I didn't think her anger would reach this point. I never thought she'd be a real danger to anyone."

"Marley's so moody. I don't know why she acts that way sometimes."

"Seeing Marley so angry was like watching her turn into a different person."

"Why was Marley acting like she didn't recognize her own name?"

Everything and more began to fall into place now. Of course I wanted to find out more about Marley's disorder and why it was kept a secret, but at the moment, I just needed to locate where Marley was before any other tragedies happened.

"Where is she now?" I inquired to them.

"I-I made her to go to the grocery store for me. She took my truck," Ophelia explained. I could tell she was starting to get shaken up and nervous.

Now, it was time to take action. God knows I didn't want to turn Marley in, but I felt like I had no other option at this point. I pointed to Ophelia. "Ophelia, call 9-1-1."

5:17 p.m.

I was actually surprised when neither Lydia nor Ophelia asked any questions. I was more surprised, however, when Marley casually strolled into the house with two, yellow grocery bags in each hand. She didn't speak a word. She glanced around at everyone, looking as if she was trying to figure out why everyone was staring at her. When her eyes locked on to me holding her opened diary, her eyes bulged. She was beginning to piece together the entire situation now.

"Marley, let us explain." I started as I reached out to her with my right arm.

She didn't give us a chance to explain. She violently tossed the bags at us. One hit Lydia and me, and the others missed. She sprinted out of the house with Lydia, Ophelia, and I following right behind her. She hopped back into Ophelia's white pickup truck and sped off.

"Come on!" Lydia ordered as she quickly entered her dark green Lexus. I hurriedly entered the passenger seat soon after Lydia did. She reversed hurriedly out of the driveway, then sped off after Marley. The next few minutes were the most adrenaline-filled and terrifying minutes of my life. Lydia and Marley were driving dangerously all through Angel City, merging recklessly, and turning dangerously on every street. Drivers blared their horns with every life threatening driving maneuver the sisters executed. Everything in our environment became a blur of sounds and colors. Our only focus was stopping Marley from hurting herself or anyone else. Our chase is now leading us to the outskirts of Angel City, very close to

TresAngeles Field.

5:25 p.m.

Marley suddenly swerves off the right of the road into a small ditch. Lydia immediately slams on her brakes, causing them to squeal a bit; and if I didn't have my seatbelt on, I would've been flung through the windshield. As our car was coming to a stop, we noticed an uninjured Marley climbing out of the car. When she saw us beginning to exit Lydia's car, she turned and began to jolt into TresAngeles Field. Without talking and without hesitation, we darted after her. Lydia's long, athletic legs effortlessly allow her to run faster than me, but I am trying with every fiber in my being to catch up to both of them. My adrenaline is pumping, my hair is whipping me in my face, and the setting sun is mildly blinding my eyes. Just as I think Lydia may catch up to her after all, suddenly, Marley stops sprinting and turns in our direction with a .45 pistol sitting proudly in her left hand. Lydia and I quickly cease chasing her and hold our arms up over our heads.

"You…bitches didn't think it would be THAT easy, did you?" Marley hisses while trying to catch her breath.

CHAPTER THIRTY-SIX

"Her blood splattered like spilled paint amongst the delicate petals of the white roses."

"Marley, please. Just let us explain," I urged.

"THAT'S not Marley," Lydia corrected, staring her sister dead in the eyes.

So, this is Jezebel. So I finally get to meet the cold-hearted person who killed my best friend. It's unfortunate that she shares a body and a mind with someone I love and adore. How do you fight the urge to strangle someone when that same person is someone you consider a best friend for life? This entire situation is just too much to handle. Lydia hardly looked afraid at all. I assumed she had been eye to eye with Jezebel many times before today. She was looking at Jezebel as if she were saying "So, it's you again."

"Why are you doing this, Marley?" I inquire sadly.

"I'm NOT Marley, you simple whore! Didn't she just tell you that!?" Jezebel snaps. "Marley doesn't have the balls to take charge of her life like I do!"

"This is "taking charge!?" You killed a pregnant woman for stupid reasons!" I yelled in return. She directs the gun at me. "Are you saying I'm stupid?"

I take a step backward in defense. "N-not at all." I need to get a grip on my emotions. It's really not a good idea to anger someone who has a pistol pointed at you, especially when that person is a few cakes short of a whole bakery.

"Isobel..Callista..Arden. Where do I begin? Oh! How about the fact that she was a big mouthed, delinquent idiot who didn't deserve to be on Nate's arm! I'm disgusted by the fact her body even got the honor to carry his child. Speaking of which, how about the fact that she willingly slept with your boyfriend and, get this, even became pregnant by him!? I must give her credit though for standing up to you, unlike Marley. You know, knocking you off that high horse you've always been on."

"You took away a sister, a daughter, a friend, and a mother. You think Dad would be proud of you?" Lydia blurted out, trying to guilt trip her.

"Dad's probably looking down at me with pride for finally standing up for myself. When she stood in the way between me and what I wanted, Callista deserved whatever came to her and frankly, Little Miss Perfect over here deserves worse." Jezebel angrily responded. Lydia's guilt trip failed miserably.

"Me?" I shockingly replied, "What did I ever do to you?"

Jezebel tilted her head back and manically laughed, just like she did after Lauralee and her got into that fight a while ago. "God, I should kill you just for being so stupid! You treat everyone around you like they're peasants! Sybil, Callista, Marley, Lauralee…instead of treating them like people, you made them feel like they were forever inferior to you. Like, you think you're top dog or something! They gave you ALL of them and you toyed with it. You've always been like that. You think Callista betrayed you without motive? You think Callista turned on you because she was jealous? Ha! Your head is so far up your tail, it's ridiculous! You hurt Marley and Callista. They loved you and all you did was sweep them into your shadow, as you got more popular. You're just like Ophelia. You're both superficial bitches! Don't you get it? It was YOU! Your overly self-centered, mean-spirited ways is what ruined your friendship with Calli, Ar-te-misss."

I wanted to just drop onto the ground and breakdown into tears. "It was me. It was me." I repeated it in my head over and over again like a mantra. All this time, I blamed Calli for stabbing me in the back when it was me who gave her the knife. A tear rolled down my right cheek and gently fell in between the roses and into the blades of grass.

"Don't start with the crocodile tears, Artemis." I'm not Marley, I'm not the one to give sympathy. Every time something happens, you ALWAYS play the victim. Callista told Marley things that she would never tell you because Marley and her knew you wouldn't understand. Callista didn't "betray" you because she hated you. She loved you dearly…like an idiot. She did it to prove a point to you. Sure, her plan went a little astray, but she did it so you'd learn you can't treat people the way you do and expect them to remain by your side. All she ever wanted from you was a genuine apology! She wanted you to change!"

This was one of the few moments in my life where I was truly speechless. All I could do was just stand there with my mouth open like a fool and think about all the damage I didn't even know I caused. No wonder why the vast majority of Callista's wrath was directed at me.

Marley wasn't the one who hurt her. I could hardly look Jezebel in her eyes. I was dead wrong and it was far too late to give Callista the apology she so desperately wanted. I've never felt such a knowing feeling of guilt and regret until this very moment. When she saw that I was just going to stand there quietly like a moron, she turned to Lydia.

"You, Lydia Aprilson, don't try to guilt trip me by bringing Dad into this. This has nothing-"

"I was just pointing out that Dad would be disappointed in his little girl."

"DON'T play me for a fool, Lydia!" Jezebel shrieked, stomping her foot. "I'm not weak like Marley! Don't try to play games with me!"

Lydia lowered her arms slightly. "This anger…where is it coming from? Is it because I left for college?"

Jezebel let out a slight, sardonic laugh as she shook her head. "You know damn well it's about more than that. You abandoned us! You left us to be raised by that pathetic excuse of a woman and never looked back. You took the first ticket out of Angel City and didn't even stop to think about your little sister. You hardly ever came to visit."

"Marley, I couldn't take you with me. I wouldn't have been able to take care of you and myself at that age."

"Take care!? Dummy, we're only 5 years apart! Marley and I weren't infants! We were 13 when you left! Surely, you don't think I'm stupid enough to believe that a thirteen-year-old needed a round the clock babysitter...retard," Jezebel seethed. Honestly, she had a good point.

"Jezebel, just listen to me," Lydia pleaded.

Jezebel stepped closer. "Why do bitches like her get all the best stuff in life, while good, smart people like Marley only get dirt shoved in their face? Why does SHE get TWO parents who would do anything for her, while I get a dead dad and a drunken, superficial, abusive mother whose love is faaaaar from unconditional?"

"Daddy loved you," Lydia replied softly.

"Shut up! Why does SHE get siblings who absolutely adore her, while I get one who abandons me and didn't even give a damn?"

"I do care about Marley. You know that."

"Hush, dammit!" Jezebel raged. "Why does SHE get to be beautiful, while Marley believes she's ugly? Why does SHE get popularity, while Marley gets treated like she's nobody and an outcast? Why does SHE get to have Nate, and we get nobody? Why does SHE get the family with money, while we live in a house that isn't fit for stray dogs to live in? Just tell me why…why do people LOVE her and don't even LIKE us? Why...why...why…"

You could practically see the grief and pain in those green eyes as they began to quickly well up with tears. Like Nahaali, all Marley knew in her life was pain and disappointment. Yes, Jezebel was filled with anger and resentment but past that tough façade she put on, I saw a broken woman. I could tell Jezebel was trying to be tough and trying not to have a mental breakdown in front of her enemies. My heart suddenly grew heavy with sympathy. I truly believe Jezebel isn't completely evil. She was just an incarnation born from Marley's deep-rooted hurt and sorrow. I no longer completely feared her. I felt an immense amount of pity for her. This goes to prove how a broken family can have dramatic effects on someone. It's quite sad, really. It hurts me to see someone I love so much in this bad of a mental state.

"Don't cry, Marley," Lydia consoled. She began to slowly walk over towards her sister with her arms extended, in an attempt to hug and console her. "You idiots didn't think it would be that easy, did you? Jezebel abruptly jumped back, pointed the gun towards Lydia, and fired. Lydia shrieked in pain as she fell to the ground, holding her shoulder. She was lucky that Jezebel didn't take the time to aim the gun at her head or chest or else Jezebel would've claimed her second victim.

"Lydia!" I yelled in concern.

"I warned you! That may have worked on someone like Marley, hell, it may even work in the movies, but it won't work on me!"

I began to move towards Lydia to ensure she was okay, but Jezebel pointed the gun at me and with tears still running down her cheeks. She coldly growled, "Do…NOT…move." Off in the distance, we heard the faint sound of police sirens. A sweeter sound has never graced my ears before. The three of us turned our heads to see multiple ACPD vehicles approaching TresAngeles Field. All of a sudden, Jezebel began to groan and hold her right hand up to her temple as if she was experiencing a headache. When she looked back up at me, I could see that something was off about her. Something in her eyes had changed. Jezebel's fury seemed to be absent from those big, green eyes now.

"Minnie?" She turned and looked down at the ground. "Lydia?" She glanced down at the gun being held in her hand. "Oh my God!" She shrieked in terror, dropping the gun immediately. I took a great sigh of relief and smiled as I rushed to hug her tightly. The REAL Marley is back. She couldn't have picked a finer time to show up.

"What's going on? Why are the police here? Why are we here?" Marley inquired, obviously in utter confusion.

"Marley, Jezebel was here. She did some bad things, sis." Lydia growled, wincing from her gunshot wound.

"She shot you?" Marley solemnly asked as she pointed at Lydia's injured shoulder.

"Yeah, but I'll survive."

She turned to me. "She was going to kill you?"

"I think she would've if you didn't take over again."

Marley shook her head from left to right, as if she was in denial of what something inside of her was capable of. "It was bad enough she killed Callista."

"Wait, you knew?" I retorted in astonishment.

She began to glance off in the distance, eyeing the police who were beginning to come towards us. We knew they were coming to get me out of harm's way and get Lydia some medical attention; but we surely knew that their main purpose was to arrest Marley. Every Angelean has been awaiting for the true culprit to finally fall under arrest for the murder of Isobel Arden, I just hate that it had to be her.

"I didn't find out until one day I found a scrapped diary entry she wrote in our trashcan. However, every time I tried to confess, Jezebel would take over. I've been the one who's had to deal with the consequences of Jezebel's actions for years. Her sleeping around, her reckless behavior, and her horrible attitude. Honestly, I'm tired, Minnie. I'm tired of feeling ashamed and I'm tired of running. I'm tired of not having complete control of my own body. This is the last day that I'll just walk away."

Marley slowly bent down and used her long, slender arms to pick up the gun she frantically dropped. I began to grow extremely worried and by the expression on Lydia's face, so was she. I turned around to look back at Lydia, as if to say, "You're her big sister, stop her!" This can't end like this.

"Wait, Marley. What are you doing?" I anxiously asked.

Marley began to step backwards from us, tears flooded her eyes again.

"I love you. I love the both of you. Never ever forget that."

"We can talk about this, Marley. I know you wanted to keep Jezebel a secret, but we can still get you all the help you need. Just be rational and put the gun back on the ground," Lydia added, clutching her arm.

She continued to move backwards and cocked the gun. "I'm not gonna pay for your sins anymore. This…ends today, Jezebel Aprilson."

I was done talking. This was getting nowhere. I began to charge at her, extending one hand towards the gun and the other towards Marley's body. A part of me hoped Jezebel would take over again to stop her. Marley pressed the gun to her temple and closed her eyes slowly. "Tell everyone I'm sorry. Nate, Lauralee, the Ardens…Violet."

"NO!!!!" Lydia and I loudly screamed before Marley finally pulled the trigger. The blast seemed to echo for an eternity. I'll never forget that sound. It will echo into my dreams and jolt me out of a deep sleep tonight. Suddenly, the environment was cloaked in silence. I stopped charging, Lydia stopped yelling, and the police even stopped sneaking their way towards us. All of us were too stunned to move. Time seemed to stand still. The only sound present was the sound of nearby birds rustling leaves as they flew away, frightened from the blast. Marley's body fell to the ground instantaneously with a lifeless thud. Her blood splattered like spilled paint amongst the delicate petals of the white roses.

Katherine Rosemarley "Marley" Aprilson, my best friend, is dead. Time of death: 5:55 p.m.

CHAPTER THIRTY-SEVEN:

"My sadness resurrects, once the vision is gone."

By the time the police catch up to us, Lydia is curled up next to Marley's corpse, bawling her eyes out, and tightly holding Marley's right hand; the same hand she used to shoot Lydia and herself. Uncle Danny holds me as I break down into a fit of tears, as well. I was crying so much that I couldn't even breathe normally. I can't help but to cry more as Lydia repeatedly sobs, "No!" as officers place Marley's corpse into a large, black body bag. Uncle Danny sniffles a bit before whispering, "I know it hurts right now, Minnie, but believe me when I tell you, it's gonna be ok. Time heals all wounds. Now, your parents are waiting at the police department…are you ready to go?"

I cannot find the strength to speak. I simply nod my head up and down, my hair and some of my tears brush up against his navy blue uniform. I stare at Lydia, who was now standing up with her back turned to us and staring off into the distance. The only noise you heard from her was her nose sniffling as she continued to cry.

"Lydia, you've got to go to the hospital. That wound needs to be examined before it becomes infected," Uncle Danny advised.

Lydia gave no response. I don't think she even cared about her injured shoulder anymore. The pain in her shoulder was trivial compared to the pain she was feeling in her heart right now. Uncle Danny leaned down and whispered, "I'll meet you in the car" before patting me on the back twice and walking off. I took two steps before Lydia randomly blurted out, "Can't you see her?" I stopped walking and respond, "What?"

Lydia turns her head towards me. Her eyes were starting to become red. Absolute grief was written all over her face. "Marley, my sister, can't you see her?

Unsure of exactly what Lydia was referring to, I decide to walk towards her to check it out. What I saw had me questioning if I was hallucinating from all the sorrow and shock or just going crazy. I swear, just for a few seconds, that I saw Donald Aprilson playing with a younger, pig-tailed Marley. He held her snugly by her tiny waist as he twirled her around in the air. They were laughing and practically glowing with joy. I haven't seen Marley smile so genuinely in a long time. I blinked once and the scene had vanished. My sadness resurrects, once the vision is gone. Lydia takes a deep breath before mumbling, "She said I was forgiven. She forgave me, Minnie." She tucks her hair behind her ear and walks off without making eye contact with me. Maybe what I saw was just a figment of my imagination. Maybe we wanted Marley to be there so badly that we actually thought we saw her standing before us. Then again, they do say TresAngeles Field is haunted.

I am smothered with hugs and kisses from my parents, once I arrive at ACPD. Normally, I'd be thankful for their overprotective concern and parental support, but I just wanted some alone time. I hated to cry in front of a lot of people. My parents leave me be as they go inside to discuss the situation with my uncle, Ophelia, and other ACPD officers. I take a seat on the hard, cement steps and bury my head in my arms. I try to fight tears, but grief wins this battle. I feel so empty, yet so full of grief. I miss her like crazy already. We all take our loved ones for granted, acting as if we KNOW they're going to be there with us tomorrow, and the truth is, we never know. You never know how attached you are to someone until they're truly gone. I knew I loved Callista and Marley but I didn't truly realize it until they passed. Marley would know how to make me feel better. She gave the best hugs. Those long arms could wrap all the way around your body and squeeze you extra tight and the vanilla smell of her hair was so good, it made you take a deep breath of it and smile. Who would hug me like that now? Marley was always the smartest and most rational thinker out of the three of us. Who would be there to calm me down and think of an intelligent solution to any problem I faced? Who?

"I'm sooo sorry, Minnie," a soft voice says.

My hysterics cease as I glance up to see Lauralee and Nate standing in front of me. Both of them were looking down at me with eyes full of pity. I don't want pity. I want my best friends back. I wipe tears off my face with my wrist and mumble, "It's ok."

"So, umm, what happened? You know, with Marley and the, um field and stuff?" Nate stumbles. I can't believe he's still this tense and awkward around me.

"Lydia and I chased her to TresAngeles Field. Marley took Ophelia's gun and shot herself…right there in front of us." An expression of disbelief came upon both of their faces.

"Why did this happen?" Lauralee inquired, shaking her head. "I just went to Prom with her. Marley seemed so normal and happy."

I inhale and exhale deeply before asking, "Shortly before her suicide, I discovered Marley had Dissociative Identity Disorder."

Nate seemed confused. "What does "dissociative" mean?" He asked. Hey, he's a jock; not an Einstein.

"You might know it as Multiple Personality Disorder. Marley had a split personality. Her "other half" is the one that killed Callista."

Lauralee's eyes bulged as she covered her mouth in surprise. Nate immediately begins to take steps backwards while shaking his head. "Unbelievable" is all Nate mutters. His tone was melancholy, yet enraged.

I turn my head towards Nate. Now, I was ready to get some answers. "Marley's other personality, Jezebel, seemed awfully fond of you, Nathaniel. Any reason as to why that is?"

"That bet..." He mumbles; his head down and his fists balled. I stand up and Lauralee and I both reply, "What?"

"That bet...! That stupid freaking bet!" He loudly reiterates. "Remember the evening I came to your house and we had that argument about Callista? Well, days earlier, some of the guys bet that I couldn't get Marley "The Weirdo" Aprilson into bed. I wasn't gonna do it until you pissed me off that day. I texted Keegan before I left you to go to Marzo's house. He warned me not to do it, but I didn't listen. I should've. Come to think of it, she was easier than I thought she would be."

"You son of a BITCH!" I scream. I started to charge at him, but Lauralee held me back by the waist. The pure thought of him touching her and taking advantage of her while she was in that kind of mental state set my blood aflame. We watch as he breaks down right in front of us. I had never seen Nate cry so passionately before. The only other time I can think of Nate being this emotional was after Callista died. It was almost like the unveiling of a complete different side of him. He sobs, "I didn't know she was CRAZY! I didn't know she would kill her! That FREAK took Callista from me." He begins kicking trashcans, punching the wall, and bawling even more. It wasn't until I saw him reacting like this over the news that I realized how much he must've really cared for her. I mean, he didn't have to say much but the tears rolling down his eyes and the rage he was displaying spoke volumes. It was clear Callista was more than just sex to him. Callista had his heart and now, it was broken. Everyone has that "one who got away," but Callista was the one who was stolen from him. I just hope he can pick up the pieces because Violet is going to need him. Then, I hear Lauralee's girly sobs from behind me. I turn around to hug her and give her gentle pats on the back and whisper, "It's gonna be ok, Lee." Just like what my uncle did for me.

"I have a confession, too," She mumbles.

I pull away from her to look her in those sad, hazel eyes of hers. I gently move her hair out of her face and say, "What is it?"

"I slept with her, too," She sniffles.

Nate blurts out, "What!?" and I accompany it with a "You've GOT to be kidding me right now."

She cries harder. "Remember that day at lunch when Marley came late and our clothes were all messed up and she was acting so odd and I was all happy and stuff?"

Oh, no.

"Well, before that, she came to me wanting to apologize for the day before when she beat me up. So we went off campus for the majority of lunch period. Next thing you know, we're in my car and she grabbed me out of nowhere and kissed me and…and."

She goes into a wailing, crying, pathetic fit. She reminded me of a child who would sit there and sob and sob and sob until Mama came to comfort them. It looks like Jezebel had her way with the both of them and they didn't suspect a thing. Who knows how many other times Jezebel took over and we never even noticed? She was a true snake. She slithered undetected into our lives and now that we're aware of her presence, it's too damn late.

"Woooow! A weird nerd who's also a bisexual, homicidal, psycho freak! You guys suuure know how to pick friends. Looks like you and I both got SCREWED like a couple of chumps," Nate raged.

"Don't speak ill of the dead, Nate," Lauralee seethes.

"She's DEAD! This isn't Resident Evil. She's not gonna riiiiise back up to get me. Hell, the only reason that girl got even a shred of respect around here was because she was related to "Lethal Lefty" Aprilson!"

"Don't loop me in with you, Nate. We're totally different. I'm nothing like YOU," Lauralee growled.

"Oh, puh-lease," Nate retorted, rolling his eyes. Apparently, if we both got tricked by this half-dyke wacko, we're about as different as fire and flame. I bet you kissed that freak at Prom, too. How cute. Tell me something, could you still taste how delicious I was on her lips?

I rushed up angrily to his face. "You have NO right to talk about her that way! What makes you think you're so damn high and mighty?"

"Hmm, let's see," He mockingly replies, tapping his left index finger on his chin, "I don't stab my friends in the back. I didn't carpet munch with the Governor's daughter for kicks. I don't go around murdering pregnant women. Shall I continue, Minnie?"

"You are the reason she went crazy! Having sex with her, then tossing her aside like…like…like an unwanted pair of high heels. Then, practically ignoring her doesn't exactly help one's mental state, y'know!" Lauralee chimed inl

"HA! My fault? Marley or Annabelle or whoever the hell she decided to be was screwed up beyond repair way before I got to her! It wasn't MY fault she had a dad and a sister who left her. It wasn't MY fault, her mother was a stinking drunk. It wasn't MY fault she had no friends and no life. I'M not the one who told her to become homicidally jealous of Callista. The girl was a raging, out casted BITCH who got overly-attached after a one-time fling!"

I slap him hard across the face, just like I did when I saw him at the hospital after the accident. I know he was furious, but I refused to tolerate that kind of disrespect towards Marley anymore. He glares at me before storming off in the opposite direction while muttering angrily under his breath. I begin to walk up the steps when I notice Lauralee's slender shadow following right behind me. Without turning to face her, I stop and growl, "Lauralee, now is not the time. I don't wanna be bothered with you so go to your fancy pink car and go home. Get the hell away from me." I don't think I've ever acted so coldly towards her before this moment. I had no desire to even lay eyes on her and I certainly didn't want to hear any more about her lesbian fling with my now deceased best friend.

In a timid tone, she answered, "But, don't you want me to stay with you? You could use a fri-"

"LEAVE!" I angrily commanded. I was about three seconds from completely spazzing on her.

She pauses for a few seconds before she turns around and runs down the street. I enter the station without even taking a look back and sit there until my parents decide to take me home.

CHAPTER THIRTY-EIGHT:
"I'm sorry for being such a screw up."

The ride back home was silent and full of tension. My head throbbed relentlessly from crying and my heart ached with grief. All I needed was my privacy. Just let me cry, and scream and be angry in solitude. I just wanted to lie in the darkness and wallow into a pit of my own emotions. I opened my laptop and as expected, "The Arden Incident" being solved was breaking news. It was all over the web, like a spectacle for other people to view, while the rest of us who loved Callista and Marley must suffer. One person commented, "I hear Aprilson was on the rag when she did all of this. PMS at its finest, smh. All of this could've been avoided if we had simply given her a Midol." I don't understand how people can possibly find any way whatsoever to turn this ordeal into a joke. The Ardens, Aprilsons, Nate and myself don't find this situation humorous AT ALL. I'm sure when Violet grows up, she won't find her mother's murder so ha-ha either. It's astounding how cruel and bold people become when they're hiding behind a keyboard and a glowing screen. After that, I fell asleep in my room after skimming through the memories of my two best friends. Memories of laughing, telling secrets, sleepovers, and getting into and out of trouble together. We always said we'd take each other's secrets to our graves. I just didn't expect two of us to hit the grave before we were even old enough to buy our own drinks. Memories of deceased loved ones are tainted bittersweet. They provide a distraction and a temporary laugh or smile on your face. Then, the smile fades and the laughter stops, because you remember they won't be around for anymore "good times." That's especially if you've ever had a loved one who committed suicide. I just keep wishing that I could've been inside her mind at that precise moment. I keep running through a thousand different questions, but it all boils down to me just wanting to know why she did it. That, my friends, is the frustrating part of someone you know dying by their own hand. You never will truly know why. You can assume but you'll never get your questions answered. I haven't eaten or talked to the rest of my family in hours. I kind of want to keep it that way. Out of nowhere, there is a gentle knock at my bedroom door. I sniffle and yell out, "Who is it?"

They do not answer. They simply open the door. Near-blinding light floods my room and burns my eyes a bit. I squint. The shadow is not quite big enough to be Dite, but it's certainly too big to be Ares.

"What is it, Athena?" I ask.

In her soft-spoken voice, she replies, "Mom and Dad wanna talk to you and Apollo." Then, I see her shadow turn around and leave.

It must be important if they're still willing to summon me out of my room after what just happened. I exhale deeply and wipe my eyes with my blanket. I'm sure it does no good. I bet my eyes are as red as my hair by now. I drag myself out of bed, into the hallway and find Mom, Dad, and Apollo all standing in the middle of the kitchen. As for Dite, Athena, and Ares, I could hear their voices in the backyard. Mom and Dad must've sent them outside while "the adults" talk.

"Sorry to have to drag you out of bed, honey," Mom states. She reaches out and embraces me in a tight hug. Daddy brushes my hair with his hand from behind me. "We know you're going through a rough patch right now, but this is something we feel you should know, as well."

I look into my mother's soft, blue eyes. They're filled with worry and sympathy. "What is it?"

"That's what I wanna know," Apollo adds as he takes a seat on one of the stools in the kitchen.

"Your father and I just got off the phone with Danny. He found some interesting information in Marley's diary," Mom says.

"Let's get right to the point, Diana," Daddy interjects. "Apollo, your uncle found some evidence that you and Marley had some kind of fling."

I jerk away from my mother and turn towards Dad. Apollo nearly falls as he jumps off of his stool. "What!?" Apollo and I both yell simultaneously. I swear to God, if my own brother took advantage of Marley like Nate did, oooh, I just don't know what I'd do.

"Patrick, don't word it like that," Mom commands. "Let me clarify. Apollo, did you…have sex with anyone at the party you went to a while ago? You remember, the party Jonas DiCamillo hosted while Minnie was in Fola?"

That sentence hit me like a brick thrown in my face. I remember Apollo calling me, still hungover and telling me about some "babe" he hooked up with the night before. I love Apollo so much, but I swear if he stooped down to Nate's level, I'd rip his head off. I could feel myself glaring intensely at him and my jaw tensing up. I was ready to kick that stool from underneath him and then beat him with it.

Apollo looked over at me and then at Mom as he shifted his weight back and forth. He seemed like he was a little uncomfortable talking about his sex life in front of his family. "Well, yeah. It couldn't have been Marley, though. That girl had long, blonde hair, and her eyes were blue, not green like Marley's. I wasn't even attracted to Marley, Mom. Tell Uncle Danny he has the wrong guy."

Mom looks nervous, but Dad looks like he's about to get riled up. "Officers have found a blonde wig and a case of blue contacts under Marley's bed, Apollo," Dad informs.

"Not to mention, Marley wrote a graphic diary entry about her little tryst with you. Scribbling your name and Nate Jacobs's name in bright colors with hearts and smiley faces. Feeling "torn" because she was "in love" with two men. Feeling "selfish" because she felt she cheated on Nate and wanted to have you both," Mom finishes.

That wasn't Marley writing that stuff. That wasn't Marley who managed to get my stupid, wasted brother into bed. That wasn't Marley prancing around parties in wigs and colored contacts…

"Her name is Jezebel," I blurted out. I was no longer angry and ready to tear my brother limb from limb. I realized it was actually Apollo who got taken advantage of.

Mom looks confused and Dad says, "Huh?"

"Marley's other personality…her name was Jezebel. She's the one who did all that stuff."

Apollo looks as if he had seen a ghost before his very eyes. "I-I don't believe it." Still emotional, I turn to him and yelled. "Well, believe it!" I wasn't too happy with him at this moment. Apollo living in a carefree world has finally caught up to him.

Dad banged his fist on our kitchen table. "DAMMIT, Apollo! Didn't you learn from that pregnancy scare Melissa had when you were a sophomore!? You failed tenth grade because you got caught up in hooking up and almost becoming a father before you were 18!"

Mom places her hands on Daddy's chest. "Patrick, please calm down." The roles have been reversed. Usually, it's Mommy losing her cool and Dad needing to be the voice of reason. I think this is the angriest I'd ever seen Dad at Apollo.

"Dad, I didn't…I didn't know. Minnie, I didn't know, I swear it," Apollo says, almost pleading with someone to believe him.

"What the hell difference does that make!? You shouldn't be getting drunk to the point where you can't recognize someone you've known for YEARS. Disguised, my foot. Your mother could walk down the street in a rainbow wig and matching tutu and I'd know it was her!"

"Patrick, please," Mom says reaching for Dad's hand. Dad pulls away, not calming down one bit.

"No, Diana. I won't have children bringing home babies and DUI's and not bringing home degrees! What kind of example are you setting for your younger siblings!? Did you think about that or were you too busy screwing random girls and childhood friends?"

After that comment, Apollo's eyes became glossy. He blinks and tears fall from his cheeks onto the floor. The tears keep coming. Apollo grunts angrily, as he thrashes his right fist onto the refrigerator door. I don't think he's upset because Dad is yelling at him. I think Apollo Carlisle is finally realizing that he messed up. Dad's angry glares and tense expression subside. He instantly calms down and looks full of regret. Seeing your child cry or in distress will do that to any parent.

"I'm sorry for being such a screw up," is all Apollo musters to say with his back turned away from us.

Dad walks forward and reaches out to Apollo. "Come here, son." My eyes begin to water slightly and my mother's do too. I don't want Apollo to think he's a screw up; because he's not. I feel terrible at the mere thought of comparing him to Nate even crossed my mind. I should know Apollo better than that. He may be a girl crazy, party animal but he wouldn't take advantage of any girl. He has too big of heart to do something like that.

"I love you, son. I want you to know that. No matter what you do, your mother and I will always love you. That goes for all five of you," Dad consoles as he pats Apollo on his back. Dad slowly releases Apollo and they smile faintly at one another.

"But, Apollo, we also want you to know that what you did was wrong, and we hope it will make you decide on better decisions in the future," Mom adds. "After Melissa's pregnancy scare, we thought you'd be more safe and careful about things like this. This could've been a very dangerous situation."

Apollo wipes his eyes with a napkin. "Dangerous?" Dad places a hand on Apollo's left shoulder. Mom continues, "Yes, dangerous. Marley Aprilson wasn't your average girl. She-"

"She had a mental disorder," I interrupt. I knew Marley the best, so I feel it's my job to tell her story now. "Her alter ego, Jezebel, was emotionally unstable and had a distorted view of reality. It all started with some boy's stupid bet. Now look, two people I loved died because of it. Jezebel had no problem committing homicide to get her competition out of the way. What if she had decided to get me out of the way, too? What if she decided your old crush, Lydia, was competition that she also needed to get rid of?"

"You don't think she was THAT bad, do you, Minnie? I mean, killing her own sister? Marley adored Lydia," Apollo reasoned.

"Marley may have loved Lydia, but Jezebel didn't feel the same. You weren't dealing with a girl who was 100% in her right state of mind." It stung me a bit to even admit that about my friend, but I was coming to terms with the truth. I just feared that others might call her "crazy" or a "psychopath." Marley didn't need a straightjacket. She needed love, attention, and compassion from those around her; and she didn't receive enough of it. Honestly, I was thinking about how close our family could've been to starring in the next Angel City tragedy.

"Your sister's right. You were dealing with a girl who brought baby items for a child who didn't exist," Mom states.

"Baby items?" I repeated.

"In the grocery bags that were found all over the kitchen floor of the Aprilson home were different baby items. They found two infant outfits, one pink and one blue. They found a bottle, a pacifier, and a small, squeaky toy duck. This Jezebel that Minnie refers to was getting desperate and losing touch with the real world fast," Dad explains.

"Maybe the child did exist," I hinted, trying to defend Marley's sanity as best I could. "Maybe-"

Mom gently cups her hand in mine. "Minnie, an examiner confirmed it. Marley was menstruating at the time of her death. She wasn't pregnant, honey."

After a few seconds of silence, Apollo mumbles, "I'm sorry, Minnie." I shake my head. "She wasn't well. There's no way you could've known. None of us did."

Dad wraps his long arm around Apollo's shoulders. "We are going to get through like a family!" he exclaims. "We Carlisles always do."

"Yes, we do," Mom, Apollo, and I cheerfully agree at the same time.

"Minnie can heat up the leftovers, Diana. Apollo, why don't you pop in a good movie, and I'll find the drinks 'cause I damn sure need one," Dad jokes.

We all laugh as Mom goes to the backdoor to call the rest of my siblings in for dinner. As we're eating, I stop to slowly look around at my family coming together. Mom and Dad are holding hands as they enjoy their second glass of white wine. Apollo, who is beginning to cheer up, is discussing scenes from their favorite books with Athena. Apollo actually used to be quite the bookworm when we were younger, and Athena seemed to inherit that love of reading. Instead of being absorbed in her cellphone, Dite is doubled over with laughter as Ares and her enjoy the comedy movie and make little side jokes throughout the scenes. I'm enjoying every second of this. I love my family. I love their company and how we can always come together when we need each other most. My mind drifts off to another place for a moment. I start to wonder…maybe if Donald wouldn't have died, perhaps the Aprilsons would've been as close-knit as we are. I raise my cup gently and I make a silent toast in my head to Callista and Marley, then I take a sip of my tropical punch and continue basking in the happiness and warmth my family is providing for me.

CHAPTER THIRTY-NINE:
"No, this is an ending."

Marley's funeral was held five days later on a serene, cloudy Friday. Hmm, it looks like it may rain on Marley's funeral…how fitting. The day of Callista's funeral was bright and sunny. The sun shined as bright as Callista's luxurious, blonde hair. Most people would jump for joy and shout, "Thank God, it's Friday!" but I have absolutely nothing to be joyous or thankful for today. Before the funeral, everyone who would be attending gathered at the Aprilson household. I made sure my family was among the first few there. The last thing I needed was to walk in and have an audience staring at me, gossiping about me, and smothering me with sympathy stares. Keegan, the Giovannis, and all of Marley's family were also in attendance. Lydia, of course, was avoiding me at all costs. If I took a single step in her direction, she'd grimace, and take five away me. I decided to sneak away from the sadness that surrounded me in the living room and go upstairs to Marley's room. I couldn't take anymore pats on the back or unwanted hugs All the signs were there and the warning was clear yet I ignored them. Hanging above Marley's large, brown dresser was an "F" chain, just like the one Callista had hanging above her's. Below that, there was a photo of Marley and Lauralee after Prom. She looked so cheerful and happy. Why couldn't she stay that way forever? Maybe I just didn't notice how much in pain she was.

"Marley suure looked awfully pretty that night," A voice softly spoke.

I turned around to see Lauralee leaning in the doorway. She had a somber expression upon her face; a sharp contrast to the happy-go-lucky personality she normally displayed. Lauralee's company still made me feel tense, awkward, and angry. I…I just feel like if she had told me about being sexually involved with Marley immediately instead of trying to be all secretive and mysterious, maybe we would've caught onto Jezebel before anyone had to die. At that moment, I didn't know if she was truly there to console me. Or, just trying to kiss me where the sun don't shine, after the secret she kept from me. Today, I don't have the patience to find out.

"Lauralee…I kinda just wanna be alone."

She stopped leaning on the doorway and took a step towards me.

"I'm not here to argue," She calmly stated. "I'm sorry for keeping me and Marley's fling a secret. I just didn't know how to tell you. I didn't know how to deal with all these new feelings that came with it. I was sooo confused, Minnie, and I just didn't know how to tell anyone that I was falling for another girl."

I abruptly raised my left hand towards her and shook my head back and forth. I was completely uninterested in hearing about Lauralee's first girl-crush at a time like this. With all the stuff that Jezebel has done, I just don't understand how anyone can be dumb enough to develop feelings for someone like that. I know, I know. Lauralee didn't know about Marley's disorder, but somewhere in me, I was still feeling sour about the whole thing. "I don't eeeeven wanna hear it."

"Artemis Wilhelmina Carlisle, for once, will you PLEASE just listen to me?" She pleaded. She had an annoying habit of calling people by their full names as if she were an angry mother, something Marley didn't like.

"Lauralee Marie Giovanni, for once, will you PLEASE just take a damn hint!?" I hissed, mocking her.

I expected this to turn into a heated, emotional argument. I expected us to be throwing each other all around that room until a crowd of people rushed upstairs to break it up. I expected something I could use to release a few of the emotional demons that were pent up inside me, even if it was at someone else's expense. Shockingly, all she did was silently stare at me with her mouth slightly open. I don't think she even blinked for a few seconds. I thought she'd have a little more to say. Lauralee's always been opinionated, but she's also always been a pushover. Almost out of nowhere, Keegan popped his head into the room.

"Heeeey, you two," He greets. "What's going on in here, a meeting?"

"No," Lauralee apathetically responds. Her fists are clenched as if she's angry, but her eyes tear up as if she's going to cry. "This is an ending." She takes one last, half-teary glare at me before shoving Keegan out of the way and storming out of the room. Keegan then turns to me.

"Drama, much?"

I roll my eyes. "You knoooow how Lauralee can be."

"No," Keegan mumbles with his head facing away from me, "but I know how YOU can be."

"Whatever," I reply, brushing off his snide remark.

Neither of us speak, nor make eye contact for a few, brief moments.

The only sound that fills the room is the chatter from the guests downstairs. Keegan places his hands in his pockets before he casually glances over to the photo of Marley and Lauralee.

"God, Marley was beautiful," He comments.

I smile faintly. "Yeah, she was. She was a lot of things."

"Beautiful, classy, intelligent, humble…perfect." He adds, now smiling admiringly at the photo.

"Hmm." I say, now going suspicious. "Sounds like you thought very highly of my best friend."

"Well, yeah," He responds as he places the picture back on the dresser. "Who wouldn't? I liked that she was different from other girls. I…I would've loved the chance to, you know, get to know her better."

As nosey as I am, I never once picked up to the fact that Keegan had such a big crush on Marley. She didn't think much of herself, but here, she has this great guy who thought the world of her. It's a shame she'll never get a chance to know him. I know Keegan would've treated her well. She was truly loved, and she will truly be missed. Suddenly, Steph walks in and somberly informs us that it's time to proceed with the funeral services.

For a second, I refuse to move. Marley's death just hasn't seemed real until now. Attending her funeral just makes it so official. I remain seated on the edge of Marley's bed, with my arms crossed as I stare aimlessly of out the window. A bluebird stares back at me from the tree it's perched on outside, briefly before it carries on with its business.

"Come on, Minnie. You've got to get through this," Keegan gently says as he extends his left hand to me. I pretend I don't see it. I continue to stare out of the window.

"Miiinnie," Keegan firmly calls. "Let's not play this game. Not today."

I roll my eyes and stubbornly take his hand, and then we slowly make our way downstairs. With the exception of a few sniffles, it's mostly silent as the funeral directors inform us on how the funeral would proceed. Our names were called in groups to let us know which limousine we would be riding in. I was chosen to be in the third limo, along with my family. Daddy wrapped his arm around my shoulder, as I closed my eyes and leaned on his chest. I wish I could've just fallen asleep right then and there. I wish I could doze off and sleep through this day and wake up yesteryear and prevent all of this; but life will not grant every wish you make. The ride to St. James Baptist Church was by far the longest and most uncomfortable ride I have ever had in my life. Pedestrians stopped and stared at the long, black limos as they rode through the city. The sound of the police siren blared so much as it escorted us, that it began to echo in my head. The city seemed to sit still; the most still I'd ever seen Angel City in a while. Part of me hoped we'd never arrive at the church and that we'd just ride silently all day long. Long car rides always made me fall asleep as a child, but I don't think it would have the same effect today. We slowly pull up in the church and each limo stops one after another in front of the entrance. Church attendants are there to greet us at the door and some of them open the door to the limos for us. An uncomfortable, uneasy feeling enters the core of my body. Apollo takes my hand as he helps me out of the limousine. I lean on his shoulder as we proceed towards the entrance. I see him glancing down at me out of my peripheral vison every few seconds. I guess that's his way of checking on me. I know he dares not to ask me if I'm okay. No one speaks as they enter the church. The only sound we hear is the soft, instrumental music playing as we are walking towards the seats. Marley's casket sits directly in the center with a few lights shining above it. It's shiny and grey with gold locks. There are radiant, colorful flowers and pictures of Marley surrounding the casket. I can't take my eyes off of it. All I keep thinking is, "my best friend is lying in there." It's such a surreal feeling. Like, is this really happening? Is this just a horrible dream? I just want to believe none of this is reality and that I can snap out of this and have both of my best friends alive and well again. I hear the sound of someone breaking down and crying behind me. I must try to be strong. Ophelia, Lydia, and the rest of Marley's family are seated in the first few rows. There was nothing but silence as people continue to take their seats. The seats are hard and somewhat cold which does nothing but add to the discomfort I'm already experiencing by being here. Shortly after everyone is seated, a minister walks up to the podium and greets everyone. His voice somewhat echoes throughout the large room as he speaks into the microphone.

"We are gathered here today to show our love for dear Katherine here, whose life was cut far too short. A gentle soul was taken from this Earth. We must remember that we are here to honor the life of Katherine and not mourn over her death," He states.

That's easy for him to say. He didn't know her like we did. He didn't love her like we did. How can I NOT mourn the fact that I won't ever get to speak to her again? How can I NOT mourn the fact that her presence will be eternally absent from mines now? Hell, if he knew her at all, he'd know she didn't really like to be called anything but Marley...not Katherine, Kate, or even Katie. The minister continues speaking. He talks about Marley's life. He references scriptures and quotes from the Bible. However, I am in a different world. I zone in and out as the minister speaks. I just can't stop looking at Marley's coffin and imagining how things should be different. Beating myself up over the fact that my best friend shouldn't be lying in that casket. Everything about this day is depressing. It's a sorrow I just couldn't seem to escape. Even the birds didn't tweet their tranquil tune this morning. Maybe they feel what I feel. No song is worth singing today. Marley's aunt, Daphne, gets up to sing a song in honor of Marley. Her eyes are closed as she sings; I guess she can't bear to look at all of us. There are already tears in her eyes and you can tell she's putting every ounce of love she had for her niece into every note that she carries. Some people break into a fit of tears as the minister continues to speak. The people who truly broke my heart were my siblings. The way Ares sobbed and leaned on our mother for comfort; the way Apollo's tears cascaded down his cheeks even though he was obviously trying to be strong for me; and the way Dite cuddled Athena as she grieved just tore my heart apart. I couldn't help but to breakdown, as well. Death never really affected me as much as it's affecting me at this very moment. This day would torment me forever and play over and over in my head like a broken record. When the minister asks if anyone has any final words to say about the departed, I gather up the courage to raise my hand. Daddy walks me up to the podium and stands beside me, rubbing my shoulder in comfort. I decide to read the poem Callista wrote for Marley. With her words, Marley's casket and I, it would almost be like the three of us were back together again. Almost, but not quite.

"I wrote a short poem for Marley. It's entitled, "Katherine." I figured there would be no greater time to read it than now." I know it's bad to lie in church, but I didn't want any criticism from people. "How dare you read a poem written by someone that was killed by the person you're reading it for! And at their funeral!" I could imagine people saying that already. Angeleans never mind their own business.

"I know a girl named Katherine,
Smartest girl I ever knew.

Not only does she have class,
She has a heart of gold to top it off, too.
I sometimes teased her for being different
And her love of learning.
When I remember doing these things,
I can feel my anger burning.
I always envied Marley for her potential.
I wish I had the heart to say it face to face.
But somehow, I just never found the time
Nor the proper place.
Just remember this, Marley Aprilson, I love you
And I apologize to you, too."

I began to cry immediately after reading that last line. My Daddy embraced me and together, we walked back to my seat. Despite what we went through as friends, we never ever stopped loving each other. That is what friendship is all about.

"I love you. I love the both of you. Never ever forget that." Marley's final words entered my mind. They somewhat comforted me and helped me to calm down. Next, it was time for all of us to view the deceased one last time before we took her to the burial site. We all lined up, one behind the other. Once Ophelia and Lydia reached the opened casket, they could hardly walk straight because they were so hysterical. Church attendants rushed to alleviate the situation by attempting to get them away from the casket, but all they did was make it worse.

"MAAARLEY! My baby! NOOOO!" Ophelia shrieked, hugging herself as she fell to the ground crying. "Why is this happening to me again!?" She reminded me of when Stella Arden broke down in the middle of the hospital floor once Callista had passed. Honestly, it's the most concern I had seen Ophelia about Marley in a long time. It's too late to be her mother now. You had eighteen years to be a good mother to her, Ophelia.

"GET OFF ME! Get the hell off me! That's my sister! I want to hug my sister!" Lydia angrily screamed as the church attendants restrained her. If some of Lydia's uncles hadn't come to release Lydia from their grip, I have a feeling she would've started throwing fists instead of throwing a fit. Hugging Marley's body seemed to finally calm her down. Lydia rested her head on her chest and just laid there motionless for a few moments. She took a deep breath; then willingly walked away with Ophelia outside. She stared at Marley until she was out of sight. The way Lydia was staring at her you could tell that she would've given absolutely anything for her sister to reawaken and hug her back one last time. Like I said before, life will not grant every wish you make. Marley looked serene and so at peace once I arrived at the casket. I could've sworn she was smiling. I reached to hold one of her hands. They were so dry and cold…so lifeless. I didn't want to ever stop holding her hand. I never wanted to let go. I didn't even want to take my eyes off her. I'd never get the chance to see those lovely, green eyes looking back at mine. I began to tear up again. My life wouldn't be the same without her in it. The three of us were supposed to be "B-F-F's". That's why we brought those chains. They were a tribute to our friendship.

"Y-You and Calli take good care of each other, ok? I love you, Marley. I always will." I whispered before I gathered the strength to finally walk off.

The ride to Resting Angels cemetery was just as silent as the ride to St. James Baptist Church. The limos drove painfully slow through the cemetery. Part of me just wanted to get this terrible day over with. I had seen enough articles of black clothing and teary eyes to last a lifetime. Once again, we all slowly exited the limos. While walking towards Marley's future grave, I noticed her father's tombstone.

"Donald Lyndon Marlow Aprilson: October 9, 1971 - August 23, 2004," the epitaph read.

"My Dad died on my first day of second grade." Marley's solemn and somber testimony entered my head upon reading his date of death. He died barely 2 months before his 34th birthday. Death is sad period, but when the life of someone relatively young is taken, it just makes it sadder. Marley once said, "Everyone always said that Daddy had such a big, loving heart. It's a shame having a big heart is what killed him." I also remembered how honored Marley was to have her and Lydia named after the man they admired most. Her eyes gleamed with pride every time she told the story.

"You see, my parents were never good with names. So, they named my sister Lydia to match with my Dad's middle name, Lyndon. Mom got the idea to use his other middle name, Marlow, and the name of my grandmother, Rose, to create my middle name, Rosemarley. It's kind of sweet, don't you think?" I smiled just thinking about how proud she was to carry on his name. Lydia and her were the true definitions of "Daddy's Girls."

The minister continued to talk and pray. I'm sure whatever he said was beautiful and inspiring, but I just zoned him out again and focused on Marley's casket. Upon finishing his speech, he released four, beautiful white doves into the sky. They were meant to represent the journey Marley's soul would take on the way to Heaven. A few tears fell from my eyes. Those doves were free to fly...and now, so was Marley. You fly on, Marley. You spread those wings and soar hand in hand with Callista and your father without a care in the world. Let your hair wisp in the wind as you zip in and out of those soft, white clouds. My friends are in paradise now, free from all the pain and stress they felt on this earth. My friends are reciting poetry and serenading the angels in Heaven. I will never be alone now. They will always be here with me in my heart and in my memories. I hope they are happier as angels than they ever were as my friends. You're free, you're finally free. Isobel Callista Arden and Katherine Rosemarley Aprilson …you rest in peace, my loves.

CHAPTER FORTY:

"I wish that I could live in this moment, eternally."

Graduation day was held about two weeks after Marley's funeral. Although I was still emotionally reeling from the events that transpired in TresAngeles Field, my mood for today was ecstatic. I've waited and daydreamed about this day for so long. Since being framed for Callista's death, I was practically bouncing off the walls at the realization that I was finally getting myself rid of this intolerable place. Due to my hyper bliss, Apollo had to practically shake me by my shoulders to calm me down enough so I could eat breakfast.

"Minnie!" Apollo laughed, "I swear on all that is holy, if you don't sit down, I'm gonna force-feed these eggs to you with my bare hands!"

I settle down into my skin again and smile gleefully at him. "Okay, Apollo. I will." I took a seat in front of my untouched plate and Apollo finished fixing his food and took his seat directly to the left of me. Daddy kissed me on the top of my head as he passed by.

"You're a real jitterbug today, honey," He teasingly comments.

As jittery as a crack addict badly needing a fix, Dad strolls on towards the full length mirror in the foyer to continue to struggle with his tie and hair. Mom was dealing with the fight of curling Athena's blonde hair in the bathroom; and Ares, being the first one dressed, was happily sitting on the couch watching Teenage Ninja Mutant Turtles and snacking on a granola bar and cereal. Dite, the diva, still hadn't emerged from her bedroom since taking her shower. She was busy making the ever so importance of deciding what she should wear. As I began to chow down on the bacon and eggs Daddy made for breakfast, I glanced over and noticed Apollo was flipping his pancakes aimlessly with his fork instead of eating them like he threatened me to do a few moments ago. A big hypocrite, he is.

"You're supposed to eat them, y'know," I sarcastically retorted.

He snapped out of his daze and directed his attention to me. There was so much emotion going on in those grey eyes. "Oh y-yeah, I am. I'm gonna eat it." He then continued to shove his eggs to the edge of his plate and continued into his daze. I placed my fork gently down on my plate and reached over to grab his hand.

"Are you really that nervous, Apollo?"

He glanced over at me and gave a half-hearted, anxious smile. "What gave it away?" Before I had the chance to talk him out of his worry, Mom yelled from the bathroom, "Minnie! Can you PLEASE go help Dite with her outfit! We'll be ready to go soon." By her tone, her agitation with her diva daughter's indecisiveness was increasing. I got up from the table to throw the remains of my breakfast in the trash, and as I was passing Apollo, I hugged him tightly, his red stands of hair tickling my nose gently.

"It'll be okay. You'll see."

I strolled past Athena angrily pouting as Mom continued to deal with her thick, blonde hair. I entered Dite's room uninvited and found her hovering over her bed, hand on her chin, hip sticking out, and staring at two dresses she had laid out across her bed.

"Dite, what the hell?" I hissed as I closed the door. "Why are you still not dressed!?"

Completely ignoring my question, she replied, "Should I wear my olive dress and my brown wedges or my peach dress and my gold heels? The olive makes me look uber sophisticated but the peach...ahh, the peach goes so well with my skin complexion and hair. It's hard being so fabulous, I tell ya."

I rolled my eyes. Apollo and I were the ones graduating and we were dressed before her. Dite makes me want chug down a few bottles of Smirnoff, I swear. I rush over to her bed, shove her out of the way by her right shoulder, and hover of the dresses and point my index finger at them.

"Eeny, meeny, miny, moe. Catch a tiger by the toe. If he hollers, let him go. Eeny...meeny…miny…moe!"

Peach for Aphrodite it is. I crumple up her olive dress and hurl it back in her closet as if it were a football. "Heeeey!" Dite protests from behind me, not approving of my genius decision-making skills.

I walk back over to her bedroom door and open it. I turn and look back at her. She's glaring Hell's wrath into me. I know that one thing Dite doesn't play about is someone messing with her clothes. Oh, well. She'll get over it by the time we go meet Cassidy, his dad, my grandparents, and the rest of the family for dinner after the ceremony. I stick my tongue out at her before abruptly slamming her door. Meanwhile, in the living room, everyone has just about finished getting dressed. Athena's wildness has been successfully straightened and for once, she isn't wearing her glasses. I can tell she feels super beautiful with her hair done and all. She looks so radiant and cheerful. Mom, who is looking stunning in her red dress and matching lipstick, is assisting Dad with his tie, and Apollo and Ares are settled on the couch watching TV.

"Aphrodite Nicole Carlisle, I will not wait all day for you, do you hear me!? Mom loudly warns. It's never a good sign when your mother calls you by your full name.

Dite hustles quickly out of her room, wearing her peach dress and brown wedges, holding various brown and peach accessories in her hands. "Okay! I'm ready now!"

"Your hair's not even done. It's all over the place." Athena truthfully points out. She had taken so much time to decide on her outfit, she left no time to do her hair.

Dite glares at Athena. "Why are you wearing that tacky orange and purple dress? We're not going to a Clemson football game. You're going to make us the laughing stock of the whole city," Dite grins evilly but Athena's smile quickly vanishes. After Marley's suicide, I wouldn't stand for anyone making anyone else feel lesser than what they are. I won't let my sister's relationship follow down the same path as my friendships.

"Don't be so rude to Athena," I defended. Athena's face shows a faint smile and her big, blue eyes showed a small glimmer of hope, as if she's happy someone is finally sticking up for her. Dite looks me up and down, as if to say, "Who do you think you're talking to?"

"Rude? I was being truthful. That dress is hideous and she needs to change. There's no such thing as an ugly Carlisle, you know," She retorts, not even slightly recanting her mean statement to her own sister. I never realized how much Dite and I acted alike until just now, so mean and so uncaring about it.

Before I have the opportunity to continue this argument, we hear "Okay, Carlisle's! Let's go, let's go!" Dad shouts as he rushes and checks his watch. In a mass chaos, everyone scrambles their things and hurries out of the front door. Dite grabs her purse, Athena picks up her favorite necklace from off of the living room table, Ares gets his favorite video game, Dad grabs the car keys, and Mom slams the door shut behind all of us. The ride to Angel City Colonial Arena, the location of the ceremony, was riddled with traffic and silence. Loaded silence, like when you know everyone around you has something on their mind but they remain quiet. I fiddle with my carefully curled hair as I stare out of the passenger window.

Thinking about how, in just a few hours' time, my life would begin anew. I was eager and excited to finally have the opportunity to leave my past behind, but I was also worried. Was I ready for college and entering the real world as an adult? What if I mess my new life up just like I messed up this one? To distract myself from these stress-inducing thoughts, I peek around to see what my family is doing. My Dad is growling under his breath at the traffic. I can tell he desperately wants to blare the car horn and curse a few other drivers out, but refrains from doing so in front of us. Mom is chatting with Grandma on her cellphone and toying with her new video camera. Since we didn't have time for pictures at the house, I'm sure we'll have an exhausting photo shoot after the ceremony and at the celebratory dinner. Athena just finished helping Dite style her hair into a ponytail and in return, Dite adorned Athena with her favorite necklace Grandpop got her for Christmas when she was 9. Ares is lost inside his video game and Apollo is gazing outside of his window without a word. I wonder if he's thinking about the future the same way I am. I wonder if he's afraid of graduation or if he's afraid of what it means.

"Okay, heeeere we are. We'll see you two inside," Dad announces as he pulls the car up in front of the entrance. We all say our goodbyes as Apollo and I scoot out of the car. I watch the silver, Chevy Traverse drive off towards the parking lot. It gleamed beautifully under the May sunlight.

"Come on, kid. Let's go in," Apollo suggests as he leads me towards the door by my shoulder. The security guards scan us for weapons before we are officially allowed to go inside. To be honest, I really wouldn't be surprised if one of Angel City's graduating class decided to pull one last prank. Inside, a mixture a students and staff were socializing and getting everything prepared for the upcoming ceremony. Apollo glances down at his Rolex.

"I-It's 11:45. One hour until show time," He informs. I think the shakiness in his voice is returning which means that he's starting to worry again.

"We should go ahead and get in our places," I suggest. I had no friends to converse with so there was really no point in wandering around the building. Besides, I was in high heels and I don't think the balls of my feet could tolerate any more walking than they had to do today. Glances and whispers emerge from the socializing crowd. I'm met with an onslaught of two different types of stares on this day. One was the "I want to apologize but I'm too proud/don't know what to say" lingering glance and the "I'm surprised she even showed up" stare. Out of curiosity, I stare around at my classmates to see what they're doing. Sophia Carlos is making some weird faces as she applies some last minute mascara in a miniature mirror she must've stashed in her bra. Carmella Carson actually looks like a respectable woman today, but that's probably because she has to wear our long, royal blue graduating gown and matching cap. Judging by her super high, glitter white pumps, I'm willing to bet she has on something stripper-ish under that gown. That's just like Carmella to want the spotlight one last time.

"Stop being so judgmental, Minnie," I scold myself in my head. Hey, Rome wasn't built in a day.

I saw Sybil and Bryce Oliver keeping each other company in a cozy corner of the building, as Sybil slightly struggled to place her gold watch back onto her wrist. Bryce was looking great with his hair cut and slicked back and all dressed up. He looked like a big, handsome teddy bear. Sybil's medium brown hair fell into perfect twirls down slightly past her collar bone. Sybil and I made eye contact for a brief second. Disgusted by our exchange of eye contact, she grimaced then turned her back and finally let Bryce place her watch onto her wrist. Lauralee...well, Lauralee looked absolutely stunning. Her hair had been nestled into an up-do with bangs on each side of her face and the turquoise eye shadow and nude lipstick went perfectly with her flawless skin tone. She was laughing and happily conversing with Rayanne Greyman by the vending machine. I wanted to run up to her and hug her and squeal happily about how beautiful she looked, but after her episode at Marley's funeral, I don't think she wanted to be bothered with me. Damian, Rebbie, and Jess are sitting on some nearby chairs most likely looking at something hilarious on Jess's phone by the way Rebbie is dying of laughter and Keegan is talking with some football buddies to the right of me. How many of these "familiar faces" will turn into strangers after today? Marley and Callista should be here. They should be right by my side, basking in this moment like I am.

Apollo and I stand and talk to each other for what seems like forever. I've gone to the water fountain at least a dozen times and Apollo has straightened his tie and shoelaces for the 19th time. I was bored enough to count. I even started count the black tiles amongst the white ones. However, I got bored and lost count around the 23rd one. This is by far the longest sixty minutes of my life. This is the epitome of unbearable torment.

"Minnie?" A voice from behind Apollo and me gently calls.

We turn to see that the suave voice belongs to Nate. He's standing there with his hands in his pockets looking ever so handsome in his black and red suit and his hair slicked back. I'm curious to know what he has to say to me now, but Apollo doesn't look too thrilled with his presence.

"Yes, Nate?" I respond. He glances quickly at Apollo then back to me. He looks a little bit worried. He probably thinks Apollo's gonna jump on him right here and now; probably choke him with the tassel on his cap. I can't blame him. Apollo instilled a lot of respect/fear into some of the guys after his fight with Damian that night. His "bad boy" ego is back now and every time it gets too high, I'll remind him of the fight he lost to Uriel Arden. A little cruel, but somebody's got to keep this boy in check. That "bad boy" reputation of his won't get him anywhere after graduation.

"Can I talk to you alone for a second?"

Apollo steps forward and points his finger down at Nate. "I don't think so. Why don't you just leave my sister alone? Haven't you screwed up enough?"

Nate had no usual sarcastic comeback for Apollo's remark. He appeared to be disappointed. He looked like a child whose Mommy was too busy to play with him. Call me crazy, but I felt sorry for him. He just looked so pitiful. He began to turn away with his tail tucked between his legs, but I stopped him. I don't know what made me stop him more, sympathy or curiosity.

"Nate, you don't have to leave," I called.

Nate stopped and turned around. He looked hopeful at the prospect of talking with me without my brother trying to kill him.

"What!?" Apollo hissed. He was beginning to go enter big brother mode, which could prove very annoying sometimes. "Minnie, you can't-"

"I can and I want to," I interrupted. I love Apollo dearly, but it's time for him to realize his little sister isn't so little anymore. "Apollo, please. Just let us talk for a minute."

Apollo exhaled angrily and growled, "I'm gonna go talk to Jonas. I'll be right THERE if you need me, okay?"

I nodded my head up and down and he glared into Nate's eyes as he stormed past him. I directed my attention back to Nate. Seeing Nate still makes part of my blood boil. He was beginning to ruin my good mood and chill vibes. Maybe requesting to speak with him was a mistake.

"I truly don't know what to call you. Should I call you Nathaniel Evan, like it says on your birth certificate? Should I call you a borderline rapist for taking advantage of a shy girl with a mental disorder? How about a cheater and an ultimate opportunist? A complete idiot, perhaps? You can have many names."

He shifted his weight from one side to the other then stared deep into my eyes. "I deserve the cheater and the idiot, but I'm not a rapist. You know my grandfather's history, so please don't call me that," he politely ordered in an emotionless tone.

I forgot all about the Jacobs's dark past. My guard lowered upon remembering it. "Sorry, I went a little too far," I apologized as I stared shamefully at my toes.

"I didn't come here to have a name-calling contest or to point fingers, Minnie. I came to say…I'm sorry."

I jerked my head up in slight shock. "E-excuse me? Since when do you apologize?"

He grinned radiantly and shrugged his shoulders with his hands up. "Since I became a papa, I guess. I'm sorry for going through with that stupid bet and lying to you and disrespecting you. You're a good woman and you didn't deserve that but I'm not going to apologize for getting involved with Callista. She gave me Violet and that girl is the light of my life, Minnie. I would've loved the opportunity to raise Vi with her mother, but I know that won't be possible. I will regret for the rest of my life going through with that bet. I was just a dumb, teenage boy who wanted to win some brownie points with his friends and wanted to get back at his girlfriend who pissed him off…and I'm sorry. Callista was one of a kind, though. Just know, her death was a great loss to not only you and the Ardens, but to me and Vi, as well. She'll be missed…truly. I lo-"

Was Nathaniel Evan Jacobs beginning to choke up a little? He didn't have to finish his sentence. I already knew what he was going to say. I knew it by the way he flirted with her. I knew it by his highly emotional reaction when we were at the police station. I knew it by the way he talked about her and stared at her as if she was the brightest star his eyes had ever spotted in the sky. I think I always knew, I just wasn't ready to admit it at the time.

"You were in love with her…weren't you, Nate?" I whispered to him.

He shifted his weight again before simply responding, "Yes." To most females, their boyfriend cheating on them with their best friend and impregnating her is a nightmare. I say that it makes for one hell of a love story. I'm not angry or envious at all; I'm happy and I'm sad. I'm happy Nate and Callista found each other, but it's unfortunate that he can't be with the woman he loves because she's lying prematurely in a coffin. I will never wrap my head around why he decided to get into the bed of the best friend of the woman he loved. But, he's apologized sincerely and accepted responsibility for it; so there's no reason for me to hold a grudge. However, I'm sure a certain angel will have a lot of questions and maybe a few profanities for him when the time comes. With a smile and a watery eye, I reply, "I accept your apology, Nate."

He wipes his half-teary eyes with his sleeve before saying, "You mean it, Minnie? I felt guilty for the longest time but now, maybe we can-"

"Move on?" I finish his sentence in my head as he steps towards me and we reach out to embrace one another in a tight hug. All is forgiven. The bad is forgotten. There's no sense in holding onto a past you can't change. I can't be mad at Nate forever. I have no right to judge Nate and Callista for their indiscretions, when I have parts of my past that I'm not exactly proud of either. Those who live in glass houses can't afford to throw stones.

Teachers and staff are now rushing students into our places as it is time for the ceremony to finally begin. Nate kisses me softly on the apple of my right cheek. He welcomes me with a charming and gleeful grin as he whispers, "You look gorgeous as always, by the way." I grin happily at him before he rushes back to where he belongs.

"This is it," Apollo says to me. "You ready?" I take a deep breath before I respond, "More than I'll ever be."

Following behind each other in a single-file line, we gracefully walk down the hall through a walkway and enter the main room. We are greeted with loud, ceremonial music and the applause of our loved ones. I hear cameras shudder as we all begin to take our seats. The atmosphere is so calm, yet anxious. I want to relax but I can't. I just can't! Butterflies in my tummy erupt as my hyper bliss and anxiety return. We go through the usual expected blah-blah: some random stranger making an epically lengthy speech about his life, our lives, and life in general. I swear, he must've brought up his dog's life at a moment. Our spotlight loving Salutatorian, Carmella eagerly gives her speech next. She's obviously been awaiting this moment all year. At least she doesn't get as long winded or boring as the speaker before her. We stand for the Pledge of Allegiance, bow our heads for a prayer, and then Principal Walker speaks. I'm zoned out for the most part, but my attention was immediately captured as soon as my ears caught wind of him saying, "…We lost two great students this year."

No longer zoning out, I jerk my head up and direct my attention fully at the stage.

"Angel City High School suffered two devastating blows this year after the loss of seniors, Isobel C. Arden and our Valedictorian, Katherine R. Aprilson. By God's will, these bright, young women were taken from us sadly not too long before their high school graduation and the beginning of a new life. I'll remember Marley as a shy, intelligent woman who had all the potential in the world to become whatever she set her mind to; and I'll remember Callista as the rebel whose smart mouth couldn't keep her out of trouble if you paid her. Here to accept their diplomas today are their mothers, Mrs. Stella Arden and Ms. Ophelia Aprilson. I ask that all of you remember them as we proceed with our ceremony."

Slight laughter slipped out of the crowd at Principal Walker's small joke. A memory crept slowly into my head. I could recall it so clearly now…all of us were at Wilmington Beach…there was a souvenir store…the day we brought those BFF necklaces…

"Heyyy! You ruined my sandcastle, Marley!" Callista whines as she crosses her arms in a childish rage.

Marley turns around, the wind carefully teasing the big, brown bun of her hair. "It looked like poo anyways." A chubby Callista then chases a giggly Marley into the water in her yellow, polka dotted bathing suit. I quit searching for beautiful seashells and starfish along the shore and rush into the sea to join them. We're splashing and squealing without a care in the world. The sun is shining intensely above us and the sand tickles as it graces in-between my tiny toes under the cool, ocean water.

"Be careful, girls!" Ophelia shouts from the shore. Then she, my very pregnant mother and Mrs. Arden continue chatting. Our fathers, Lydia, Mike, and Rafe are busy playing a competitive game of beach volleyball. One and a half year old Dite is snuggled up cozily against my mother's chest. Apollo, Gabe, and Uriel are pretending to be "Sand Warriors," as they play fight with one another near some rocks with branches they were using as swords. If I remember correctly, Cassidy fell off those rocks trying to climb to the top and be "Lord Of The Sand Warriors;" and Benjamin spent 15 minutes getting him to calm down. He was such a crybaby as a child.

Marley ceases her splash attack and blurts out, "These necklaces are the best, Minnie."

Callista stops as well and glances down at hers. "Yeah! They rock. I'll keep mine until I'm old like your mom." I kick water playfully at her before I say, "We should wear them forever. You guys are my best friends."

I release a gap-toothed smile at the both of them and they both return the favor.

"Best friends?" Marley reiterates as she reaches out for my left hand.

"The bestest!" Callista loudly shouts as she takes her right hand and grabs Marley's hand, as well.

A powerful wave sneaks up on us and hand in hand, we all fall over into the seawater and sand. We laugh and Marley laughs so hard, she snorts. Her unexpected snort causes us to laugh so hard, we are unable to get to our feet again. So there we are, a gap- toothed red head, a loud, chubby blonde and a soaked, giggling brunette rolling over in the sea and sand, squealing with delight.

A single tear falls forth from each of my eyes and rolls off the apples of my cheeks. I can't explain to you how much that memory just means to me. I swear that I can feel my heart smiling. That memory reminded me that we were best friends and we did love each other; no matter how hard our friendship was tested. Once upon a time, things were good. Once upon a time, before puberty, before the boys, before Donald's death, life was easy and good for all 3 of us. I wipe away the tears. Today is a day for pride and joy, not crying. They wouldn't want me to cry. From now on, I'll welcome their memories with smiles and not sadness. The applause for Callista's name was three times as big as it was for Marley's, but I expected that. Of course everybody claps for the victim but nobody wants to applaud the one who did it. Before I knew it, it's time for our row to stand and walk towards the stage. This is our big moment. Apollo's name is next and before the announcer calls his name, he glances back at me with a smug grin. I can't help but to smile back at him. He eases some of my nervousness.

"Apollo Montgomery Carlisle!" the announcer shouts.

You wouldn't have even known Apollo was nervous to the point that his voice was shaking and he couldn't speak, by how casually and smoothly he strutted across that stage. I hear my family yell proudly for him somewhere within the crowd. He shakes hands with Principal Walker, takes his diploma cover, and finishes his show, as he walks down the other set of stairs on the opposite end of the stage. Upon officially realizing that I'm next, I think my heart fluttered over a few beats. What if I get booed? What if no one claps? What if-

"Artemis Wilhelmina Carlisle!"

There's no time for worry and what-if's now. I exhale and begin my walk across the stage. Thankfully, there is applause, but I still refuse to look at the crowd. I stare directly in front of me until I get to Principal Walker. As I'm shaking his hand, Ophelia and Stella get on the mic and turn towards me.

"Minnie, we've known you since you were in kindergarten. You and Callista were my daughter's very best friends. I'm sure she thought of the two of you as sisters. You three always seemed to be there for one another," Ophelia states.

"It takes a strong woman to overcome what you went through. I know you loved my daughter dearly," Stella adds. "Can we give Minnie another round of applause, please? Lord knows this city didn't take it easy on her. We weren't the only ones who suffered from the loss of Calli and Marley." The applause starts off slow but gradually increases until it's almost thundering within the auditorium. I stare at the crowd in shock. My classmates, teachers, staff, Ophelia, Stella, and people within the crowd all stand as they continue their applause. I look over at Apollo, whistling and cheering proudly over by the stairs. I truly don't know how to take all of this in.

"Don't just stand there like a bump on log, Artemis. Show them your appreciation," Principal Walker teasingly whispers to me. I snap out of my in-awe daze, take my diploma cover in both hands, and with a smile stretched from ear to ear, I raise it high above my head. The applause reaches a new pinnacle of volume. It's practically echoing off every wall of the room. This overwhelming pride, relief, and joy I feel at this moment is almost indescribable. You'll be lucky if you feel this much love and positivity flowing simultaneously even once in your lifetime. I'll be rewinding this moment in my head for many years to come. I'll surely tell my children about this someday. This is for you, my friends. I wish that I could live in this moment, eternally.

CHAPTER FORTY-ONE

"Once again, the biggest idiot in the conversation always has the most to say!"

Before I went off to college that August, I wanted to make everything right in my life. Marley's and Callista's deaths taught me that I should not take life for granted and that I should take action while I have a breath in my body to do so. That day, I visited Marley's and Callista's graves and as I laid a bouquet of white roses from TresAngeles Field and blue Forget-me-nots at each of their tombstones, I made a promise to them that I'd go back and apologize for the damage I had caused any of my peers and/or friends over the years. I don't want a medal. I don't want a reward. I don't want praise. I just want forgiveness.

Sybil Mallory Florentine:

I slowly drive to Sybil's house, ready to swallow my pride, and apologize. I never thought I'd be so nervous to do something like this. Butterflies are fluttering in my stomach and my heart begins to beat slightly faster. Why couldn't I have just been a good person from the get go? An apology is by far the hardest thing to give someone. I take a small breath of relief when Mrs. Florentine informs me that Sybil took her brother and sister to the local pool, probably to cool off from the summer heat. That means I get to go at least a little longer before I have to face her. I smell something sweet baking from within the house and I see bright colored balloons of various colors on the floor. I can't help but to wonder what they're celebrating today. Park Street Recreation Center luckily isn't too far from their house so I drive there. Inside, I find Bryce, Sybil, and her younger siblings, Hector and Chelsea, having a blast swimming and splashing around in the pool. They looked so happy. I almost don't want to disturb them, but I have to get this off my chest.

"Sybil!" I bellow out.

Sybil stops splashing water on a giggling Chelsea and turns in my direction. Her smile quickly vanishes. The pure sight of me makes her happiness disappear. She tells Hector and Chelsea to wait in the pool, as she steps out and begins to walk towards me.

"What do you want?" Sybil hisses, violently tossing her hair out of her face.

Man, I must've been more evil than I thought. Sybil's already pissed off at me and I haven't even started talking to her yet. I bring my fist to my mouth and clear my throat.

"I just wanted to apologize to you." She tilts her head slightly before she responds, "Excuse me?"

"I'm sorry for calling you "Piggy Florentine" and "Big-Boned Barbie" and playing all those pranks on you. They were cruel and I had no right to do them."

She didn't look phased at all. "Are you sorry for having Callista beat me up in front of everyone?"

I had almost forgotten about that. It was 8th grade and a football game had just ended. I was in one of my usual "mean girl" moods so I started antagonizing Sybil. At the time, she had Chelsea and Hector with her so I guess she didn't want her little brother and sister to see her get degraded (as she usually does). She challenged me to fight her, right then and there with everyone watching, instigating and waiting eagerly to record. I'm not proud of this, but I had Callista fight my battle so I wouldn't have to get my hands dirty. I persuaded Calli to fight Sybil and with Callista being loyal to me and loving a good fight, she gladly accepted the offer. That was the easiest win I'd ever seen Calli take. Sybil went home with a busted lip and a limp that night. I wonder if her siblings remember that, too.

"You know, Chels and Hector were only six years old when that happened. You know how terrifying it was for them to watch that!? You could've broken it up, but you DIDN'T. Everyone preferred to sit back and watch and record it! You're all like animals! All of you just itching to put someone else's misery on social media for your own entertainment. Chels and Hector screaming and pleading for Callista to stop didn't even phase you. You know, today is their tenth birthday, and I don't want you to ruin it for them."

"I'm not here to argue," I whined.

"Then leave us al-"

Before Sybil could finish her statement, her adorable, freckle-faced brother came over to join us.

"Sybs, when are you coming back in?" He asked.

Maybe I couldn't make nice with Sybil but I doubt little Hector even remembers that day. He's just a kid. He probably doesn't even remember what he had for breakfast yesterday.

"Hi! I hear I need to wish you a Happy Birthday, Hector," I greeted in my happiest voice.

He looked tense and afraid. He moved to stand behind Sybil, as if he was looking for her to protect him.

"What's wrong? I won't hurt you," I stated.

"You hurt Sybil. You're the girl from the football game that night. I don't like you. You're mean…like Aphrodite."

I was taken aback by him insulting my sister. "Dite? What did she do?" He broke eye contact with me before mumbling, "She picks on people."

Sybil glared at me. "The cycle repeats. Dite is going to grow up to be just as mean and as vicious as you. I don't want your apology, Minnie. I just want you to leave. Let my boyfriend and I enjoy this day with Hector and Chels."

"Sybil," I whined. I desperately wanted her to listen to what I had to say.

Sybil shook her head furiously, causing brown hair and water to fly all over the place. "Don't "Sybil" me. You weren't thinking about apologies when you were laughing at me getting beat up, or when you were calling me "Piggy," or when you were playing pranks on me in class. You weren't feeling very apologetic when you'd join in on calling Bryce "B.O." or talked about his size. You know, you're the reason I had such low self-esteem. You're the reason why I felt like I needed all those hair extensions and makeup and fake stuff. I still remember the days I used to idolize you and Callista"

I never knew that. I mean, I thought everyone wanted to be me. But, no one ever ADMITTED it to me, especially not someone who seems to hate me so much. I was a bit thrown off.

Sybil smirks. "Oh, are you surprised? Yeah, I hated myself and all I wanted was to be popular and liked and pretty. The two of you had everything I ever wanted then. I remember the day I was given the nickname, "The Wannabe." I remember when I stupidly persuaded my mother to buy me those grey contacts, all so I could be just like Minnie-Carlisle. I remember when I got desperate and stole some hair dye from the local Wal-Mart just so I could have red hair like you. Good God, I was so lost in self-hatred."

Looking back, that was the main reason she was given that nickname. Her terrible red dye job and grey contacts and copying me made her a target. First, she was a Wannabe, then a Piggy, then a Big-Boned Barbie. Sybil's middle and high school years must've been pure Hell. Although her eyes were glaring flames into me right now, looking at Sybil so up close made me realize, she's really a very pretty girl. I'm not sure complimenting her on her looks would make her feel any better since I've made fun of them for years. She'd probably get even more pissed off. I want to tell her that I'm genuinely happy she and Bryce Oliver have found each other, but I don't think she no longer cares about what I do and do not approve of.

"I'm sorry, Sybil. Really, I mean it." I mumbled. I felt like the most despicable person on the Earth at that moment.

Sybil exhaled deeply. I think she knew I was sincerely trying to make things right, but she just didn't want to hear anything from me anymore. "I don't want your apologies, okay? Peace is all I want from you and the only way you can give that to me is to leave me alone for good. Have a nice life," she says before turning around with Hector to get back into the sapphire pool water.

Sophia Janine Carlos:

I spotted Sophia at the gas station as I was filling up my car, after I had left Park Street Recreation Center. She was wearing a low-cut, zebra printed, mini dress with neon pink pumps, strutting proudly with her zebra print clutch and pink feather earrings. Sophia always was an eccentric dresser. You could spot her from a mile away.

"Sophia!" I yelled.

Her ridiculously long, auburn ponytail whipped around as she looked to see who called her name. Her facial expression didn't change when she saw it was me. I'm surprised she didn't look angry like Sybil did. She didn't look phased whatsoever.

"What is it, Minnie?" She asked in her slightly nasally voice. I must say, that black eyeshadow and pink lipstick didn't look too shabby on her at all.

"You mind if I talk to you for a minute?" I asked once I caught up to her.

"I don't care," She responded, batting her long, dramatic eyelashes.

"Oh. Umm, well," I started, thrown a bit off guard, "I wanted to apologize to you."

She seemed confused. "Foooooor?"

"You know, putting that picture up on your locker of you with that lazy eye and calling you "Lazy Eyed Sophie" and-"

"Pssssssh, girl please," Sophia interrupted, waving her hand at me. "That bull didn't bother me in any way shape or form. We Latinas don't get our feelings hurt that easily. I took that picture home, laughed at it, and then burned it in my backyard with my Papi's lighter."

Sophia always was a bit off. Crazy or not, I'm happy she wasn't mad at me for what I did. I was happy that this encounter was going much better than the one I had with Sybil a little bit ago. I sighed and smiled with relief. "Oh, Thank God."

She leaned on the side of her teal blue Honda and looked me dead in my eyes. "I mean, what is a poster compared to what you lost?" My smile slowly faded. "Excuse me?" Did she really just go there?

She rolled her dark brown eyes. "Don't get your panties in a bunch, Minnie. It would be petty of me not to accept your apology. I can get rid of that poster and the damage is erased, right? Callista and Marley are NEVER coming back. I may have a lazy eye, and yeah, it was really not cool for you to tease me about it. But, what you said to me years ago is nothing compared to what you went through this year. I accept your apology because karma did my dirty work for me. Not saying that anyone deserves to lose people they love over a stupid taunt, but hey, if you dish out negative, you never know how badly it'll come back to you."

I didn't have a single thing to say back to that. Sophia may be a bit off, but she's absolutely right on this one. She sleeps peacefully at night; I don't. I had to learn the hard way that what goes around comes back around. She opened her car door, sat down in the driver's seat, and started the engine. Latin music began to fill the car. She reached over into her glove compartment and got out a pen and a yellow sticky note. As she was writing, she said, "I didn't know them all that well, but I am sorry for what happened to them. I didn't need to hear your apology, but there is someone who I think does."

She handed me the sticky note with her French tipped nails. "Phyllis James. 477-2638," the note read.

"Phyllis James?" I said. Sophia puts on a pair of white and gold sunglasses.

"You say that like you didn't totally expose the whole shebang about her having a STD. You say that like you didn't basically run her out of Angel City High. Maybe this will teach you to think the next time, before you stick your foot in your mouth, hmm? Now if you excuuuuse me, I have some shopping to do. Adios!"

She drives off, leaving me behind with my thoughts and her note. I head back to my car. As I'm filling it up with gas, I reluctantly swallow my pride for the second time that day and call Phyllis. Lord, please help me through this.

Phyllis Claire James:

"Hello?" Phyllis answers.

"Hey, Phyllis. It's me…Minnie Carlisle," I respond.

Silence is all that's returned to me. The only thing I heard was her breathing. "I just wanted to apologize to you for what I did. I was wrong. I don't want to start anymore trouble with you. I'm just trying to make things right."

"Bitch! You went behind my back and snuck and got a look at my personal medical records just to get an upper hand on me! You blabbed to the entire school about my business! You're so flipping EVIL, do you hear me!? Sophia's told me everything that's been happening at Angel City High. I've never laughed so hard in my life! I hear you and Giovanni's daughter got your asses whooped. I wish I hadn't moved, because I would've loved to have seen that. The guy you did aaaall of that dirt to me for, ends up cheating on you with that loudmouthed, blonde bitch and that weirdo. I hear she went straight mental."

"Shut up!" I screamed, alerting the attention of everyone around me. "You don't know anything about Callista and Marley! She wasn't mental! She was sick and don't you DARE call Callista out her name again or-"

"OR ELSE WHAT!?" She shrilled into the phone, hurting my ear. "What are you gonna do to me!? This isn't high school anymore so your petty threats don't mean CRAP to me! I don't want your flippin' apology! I want you to go to Hell. I'm glad your friends died. If you call my damn phone again, you'll end up just like them."

Click! I enter my car and I go absolutely psycho. I scream, I kick, I punch the armrest, I punch the door, and I banged on my steering wheel, accidentally honking the horn. I actually did try to call her again, but it went directly to voicemail. She probably blocked my number soon after the call ended. After that conversation, I hated her with a burning passion. I regret ever taking Sophia's advice and calling her. She's a waste of my time and a waste period. She always was and always will be. Sorry, Calli and Marley, but after that, I don't regret at all what I did to SPHYLLIS James. She wasn't worth my apology anyways.

Lydia Vanessa Aprilson:

After Lydia had taken some of Marley's cherished possessions and made a vow not to ever return to Angel City, I had to get in contact with her over the phone. She wasn't too eager to speak to me. I expected that. However, Lydia was Marley's only sibling and making things right with her would be almost as equal as having a piece of Marley back in my life. She went ballistic when I said I wanted to make amends. She blames me just as much as she blames Ophelia for Marley's mental demise, saying that she's an only child now because of us. Lydia says that Marley's coffin will forever lay on my conscience. She cussed me out five ways from Sunday and told me I was "the Devil reincarnated." I admit, I'd never heard anyone call me that before and I'd been called a lot of things over the years.

"Oh, yeah. It must be so easy for you to be able to point fingers and call names. You had it easier than Marley. At least you were Mommy's Favorite. Hell, you were everyone's favorite," I pointed out.

"Typical!" She exclaimed, her tone tinged with attitude. "Once again, the biggest idiot in the conversation always has the most to say! You think I liked being Ophelia's little trophy? You think I took pleasure in the fact that my mother only seemed to value me for what I looked like or because I was popular? I just wanted to be left alone. All she ever wanted to do was strut me around, proud of me for mess that didn't matter. I never got compliments on my character from her. I felt that my own mother didn't like me for ME. She favored me because I was more like her than Marley. You think I enjoyed watching Ophelia degrade Marley on the daily? The constant comparisons, insults, and whatnot? I knocked on her a few times for that! I never enjoyed people poking fun at my baby sister, Minnie. You may have known my sister and me for a long time, but you're still an outsider looking in. Only Ophelia, Marley, and I know EVERYTHING said and done in that home. Next time, keep your mouth shut." After shutting me up, she warned me to never call her again, but before I thought she would hang up, she said to me, "You wanna know why Marley begged Ophelia and me to keep her disorder a secret? It was because she already considered herself a disappointment; and her peers already thought she was a weirdo; and she didn't want people like YOU constantly brandishing her as a maniac, as well. She didn't want to be defined or confined by her disorder. She just wanted to be normal!" With Marley gone, she said that she no longer had a reason to communicate with me. Sniffling, she then hung the phone up in my face. Hmph, I feel it's a little unfair and hypocritical of Lydia to just blame Ophelia and I because her leaving out of state for college affected Marley also. Yes, I was a bad friend and Ophelia was an even worse mother, but Lydia wasn't the best big sister around. Like Jezebel said, she selfishly left Marley behind. However, I wasn't concerned with playing the blame game, I just wanted to make things right. I tried to call her back to continue my attempt to make amends, but no one answered. I don't think Lydia is the type to care about resolving a grudge; and I really don't think she wants to hear the truth about her part in Marley's illness. With Marley and Donald deceased, Lydia hating me miles away with no intent to ever return home, and Ophelia living in Tennessee with her brother now, I no longer had any ties with any members of the Aprilson family.

Lauralee Marie Giovanni:

I thought Lauralee would surely accept my apology. I arrived at the Giovanni mansion, eager to see Lauralee again. I hadn't really seen her or gotten the chance to really talk to her since graduation. She's pretty good at avoiding people. Darla, bouncing baby D.J. in her arms, let me in and gave me permission to go upstairs to Lauralee's room. I said a quick hello to Stephanie on her way to one of their many bathrooms, before I finally made it to my destination. So much had changed since I'd last been in her room. Instead of the cotton-candy pink it used to be, the walls were now painted a dark grey. Loud, metal music filled the room. There were rock band posters plastered everywhere and a skull shaped lamp in the corner of the room. What in the world happened? A young woman was rummaging under the bed, apparently searching for something.

"Excuse me, have you seen Laur-"

Before I can finish, she looks up at me. There's no mistaking those hazel eyes. This woman is Lauralee. Her long, brown tresses had been dyed a darker brown and were now styled into a short, shaggy haircut. She now has her eyebrow pierced and has added two more ear piercings and tattoos to her body art collection. Her nails are long and blood red. She's wearing black shorts, a red shirt that cut off above her stomach to show off her flat tummy and belly piercing and black, red and white tennis shoes. Her earrings are dark red and shaped like broken hearts.

"Are you just gonna sit there and freakin' STARE all day?" She growled, as she walked over to the dresser.

She doesn't even talk the same way. Who is this girl? Where's the happy, energetic, prissy Lauralee I've always known? Where's the Italian bombshell who used to catwalk down the walls of Angel City High School in high heels and colorful dresses? What the hell happened?

"What happened to you, Lauralee?"

"First of all, I go by just Lee now. Lauralee is too girly for my tastes," Lee corrected as she finished applying some mascara. After that, she reached for a tube of dark red lipstick.

"When has anything EVER been to girly for you?"

"Things change, girlfriend. People change. Get over it. This is me now. It always has been. I'm a bisexual, tattoo loving, girl who likes Rock music, piercings and smoking a little weed every now and again," She chuckles. "I'm living the liiiiife."

I shook my head in disbelief. This couldn't be Lauralee. It just couldn't be. I almost slapped myself just to make sure I wasn't dreaming. "What happened to-?"

"What happened to what!?" Lee angrily interrupted after finishing with her lipstick. "The Lauralee Marie you used to criticize and pushover and bully? The ditsy, rich girl who followed you around like an orphaned puppy? THAT GIRL IS GOOOONE! Do you hear me?"

"Bully? What are you talking about? I never bullied you."

Lee stuck her hip out and rolled her eyes. "Oh, yeah. Play dumb if you want to, Artemis. You were always so mean to me. Always calling me a name or treating me like a stupid child. I figured since you were already popular, beautiful, and your family had money of their own, you'd be a perfect candidate for my best friend. I thought that you'd actually like me for me and all would be peachy, but boooy was I wrong. Even when Marley died and I tried to be there for you, all you did was toss me aside like yesterday's garbage. I have feelings, you know! You know how hard it is being the Governor's daughter!? Having to put on a fake image every time you go out? I tried to be "perfect" and nobody liked it. All I wanted was a friend! I wanted a genuine friend who didn't want me because I was attractive or who didn't want my money or my status. It was lonely for me being an only child and even when Steph came to live with us, we never could see eye to eye. All I ever wanted was to find a best friend. You're so damn insensitive and so much of a BITCH that you couldn't even see that!"

No wonder I can't keep friends. I had three great friends and now they're all gone because of me. There was so much hurt in Lauralee's heart and tears in her eyes. I don't deserve to have friends. All I seem to do is ruin their lives. Lee's guard lowered and the old Lauralee came through for just a moment. She glanced down at the light grey carpet as she softly stated, "I know it's wrong, but even after Marley and Callista died, I thought that we'd, you know, become closer as friends. I know it's selfish, but I guess I was kinda hoping to fill their spot as your best friend."

That statement truly stunned me. I never knew she felt that way so deep inside. Then again, as self-centered as I was, if she had told me, would I have even cared?

"I'm soo sorry, Lee." I consoled as I began to walk over to her, my arms extended in preparation to hug her. Lee pointed her finger at me and took three steps away from me.

"Oh, no you don't. I don't want to hear an apology. I don't want anything from YOU anymore. You can take that apology and eat it and get the hell out of my house."

"Lauralee, please," I whined. After losing Callista and just recently losing Marley, I didn't wanna let go of her either.

"What's the matter? Can't handle my 'Italian, mob-wife assassin temper'?" Lauralee's snide remark hit me immediately with shame and regret. I was ashamed I ever even said that to her. She was giving me the side-eye with a mischievous grin.

Once again, I was rejected. I just stood there and stared her in the eyes. I know my eyes were pleading with her to take me back. I just wanted a second chance. She turned back towards her mirror and prepared to apply some black eyeshadow.

"The only thing I will say to you before you leave is thank you. Thanks for telling me about Erica. If it weren't for you, my bastard, unfaithful

Daddy probably would've never come clean to us."

"Anything for a friend," I replied. I must sound so desperate to her right now.

She shot me a skeptical look before she coldly stated, "I have a date. Goodbye, Artemis."

Rayanne Susannah Greyman:

I decided to meet Rayanne in the park that evening after my meeting with Lauralee. I may not have picked on her as much as I did Sybil, but I still felt the need to make amends with her. The sun was beginning to set and the wind was blowing so perfectly. I closed my eyes just for a second to enjoy the breeze lightly caressing my body and twirling my hair. Next to February, autumn was my favorite time of the year. The weather is so tranquil and relaxing that it actually makes you want to stay outside and linger in the sun's warm rays. I used to watch the birds migrate in a V-formation and wish that I could fly away with them. But, I am not a bird. I cannot just fly away from my problems. I must stay here and deal with them head-on no matter how hard it may be.

"You're really enjoying that wind, aren't you?" a voice spoke.

I opened my eyes to see Rayanne Greyman standing right in front of me. She was wearing faded blue jeans, black flip-flops, a white t-shirt with a brown Peace symbol on it, and a red hat sitting atop of her long, wavy, brown hair.

"Hi, Ray." I greeted.

"I know you didn't call me here to say hello and sip tea by the sunset, Minnie," Rayanne blurted out in her Southern accent. I see she wanted to get straight to the point. "What is it?"

"I wanted to tell you that I'm sorry."

Her facial expression slightly changed. It looked as if she was taken aback by my apology. She didn't take her eyes off me, not even for a split second.

"I'm sorry for everything I did to you while we were in school. I know I said some little things-"

"You mean callin' me a "trailer trash tomboy" and givin' me the nickname "Rayanne GAYman?" She interrupted. "You and your stupid rumors got me picked on all seventh grade year for being gay! How homophobic can you get, you damn bimbo."

Man, I just couldn't get a break today. I guess I didn't deserve one after all I had done over the years. God sure wasn't going to make doing the right thing so easy for me apparently.

"I was childish."

"You were stupid. All I did was compliment you a few times and you used that as "proof of my gayness." Seriously, do you have nothin' better to do with your life?"

"I'm TRYING to apologize." I growled. I was trying to be the bigger woman and I kept getting dirt thrown back in my face. Rayanne waved her finger and shook her head at me.

"Oooooh, no. This ain't middle school anymore. You can take that attitude out of your voice, sweetie. I won't tolerate that crap from nobody." She threatened, as her blue eyes staring angrily at me.

I truly don't know what came over me but I all of a sudden felt big and bold. The old Minnie Carlisle decided to come out for an encore and show her ugly head again. "Yeah, well what are you gonna do about it, Rayanne GAYman? Huh? I'm TRYING to apologize to your hillbilly rump and all you're doing is acting like trailer park trash! You're all talk! You're not even gonna do any-"

With god-like agility, she rushes and tackles me to the ground. I squirm, but Ray's athletic build easily dominates mine, and she sits on top of me. She pins my arms down firmly and then gazes down at me with a smug grin upon her face. Brunette strands of her hair are dangling annoyingly close to my nose and eyes. It's like my fight with Jess happening all over again. I feel like a gerbil trying to fight off a Rottweiler. If Hercules and Wonder Woman had a daughter, it would've been this girl for sure.

"You were saying?" She taunted.

"Get off of me!" I demanded, still trying to squirm away. With Rayanne having the weight and strength advantage over me, it almost hurt trying to squirm away the lower portion of my body from under her. There was no way I was getting off that ground unless Ray let me.

"Callista and Marley are gone now, Minnie. It's time for you to grow a pair of ovaries and fight your own battles. Be a real woman for a change. You need to be careful of the mistakes that you judge people by, because now it's YOU that's askin' for forgiveness," Rayanne advised in a softer, more feminine voice.

I stopped fighting and just stare at her as my epiphany strikes me. I've never had anyone say truer words to me. I need to be a woman. I need to grow up. Acting childish, immature, and stupid is what got me into all this mess in the first place. Ray is 100% right. Never judge someone too harshly for screwing up because it may be you seeking forgiveness for something the next time. Rayanne slowly stands up and offers her hand to me. I take it; and she assists me up to my feet again. We never break eye contact except for when she goes to retrieve her hat, which had been displaced just a few inches away from us because of the struggle.

"Now, that you've calmed down a bit and now that the big bang about Marley's disorder is out, I feel like there's somethings I should tell you," Rayanne stated.

I dust grass, dirt, and other debris off of my jeans before looking up at her. "What is it?"

She steps a bit closer to me so that I can hear her better. "Something went down between your friend and Carmella Carson."

I give her a skeptical look. "Carmella Carson? As in the-daughter-of-the-police-chief, Carmella Carson?"

Rayanne nods her head up and down. "The very same. I was joggin' in the park one day and I came upon Carmella and Marley havin' an exchange of words. When Carmella tried to walk away, Marley grabbed her by the arm to stop her. That's when Carmella turned around and used her nails to scratch her right in the face. I knew it put a hurtin' on her because you know Carmella always got them long, bright colored claws for fingernails."

The gears in my mind slowly began to turn and piece this situation together. The scars on Marley's forehead and Carmella's broken nails, it was all falling into place now. Once again, Jezebel takes over and Marley is the one to pay the consequence. "Do you know what they were arguing about?"

Rayanne placed her red ball cap back atop her head. "Well, I caught up to Carmella after she ran for dear life away from Marley. Seems like your ol' pal tried to put the moves on Carmella. I almost didn't believe it. I knew she didn't ever go out with any fellas, but I didn't think 'ol Aprilson was swingin' off that side of the plate."

Hell, I hardly believed it, but I guess I have no choice. Truth was being laid out in front of me right here in plain sight. Well, Jezebel did sleep with Lauralee so I guess it's not too farfetched that she'd go after someone who's also very feminine, like Carmella.

Rayanne scratched her head, as if she was still trying to figure it out herself. "I don't know. The way Carmella described it, Marley wanted her baaad. I guess that was the first signal that Marley "wasn't herself," y'know? Marley's not the type to be that aggressive, let alone put her hands on someone. I shoulda told you earlier."

"Did you tell anyone else?" I inquired, hoping for the answer I desperately wanted.

Rayanne looked me dead in the eyes and smiled mischievously. "Hell no. I, unlike some people, know how to keep my mouth shut."

I jolt my eyes down towards the ground in shame and fiddle with my fingers. I feel like a child who had just been scolded. "I really am sorry, Ray."

She shrugs her shoulder up and down quickly and gives an apathetic look. "It's whatever. Now, if we're done here, I have a movie date with a smoooooking hot Italian."

She grins smugly at me again before turning to walk back towards her dingy, white pick-up truck.

Rebecca Baylee Hardwick:

By the time I was about to begin my drive to Rebecca Hardwick's house, the peaceful weather turns into a sudden downpour. Great, now the weather fits my mood. I know that after what they did at that party, I shouldn't even want to speak with Rebbie. Somehow I believe that part of what drove Rebbie to participate in those cruel events was the cruel rant I said to her that day at her locker when I lost my temper with her. We'll never know, but maybe if I hadn't made her feel so damn bad about herself that day, she would've talked Jess and Damian out of throwing that setup party. Rebbie's not as wild as Jess or as aggressive as Callista. It was out of her character to be that mean. I find Rebbie happily playing a card game with Jess on her front porch where it's dry and the weather can't dampen their fun. Jess is first to spot me as I start to approach them.

"Well, look what the cat dragged in." Jess teased as I hurried to get out of the rain. I see she got rid of her blonde hair and reverted back to her natural hair color, a luxurious, dark brown.

Rebbie said nothing. She didn't even acknowledge my presence as she silently shuffled the deck of cards.

"Jess, I'd like to speak to Rebbie alone. Is that okay?"

Jess shoots a look at Rebbie who glances up at me then nods her head approvingly at Jess. Jess puts her cards down on the floor of the porch and stands up.

"Rebbie, I'll be in the house if you need me." In Jess Ward lingo, that means, "I'm here in case you need me to beat her down again." My sides were already hurting from being tackled by Rayanne and I was mentally exhausted from my interactions with Sybil, Lydia, Phyllis, and Lauralee. I really wasn't looking forward to any of Jess's antics. I was in no mood to be slipping and sliding in rainwater and mud with her.

Once Jess had shut the door, Rebbie got up off the floor of the porch and walked towards the dark green and white swing that was behind her. She took a seat and began to slowly rock back and forth in it before she asked, "What do you want, Minnie?" She didn't say it like she was aggravated. She said it like she was preparing for me to say something horrible to her again.

"Rebecca, I'm sorry."

She abruptly stops swinging and blurts out, "Huh!?"

"I'm sorry," I reiterate. "What I said to you in the hallway that day was totally out of line and mean. I was just angry and emotional and I guess I took it out on you. I shouldn't have said those things and I apologize for them."

"When does the infamous Artie Carlisle EVER apologize? Are you high or something?"

I smiled faintly. That sounded like something Callista would've said to me. "No, I'm completely sober, Rebbie."

She pulls her hair over both her shoulders. "Callista was more than my friend. She was like my protector. She and Jess....they are like my guardians. I know I'm not too smart, Minnie. I'm gullible, naïve and a pushover and people like to take advantage of that. Callista and Jess made sure things like that didn't happen. Now that Calli's gone, all Jess and I have is each other. She won't admit it like I will, but she misses her, too. Calli was like the sister we both never had. At least I have Jess, though. You...you have nobody."

That last part stuck a soft spot in me. I was so taken aback by it; I think my heart skipped a beat. I guess this is karma's way of making me feel just a small sliver of how I made Rebbie feel in the hall that day at school. Rebbie was right. I had nobody and it was my own damn fault. "I miss her, too," I softly spoke. I knew I was about to cry.

She turned her head towards me. Her eyes were watering, as well. "Well, for the sake of Calli, let's just forgive and move on. She'd want that."

She got up off the swing and walked over to embrace me in a hug. It was the best hug I had gotten in a while. Jess suddenly opened the front door. It was obvious she had been eavesdropping because tears were flooding her big, brown eyes. She wiped them away with the bottom of her purple shirt.

"Look at the two of you crying like a bunch of punks," She was half crying, half laughing.

Rebbie and I smiled at her, still with tears in our eyes. "Jessica, come over here, you big crybaby." Rebbie playfully commanded.

Jess casually walked over to us and joined in our hug. Callista's somewhere smiling right now, I'm sure of it. Maybe Marley's smiling as well, watching me as I finally grow up. I had finally gotten the forgiveness I was searching for all day. After we had enough of bonding, Jess rushes off the porch and sang out into the sky, "I miss you, you crazy girl! You hear me, Callista!? We miss you!" She didn't care about the occasional flashes of lightning, the thunder roaring above the house, or the fact the rain showed her no mercy as it poured heavily upon her brown skin, soaking her clothes and her kinky, brown hair in a matter of split seconds. Jess shows no fear; I must give her credit for that. I'm sure Callista heard her. She's probably tickled pink right now, as she watches her best friends make a truce and come together for her sake.

CHAPTER FORTY-TWO

"A blemish on our once innocent friendship."

I began attending the University of North Carolina that autumn. It's done me well to be in a new environment with new people and new challenges. However, there are some familiar faces. Cassidy, Nahaali, and Keegan also attend this university with me. I even apologized to Nahaali, although she only partially deserved it. Surprisingly, she eagerly accepted my apology. She even gave me a hug. I think she was just happy to have her first possible friend. However, she has more than that now. She and Keegan have started dating. Keegan says all is going well and that Nahaali's therapy sessions have really helped her to have a more stable mind. Nahaali's so happy that she's already planning double dates. I'll have to talk with Cassie about that one. I'm happy things have turned out well for her. Underneath all of Nahaali's emotional issues is a sweet, loving girl and she's finally letting that side of her come out to play. The Arden brothers and I have made amends. I'm happy that I have made peace with everyone Callista was connected to. Even Uriel and Apollo can stand to be in the same room now. Shocking, isn't it? Speaking of Apollo, he's decided to attend a technical college right in Angel City and is working on saving money so that he can get his own apartment. I'm proud. My carefree big brother is becoming a man. Stella Arden and my mother have slowly began to repair their friendship. It's refreshing to see them able to rekindle what they had like mature adults after everything that happened. However, Stella still has a large amount of contempt towards the Aprilson family. I guess she was just being cordial with Ophelia for graduation. I understand she's still looking for someone to point the finger of blame for the murder of her only daughter. But, maybe one day, she'll understand that Marley was a victim, as well. At least she won't have to deal with them anymore since Ophelia decided to move to Tennessee with her brother, Terrence. She left me Marley's diary, her "F" chain, and some other of Marley's small possessions. Marley's diary gave me further insight into the pain she was going through at home.

Marley was picked on as a little kid in school. As soft-spoken and as timid as Marley was, she was afraid to speak up for herself. "The kids in school always called me names and whisper whenever I walked into the room. I used to be afraid to even speak in class. I'd feel more worthless with each day my mother forces me to go to the hellhole the government calls, "school." I remember the day Julia pushed me off the swings and I got sand in my eye and I scraped my knee. I cried and they laughed. Then, Albert took my lunch money which meant that I didn't get to eat lunch that day. I hated that place."

Marley was raped by one of Ophelia's many, scumbag boyfriends.

"I really wish Bill would stop doing this.. He looks at me like I'm a slab of fresh meat. He practically drools. I'm afraid to wear shorts or even a tank-top. Wednesday, I wore a dress and he raped me on the bathroom floor. I'll never wear a dress again. Ophelia is, of course, no help. She's either drunk or too busy recovering from a bad hangover. She'll never believe me."

Before Lydia left for college, Ophelia and her would get into heated arguments almost every day and often, they would even turn physical. "Lydia gave Ophelia a mean beating today. Ophelia threw a small lamp at Lydia and she fell unconscious. Now there's glass all over the floor and Ophelia demanded I clean it up. I cut my foot trying to do so. No one else will bother to help me. Ophelia is always pressuring Lydia to be like her and criticizing me and her for any little thing. I just want the people I love to get along—Lydia, Ophelia, Callista, and Minnie. I'm tired of all the fighting. I wish Dad was here. He was always the peacemaker."

I knew Ophelia became an alcoholic after Donald died, but I didn't think the bottle would make her abuse her own children. "Ophelia gets so frustrated when she's drunk. The alcohol makes her hate me, I know it. I can't let her use me as a punching bag anymore. Today, she broke my arm because she thought I was trying to raid her booze stash. I was really trying to get a snack, since I hadn't eaten all that day. She didn't even care enough to take me to the hospital. Today is the last day I call that woman, 'Mom'."

There's one entry about Callista and I that really caught my eye. "Callista's been really mad at Minnie lately. I know Minnie can be a little bit difficult to deal with, but that's no reason why we can't stay friends, right? Callista has a plan to break off her friendship with Minnie to teach her a lesson. She wants me to join her. She says she loves me too much to watch Minnie make me feel inferior to her. I can't. I don't have heart like Calli does. I can't rebel against my best friend. Callista's disappointed, but says she understands. She informs me that she'll "end" the friendship with me too, but she'll only be pretending to hate me. Minnie is her real target."

Ophelia also left me a video she recorded of Marley singing to Donald and her. Who knew that underneath that soft-spoken tone and humble demeanor was such a lovely, singing voice, especially for someone that age. She must've inherited it from her Aunt Daphne. Both Callista and Marley seemed to have hidden talents that they were too shy to inform me of. Ophelia realizes that Donald's death, stress, and alcohol caused her to resort back to the superficial, selfish, and cruel person she was many years ago. She blames herself for Marley's condition and therefore, she cannot bear to live in that house or Angel City anymore. I think it's for the best that she moves because she has started to become the target of some cruel pranks around here. Someone spraypainted, "Killer" on her house just recently and slashed her tires. The city turned on her, just like they did me. Violet and Nate are doing well. Up until his parents and I persuaded him to remain in Angel City, he considered taking Violet and moving down to South Carolina with some of his other relatives. Vi is half of Callista and I just couldn't bear to see her go, especially since I hadn't gotten much time to bond with her. I've only gotten to see her once since Callista's death. When Violet wrapped her tiny palm around my index finger and cooed at me with her baby blue eyes, adorable giggle, and toothless smile, my heart nearly melted. I wanted to cry, because I see Callista, that heart shaped face, and bubbly smile. But, at the same time, I was happy because she is a blessing; and I'm happy a major part of Calli is here to live on. Nate's broken heart is healing. He seems to finally accept the conditions around Callista's death. He spoils Violet like a princess so I know he would've spoiled Calli like a queen. We keep in contact for Violet's sake mostly, but I must admit, after all we went through, it's nice that we can be cordial. He says it's nice having me around to talk to when he wants to vent about Callista because I understand. Cassidy is not so understanding though but I'll get him to come around. Although I have tried to regain contact with her, Lauralee, or "Lee" as she now likes to be called, still wants nothing to do with me. I guess I had it coming. I don't deserve her forgiveness after how I treated her. She does talk to Cassidy occasionally, since they now know that they shared a sibling. Cassidy says she may have her emotional scars, but all in all, she's stable and that on a more positive note, Steph and her have become closer. This is most likely due to Lauralee's attitude adjustment. Although she was once a Daddy's girl, she now has a rocky relationship with her father because he kept the truth about Erica from her. Rebbie emailed me a photo of her proudly holding her belly and soon-to-be Aunt Jess pointing at her with a wide, silly smile with a caption that read, "Guess who's preggers!?" I truly wish Rebbie and her new baby all the luck the world can give them. Jess, too. I'm sure she'll make a great aunt. Jess will be a protective aunt, that's for sure. Recently, I decided to change my major from nursing to psychology. When my counselor inquired why I now want to become a youth psychologist instead of a registered nurse, I answered, "Because of some old friends. I want to be a listening ear for all of those who cried out for help and no one even offered a tissue." Times have changed and I'm happy to say that I have too. I am no longer the Minnie Carlisle that I used to be. This time, Artemis has grown up and sees life from a different pair of big, grey eyes.

"You mind if I sit here?" A voice softly inquires.

I pause the song I was listening to and turn to see a girl carrying a hand full of books against her chest. She is short with a pear-shaped figure. Her hair is long, luminous, and blonde. She has fair skin, an adorable, heart shaped face, and dark red glasses that she wears over her enticing, arctic blue eyes. She's wearing a long, pink colored dress with pink flops and a pink flower in her hair. The only other girl I knew who loved pink as much as this girl was Marley.

"Sure," I replied.

She takes a great sigh of relief as she placed her books and neon green backpack down on the table. "Oh, thank God. These books are killing me." Once she is seated and situated, she reaches into her purse and begins applying another coat of what smells like berry-scented lip-gloss.

"I'm Minnie," I say, introducing myself. Normally, I would've just went back to doing what I was doing but something intrigues me about this girl. Was it her beauty or her style? Maybe I was just looking for a new friend. Maybe she subconsciously reminded me of someone I already knew.

She grins radiantly. She has a picture perfect smile. "Hiiii! I'm Megan Katherine McKinley, but you can just call me Meg. You're awfully pretty, by the way," She greets in her cheery, yet soft-spoken voice.

She extends her arm happily and eagerly, waiting on me to shake her hand. I think I'm gonna like this girl. Her perkiness and dorky adorableness reminds me of Lauralee…well, the OLD Lauralee. We sit down and chat for a while. Turns out, Meg is a straight-A student who plans on becoming a doctor one day. She told me about how she was eager to get her braces finally taken off in about two months and how she absolutely loved animals, especially dogs. I greatly enjoyed talking to her. Every time I looked at her red glasses or pink braces, I was reminded of Marley. Maybe that's why we got along so well.

"There you are!" a girl calls out as she suddenly approaches the table.

My first thought was, "Maaan, this chick is tall." She had to stand at 6 feet. She was petite and had short, dark brown hair cut into a chic bob that was frizzy at the moment due to the breeze that continuously flowed through here. Her style bleeds "Callista." She was wearing a bright yellow, spaghetti strap top with a camouflage hat, combat boots, and camouflage shorts that showed off her long, slender legs and a diamond stone was shining beautifully in her nose. The color of the gemstone in her ring soon captures my attention, it's a beautiful shade of violet. Callista would've loooved that outfit. Only thing missing to top it off would be those "grim" earrings Callista gave to Marley that she, of course, never wore.

"Minnie, this is my tomboyish and rude cousin, Elizabeth McKinley." Meg introduces jokingly while she places her right hand on her hip and flips her hair dramatically over her shoulder.

Elizabeth sticks up her middle finger and crosses her eyes at Meg before turning back to me. "Ignore her. You can call me Beth." Her eyes are so green and striking.

"So, where ya from, Moon Eyes?" Beth asks as she puts away her canary yellow phone and she takes a seat at the bench.

Her calling me that makes my heart skip a beat. "M-moon Eyes?" I hadn't been called that since Callista died.

She takes a bite out of her green apple. "Yeah, Moon Eyes. You know, because your eyes are big and grey…like the moon."

"She has a habit of giving people nicknames. It's one of her many quirks," Megan explains.

I take a small breath of relief. I didn't want to seem too startled by her calling me that name. "Well, what's yours?" I ask Meg, diverting her attention for a bit.

"Nutmeg!" Beth laughs, causing Meg to playfully push her.

"To answer your question, I'm from Angel City," I finally stated.

They both look at me with eyes bulged. "Seriously!? We're from there, too! Yaaaay! That must mean that we're like meant to be friends." I don't recall seeing or hearing about either one of these girls in Angel City. Then again, I also didn't know Damian and Jess were cousins. Maybe that city isn't as small as I thought it was.

"You're such a weirdo," Beth mumbles, munching some more off her juicy apple.

We continue chatting. Talking with Beth and Meg is like talking with Marley and Callista all over again. They look like them, talk like them, and act like them. Meg even has three ear piercings like Calli did. I feel an instant connection and nothing but positive vibes with these two. I feel like I've already known them for forever. Meg then invites Beth and me to the local coffee house to munch on some sweets and I gladly accept. I'm feeling so good, I'll even invite Nahaali to meet us there. I just can't believe I have friends again. It's almost too good to be true.

"You comin', Moon Eyes?" Beth asks as I rush to put my things back into my book bag. "Yeah, in a minute, Callista."

I catch my mistake instantaneously. Great, I haven't had friends for a half a day, yet and I already mess it up. I didn't mean to call Beth by Callista's name. It's just that she reminds me so much of her. Now, I was going to have to explain who Callista and Marley were and all of my Angel City drama. I can see it now. I was going to be resorted to being nothing more than "the egocentric mean girl that caused it all." Callista's loveable, rebellious spirit was going to be reduced to her being "the killed pregnant girl" and Marley's class and intelligence were going to be overshadowed by people calling her "the psychopath that got too jealous." I was so not ready for that kind of drama again.

"How did you know my middle name is Kallista?"

I paused and just stared blankly at Beth for a second. I know I must've looked like a total buffoon at that moment. "Huh?"

The cousins exchange glances. "Kallista. You called me by my middle name. How did you know what it was?"

That name is NOT common. Now, I know meeting these girls was more than coincidence. "Umm, sorry. It's just that you reminded me of someone I knew who had that name. Sorry."

Beth shrugs it off. "It's alright. I think it's a pretty cool name anyways. I don't mind."

I am extremely thankful that they do not ask any more questions and that they weren't too weirded out by it. There's something about these girls. I lose both of my best friends within 6 months of each other and all of a sudden, Beth and Meg pop up in my life and they're similar to Callista and Marley in so many ways. Their names are somewhat similar, their appearances, their fashion sense, and even their personalities. Is this God giving me a second chance at friendship? Is this His way of giving me another opportunity to make genuine friends and do it RIGHT this time? I don't know, but I'm dyiiiing to find out. This could be the start of a beautiful friendship. I can see it now.

Oh! I got so tangled up in my drama and engaged in my conversations with Beth and Meg that I almost forgot to read Callista's last poem. I sit in the backseat and read it silently to myself, as Meg drives on a new level of slow and Beth dances wildly in her seat to "Breaking The Habit" by Linkin Park. Calli's final masterpiece is titled, "My Roses."

"My best friends are my white roses.
They represent the purity and the serenity that I desire in my life.
Years later, I find myself in love and impregnated, so now my stupid plan's gone awry.
I accidentally became the black rose
That grew many thorns
That painfully prickle so that no one can reach my heart.
With my thorns, I have managed to prick both of my best friends
And now they bleed.
One could say I caused there to be blood on white roses;
A blemish on our once innocent friendship.
Is it possible for a black rose to erase its sins
And become white again?"

I'm not saying that Beth and Meg could ever take the place of either Callista or Marley, but maybe they can fill some of the hole that's here in my heart. Maybe they can help fill the void I feel and help me to cure some of this guilt and regret. I really believe that Elizabeth and Megan are angels that God sent to me to teach me how to be a real friend this time around and not take the people I love and cherish for granted. This is my chance to start over and to have a clean slate in a new environment with a new boyfriend and with new friends. As Calli and Marley are looking down at me, I want them to know that Beth and Meg won't we taking their place, but filling their space. I especially want Callista to know that she is not entirely to blame for our friendship's demise. I'll love them forever, but I'm still lonely. You ever missed someone so much that you could feel your body craving their presence? That's how I feel every day; and it's absolute torture. It's the little things that make me miss them the most. Sometimes, I'll get ecstatic because I got a good grade on a difficult test or had a great date with Cassidy and I'll want to call them…forgetting that neither of them will answer. I yearn to be the friend to Beth and Meg that I should've been to Calli, Marley, and Lauralee. God does give second chances and don't ever, ever doubt that for a second.

EPILOGUE

There are traits in my character that I am deeply ashamed of. There's a dark side of me; and it's a side I hope to keep buried from this day forward. I assisted in the bullying of some of my fellow classmates. Some of them will probably hate me forever. I've probably scarred them. I left Nahaali fighting for her life in a pool and only cared about my own selfish needs. Her possibly drowning didn't even cross my mind. I made fun of Sybil for her appearance; and it caused her to develop very low self-esteem. Her siblings will remember my part in Sybil's middle school beating for the rest of their lives. Rayanne was deemed the "homo" of the school for years because of me. I had no right to call her "trailer trash" just because of her accent and where she was from. Developing fast and climbing higher in social status changed me and it definitely wasn't a change for the better. All Lauralee wanted was for me to be a genuine friend to her and I gave her my butt to kiss. I took advantage of her kindness and took it for granted. My best friends were dealing with internal conflicts; and I didn't even take the time to notice. I was too wrapped up in my own superficial lifestyle. God, I wish I could rewind time. I'd be a totally different person and love the ones I cherished a little stronger. All I can hope for is that my sister no longer decides to follow in my shallow footsteps. Maybe, I can get her to see the error in her ways before it's too late. I'll never forget Callista, Marley, and Lauralee. Never in a million years. The memories I have shared with them will stay with me for as long as there is a beat in my heart. It's because of me that they are gone now. It truly does hurt me to see our friendship wither away and die like vibrant trees under the cold of December. There's no feeling worse than regret. Please, do not make my mistakes in your own lives.

-Artemis Wilhelmina Carlisle

ABOUT THE AUTHOR

Kimberly Thompson was born in suburban, Columbia, South Carolina

on December 7, 1993. She was born into a large family. Her mother was the 13th of 14 children. Despite their ups and downs, the love they had for one another remained constant. From the time she was young, she had always had a gift for writing. She believes her vivid imagination gives her the ability to create great plots and interesting characters within a story. Kimberly always loved to make up stories. She began working on *Blood On White Roses* when she was a junior at Irmo High School. She then took a hiatus on writing this novel until sometime in her senior year. Though it was sometimes challenging, Kimberly became more devoted to completing it. Kimberly considers *Blood On White Roses* her masterpiece. Although it is her first story, she takes great pride in the time and effort she has placed into it over these few years.

BLOODON WHITE ROSES:
BEHIND THE SCENES
Interesting Tidbits

1. The first name of Cassidy's mother is Arella, which means "Angel Messenger." Arella's middle name is "Rosalba," which means "White Rose."
2. The names of Callista's older brothers are also the names of the Archangels: Michael, Raphael, Gabriel, and Uriel and each of the Carlisle children is named after a Greek diety.
3. TresAngeles means "Three Angels" in Spanish. The title of the field is a dedication to Minnie, Callista and Marley.
4. Fola, the small rural town Cassidy lives in, means "Blood" in Irish.
5. Nahaali's last name is the word "drama" spelled backwards.
6. If you take Chief Marshall Carson's phone number, "737-8378," it spells the word "pervert," using the letters on the number keys.
7. Sybil's middle name, "Mallory" means "Unlucky," which describes her perfectly given the treatment she received during her middle and high school years.
8. Originally, the story behind Marley's middle name "Rosemarley" was supposed to be that her mother is such a screw up that she even screwed up Marley's name. She meant to name her "Rosemary," but was partially inebriated and therefore, pronounced it wrong. When her father arrived at the hospital, he didn't ask any questions and just assumed Ophelia intentionally named her that. Later, I decided to give Donald Aprilson two middle names, Lyndon and Marlow, and have each daughter named after him with the eldest daughter, Lydia, being named from Lyndon and Marley's middle name, Rosemarley being derived from Marlow and the name of Ophelia's mother. Marley's original full name was "Rosemarley Genevieve Aprilson."
9. Marley is the "tall, hot brunette that was surprisingly wild in the sheets" that Damian was referring to.
10. Originally, Marley was meant to make an attempt to murder Minnie also and commit suicide so she would not be sent to jail. She was

supposed to pretend to be Minnie's best friend, so she could secretly seduce Nate and sabotage his relationship with Minnie. Also, she was meant to be unsure about her sexual orientation.

11. Originally, Callista began sleeping with Nate as a childish attempt to upset Minnie; because she had a level of jealousy, animosity and hatred towards her for being beautiful when they were growing up but she was unaware that Marley was also sleeping with him.

12. Jess Ward and Damian Abernathy were originally planned to be Caucasian.

13. I once thought to give Lydia I.E.D. or Intermittent Explosive Disorder.

14. Megan was almost named "Minerva" so that she, too, could go by the nickname "Minnie."

15. A scrapped mean girl moment: Minnie was meant to call some girl fat in front of everyone in gym class and humiliate some boy in public.

16. Callista was supposed to key some girl's car for calling her a "degenerate whore."

17. Lydia was meant to get into a verbal altercation with her mother and a physical altercation with Minnie at Marley's funeral.

18. Because it was originally planned that Nate and Marley have a long affair instead of a one-time thing, in Marley's diary, Jezebel confessed she poked tiny holes in their condoms in an attempt to trap Nate. It worked because she became pregnant with their son but committed suicide.

19. Sybil was originally meant to push Minnie into the pool at the end of the story when Minnie went to apologize to her.

20. Donald Aprilson died from complications of cardiomegaly, a medical condition where the heart is enlarged.

21. Although she is only involved with women in the story, Lauralee is actually bisexual. She expresses physical attraction towards Cassidy Paris in Chapter Seven but is looking to pursue a relationship with a woman. This is subtly hinted when she told Minnie "Maybe I'm not looking for a man, Artemis. Did you ever think of that?" in Chapter Seven. At the very end of the story, she begins going out with Rayanne Greyman.

www.ingramcontent.com/pod-product-compliance
Lightning Source LLC
Chambersburg PA
CBHW020948310726
48980CB00001B/98

* 9 7 8 0 6 9 2 9 6 5 6 5 8 *